MIDNIGHT FEVER

LISA MARIE RICE

Midnight Fever ©2017 by Lisa Marie Rice

Published by Lisa Marie Rice

Cover Design & Formatting
by Sweet 'N Spicy Designs

All rights reserved. Without limiting the rights under copyright reserved above, no part of this publication may be reproduced, stored in or introduced into a retrieval system, or transmitted, in any form, or by any means (electronic, mechanical, photocopying, recording, or otherwise) without the prior written permission of both the copyright owner and the above publisher of this book.

This is a work of fiction. Names, characters, places, brands, media, and incidents are either the product of the author's imagination or are used fictitiously. The author acknowledges the trademarked status and trademark owners of various products referenced in this work of fiction, which have been used without permission. The publication/use of these trademarks is not authorized, associated with, or sponsored by the trademark owners.

One

Portland, Oregon

"You're a hard woman to catch, Dr. Hudson," Nick Mancino said, smiling. Well, not really smiling, more like a baring of teeth. His dark eyes seemed to penetrate her head. "Missed you by five minutes in DC."

Kay Hudson suppressed a sigh as she looked at the handsome face scowling at her. It would be easier if he weren't right. She had been avoiding him, though not because she didn't want to see him. Nope. He'd featured in many erotic dreams. They'd been dancing around each other for months and it was entirely her fault that this was the first time they were actually together in the same room.

And what a room—elegant, hushed, candlelit. The Lounge offered the finest food in the Pacific Northwest. She'd eaten here several times before with her good friend, Felicity Ward. They'd laughed and eaten superbly well.

Not that she was hungry. Her stomach cramped with anxiety and the thought of food was slightly nauseating. She hadn't even been able to order her meal, something she usually enjoyed.

Nick had missed her by five minutes in DC. Yeah. She'd gotten word that Nick was arriving and had escaped out the back door as he walked in the front. And she'd deliberately come into Portland last month the day after he'd left for a job. She'd been avoiding him for a while now.

Not because she wanted to. God no. Who wouldn't want Nick Mancino? *Just look at him*, she thought. He was elegantly dressed—definitely in her honor because she knew he preferred sweats and jeans—but the white Armani shirt, Versace tie and blue-black Hugo Boss suit couldn't hide the fact that that hard body wasn't meant for boardroom suites. It was meant for midnight raids.

And sex.

Nick exuded toughness and self-reliance, the kind of guy who wouldn't back down from anything. More than capable of defending himself. No one needed to protect Nick, least of all her.

In ordinary times, at least.

There wasn't any physical danger Nick would refuse to meet, but there was the question of fairness. Nick had had a brilliant career by being smart and brave and amazingly hard-working. He'd become a Navy SEAL and then a member of the FBI's elite Hostage Rescue Team.

Such hard things to do. They were things he'd earned a million times over. She didn't want to hurt a career he'd worked so hard for.

As long as he was in the FBI, she could ruin his life with what she was doing. If things went south, she might have to run for her life, and every single person she'd had dealings with before disappearing would have their lives turned inside out. He'd live under a perpetual cloud. It would ruin his career.

But Nick wasn't with the FBI anymore. As of last week, he was with Alpha Security International, a big security company in Portland. A good place to be, with good people. Felicity worked there, and said that the bosses at ASI were reasonable men. Nick would definitely not be penalized by an association with her. Not at ASI. They'd be on her side, and his. So now she could allow herself contact with him. Briefly.

Nick was still airing his grievances. "And I missed you by about an hour in New York last month."

"Mm." That had been careful timing, too. Nick had been on a job and had found out from her grandfather that she was in New York. She'd checked out of the hotel early, missing him by half an hour.

"I could almost think you're avoiding me, Dr. Hudson."

His tone dripped sarcasm. The "Doctor" was overkill. Particularly considering the incendiary kiss they'd shared back when Nick was helping to save her beloved grandfather, who'd been kidnapped by a former Russian FSB officer. He'd moved his lips to her ear and breathed "Kay," and every hair on her body had stood up. It would have gone beyond that kiss—which had almost been enough to give her an orgasm—straight into sex, but she had put a stop to it. Wrong time. Wrong place. She'd been worried sick about her grandfather.

But sex was definitely in the cards.

They were off to a good start. He was interested, she was interested.

As a matter of fact, she'd never been as aroused and attracted to a man like she was to Nick. He fascinated her. And—icing on the cake—she liked him. A lot. And—the cherry on the icing on the cake—he wasn't a jerk. So, she made room to have Nick Mancino in her life.

Then her professional life blew up in her face. Each time she ran away from him it was because something scary was happening. Something that showed that things were very wrong in her world.

"Not avoiding you, Nick," she lied, looking him straight in the face.

His eyes were mesmerizing. Dark and intense, set in a dark and intense face.

He stared at her as if she were under interrogation. He was good at interrogations, too, a master. She was a scientist and had no clue how to dissemble.

Too much. His intensity was too much. Kay dropped her own gaze and watched the patterns her fork tines made in the damask tablecloth. This was painful. She could actually *feel* her heart hurting, like someone was crushing it under an immense weight.

Nick reached over and placed his hand on hers, stilling it. His hand was fascinating. Dark and calloused and sinewy with strength, nicked with scars. He'd already had two careers as a warrior and was starting a third. He was a warrior in every line of his body. He was walking testosterone and oozed it out of every pore. Even his hands.

Kay was under intense pressure, about to do something that would blow her existence to smithereens. These past weeks, as she'd contemplated steps that would ruin her life, perhaps forever, she'd remained calm. All the permutations of the steps she had to take had been slowly and carefully considered.

Her job sometimes required that she hold pipettes of nature's most dangerous creations in her steady hands. In a level-4 biolab, with clumsy, thick rubber gloves, she handled life's worst enemies—pipettes of Ebola, Marburg, rabies. It was possible that one day she'd be asked to handle smallpox, and she'd be okay with it. But this? Nick Mancino's rough, scarred hand over hers? It made her tremble.

She finally looked up, met his eyes.

"You *have* been avoiding me, Kay," Nick repeated. His jaw muscles clenched. "Don't deny it."

She couldn't deny it anymore, because it was true. There was nothing she could say that wasn't a lie. Nick was a walking lie detector, anyway. He could smell lies at a hundred paces, like sharks could smell blood in the water.

Kay opened her mouth and then closed it. She huffed out a breath, tried to smile, looked him in the eyes. "I'm here now."

Nick blinked and a slow smile grew on his face. He lifted her hand to his mouth and kissed the back of it. "Yes, you are."

He could feel her hand trembling, she knew. Nothing escaped his notice. He'd been a SEAL and then a member of the FBI's elite Hostage Rescue Team. He wasn't going to miss the fact that the hand he was holding was shaking.

Looking away from him was impossible.

"May I top you up?" Kay jumped at the intrusion. The waiter, hovering. He'd introduced himself when they'd arrived, but she couldn't remember his name. She could barely remember her own.

"Thanks." Nick leaned to one side as the waiter poured another glass of an excellent merlot and waited for Kay's glass to be filled again. She took a sip, barely tasting it, then another. And another. Dutch courage, her grandfather called it. God knew she needed any kind of courage there was on offer.

"Your *antipasti* will be coming shortly," the waiter offered in a delicious Italian accent that might even have been real. You never knew. He had Italian good looks—thick black hair shaved at the sides and luxuriant on top, sharp cheekbones, a soul patch, brown eyes with ridiculously long lashes, which he actually batted at her. His eyes twinkled.

A real hipster hottie.

She looked from him back to Nick, whose eyes weren't twinkling at all, and who had absolutely nothing trendy about him. Clean-shaven, short-buzzed hair and he definitely wasn't batting his eyelashes at her. As a matter of fact, he was staring at her narrow-eyed.

It wasn't even a contest, she thought. The waiter thought he was cute, but he looked like a puppy next to Nick. Maybe even from a different, wussier species.

"Fine." She smiled, forcing the edges of her lips up, trying to remember how to smile. She'd almost forgotten how. There hadn't been much to smile at these past weeks.

The server glided away and reappeared two minutes later, sliding long white porcelain rectangles filled with tiny bruschette, fried stuffed olives, sage fritters, ramekins of goat cheese soufflé and tiny pesto-filled mozzarella balls. Nick didn't say a word and didn't break eye contact with her as the plates were placed in the center of the table.

They sat there, staring at each other, until the server discreetly coughed. Kay glanced away from Nick. It was surprisingly hard to do, like wrenching something that was stuck. Nick was an eye magnet.

Two small square hors d'oeuvre plates appeared in front of them. "Enjoy," the server said, a trace of irony in his voice.

Enjoy.

Yeah, that was the kicker. She'd been avoiding Nick, trying her best not to even think of him, and by rights, she shouldn't even be here this evening. She had something dangerous to do tomorrow morning, and then she would probably disappear forever, and why the hell had she agreed to dinner with Nick?

Because, well, she enjoyed the hell out of him. Her grandfather was FBI, her father had been a judge, so she was used to tough guys, but Nick was something else entirely. Like he'd invented the tough guy persona—super tough, capable, absolutely mesmerizing. When she was with him, he threw a force field of sex and protection around her. It was as if he bent gravity. She'd loved every single second she'd ever spent with him and she'd thought of him constantly, even while running away from him.

Nick picked up his fork, speared a mozzarella ball and frowned at her. "Eat," he growled.

She sighed, picked up her own fork, put a hot stuffed olive on her plate and pushed it around. Her stomach was closed, there was no way she could eat anything. Every muscle in her body was tense, tightly knitted. It felt that if she put food down her throat, it would just bounce right back out.

He made a gesture and she put the olive in her mouth. Chewed. Swallowed. It was delicious, a little ball of warmth sliding down her gullet and into her closed stomach, which opened, just a little.

"Drink," he growled, and she took a sip of wine, which tasted like sunshine and joy.

He narrowed his eyes at her, only gleaming darkness showing. "That wasn't so hard, was it?"

Yes, it was hard. This whole thing was hard.

God, he looked so amazingly sexy. The soft overhead lighting picked out the edges to his face, his hair so black it looked faintly blue. He was so fixed on her it felt like a spotlight had been turned on. Kay wasn't used to being under the intense focus of a man like this—usually she was the focus of bland attention by bland males. Fellow scientists, the odd pharmaceutical company executive or CDC manager. All men who basically found money or power or science more interesting than she was.

Nick was hotly focused on *her*.

Nick was the most fascinating man she'd ever met, she was half in love with him, and she was going to take a leap into an abyss from which she might never return.

"Whoa there."

She looked up, frowning. Nick had put down his fork and gently pinched her chin. He rotated her head left and right, checking her out. His scowl was gone, replaced by something that looked like worry. Only that was crazy. Nick Mancino didn't do worry. Everything in his world was under his control.

His eyes held hers. "What's wrong?" That deep voice was gentle, and for some insane reason, she had to blink back tears.

She tried the smile again. Practice makes perfect. "Nothing." She lifted her head, hoping to escape those strong fingers, but he held fast to her chin. He wasn't hurting her but he wasn't letting go either.

"Bullshit," he said, his voice still gentle.

This was a very bad mistake. She should go before she broke down in tears and told him everything. Which would be an even worse mistake, because Nick Mancino would not approve of what she was about to do, and when he disapproved of something, there were consequences.

So—get out of here, fast, she told herself, running through possible excuses that didn't sound insane. Headache, stomach ache, vague female complaint. That last one should do it. No guy wants details on female problems.

"I, ah." She coughed to loosen a tight throat. "I don't feel too well. I think I should go."

Nick barely registered her words. He was studying her face the way a sniper studies the battlefield. "You don't look well," he said finally. "You've got bags under your eyes and you're very pale underneath your makeup. God knows you're still beautiful—nothing less than a gunny sack over your head would change that—but there's something wrong." He drew his hand away slowly, making it a caress. "What's wrong, honey?"

Kay blinked. Her heart had given a huge thump in her chest when he'd used the term of endearment. Oh God. This was getting out of control. She should get up right now and walk out. Nick wouldn't follow her if she made it clear that she didn't want him to. But that was the thing—she wasn't capable of simply getting up and leaving. And she was certainly incapable of pretending she didn't care about him. In her state, nerves on edge, with sleepless nights and worry gnawing at her every single moment, she didn't have the strength to pull it off.

But she had to do *something*. She'd found it possible to resist tough-guy Nick, but this gentle Nick, dark eyes watching her with sympathy and something else... Nope. Couldn't do it. The truth was out of the question, but she could skirt it.

"Work," she said, her voice slightly hoarse. She cleared it. "Work. I'm having some issues at work."

His black eyebrows drew together. "Considering what you do, that's really alarming."

You have no idea, Nick, she thought. "It's more admin stuff than anything else," she lied. "My boss is being...difficult and is making my life hard. It's a little depressing."

Depressing didn't begin to cover it. She might have stumbled upon a plan to burn down the world.

"I'm good with guns," Nick said. Which was an understatement. He'd been a sniper as a SEAL and as an FBI HRT guy. "Want me to shoot that son of a bitch who's bothering you? Say the word and consider it done." His face was entirely deadpan, as was his voice.

Kay hesitated a beat then smiled. It was shaky, but genuine. "That was a joke," she said. "Wasn't it?"

"Nah." He speared a mozzarella ball and put it up to her lips. "I meant it, but let's pretend I was joking. Though whoever your boss is, he has worse weapons at his disposal than I do." He shuddered. "Any guy who deals in smallpox and Ebola scares me more than I could scare him." He nudged her mouth. "Open up and eat."

Kay opened her mouth and he gently placed the ball on her tongue. It was delicious and went down like a dream. Her stomach had been closed for weeks, but now it just opened up like a flower.

The entrée arrived. Beef ragout on a bed of pappardelle for Nick. Gorgonzola cheese risotto for her. The dishes looked amazing and smelled even better.

Nick wound strands of pappardelle with ragout around his fork and put it next to her lips. She chewed and swallowed. God. Food like that should be illegal.

It was the food but it was also Nick himself. He'd offered to off the bad guy and it was such a tempting thought, except she wasn't too sure who the bad guy was here.

But beyond that, Nick was definitely someone to take your woes to. She couldn't take this particular woe to him—that was her burden to bear—but in general, he was made to lift burdens from people, and not just with his sniper rifle. There was something about him—that tough guy, protective attitude—that made her feel better.

"Attagirl," Nick said approvingly when she began to eat. "See what the thought of me whacking your boss does? Brings your appetite right back."

Kay smiled.

"That's more like it," he said. "I thought you'd forgotten how to smile."

She'd thought that, too. "Haven't forgotten," she said. "Just not much to smile about lately."

"You shouldn't have avoided me." Nick shot her a dark, intense glare. "I'd have made you smile. Guaranteed."

And just like that, heat shot through her, a scalding wave from head to toe, like a sun blossoming inside her, under her skin. She had very fair skin, and she knew beyond a shadow of a doubt that she was blushing bright as a stoplight. Though in childhood her skin showed exactly what she was thinking, she'd learned to control it. Or thought she had. And now, just when she needed control most, her fair skin betrayed her.

"You like that thought." Nick leaned back in his chair, never taking his eyes off her for one second.

Kay closed her eyes and drew in a deep breath, let it out.

"Yes," she sighed. "Apparently, I do."

She didn't dare open her eyes because she knew what she'd see—a smug male face. After a long moment's silence, she finally opened them and saw Nick looking at her soberly. Not smug, not smirking, even though he'd alluded to...well, to sex. The eight-hundred-pound gorilla at the table.

He drummed his strong, thick fingers on the tablecloth once, eyes dark and serious. "What's wrong, Kay?" he asked, that deep voice gentle and controlled. "And don't say you don't know what I'm talking about."

No, he understood far too much, was way too perceptive for her to lie right now. "I can't—I can't talk about it," she said finally, after a long silence.

He drummed his fingers once more, thinking about it. If there was one thing a former Navy SEAL, former FBI HRT guy understood, it would be what he'd call "opsec". Operational security. What she knew and what she suspected hadn't been classified as secret because it didn't officially exist, was pure supposition, but it was a bombshell nonetheless. And certainly not something she could share now.

"Okay." Nick continued watching her, face expressionless. "I can't argue with that. So, you won't tell me—"

"Can't," she interrupted. "Can't tell you."

"All right." He bowed his head in acknowledgement. "Can't tell me. I respect that. God knows I've got enough stuff of my own I can't talk about."

I bet, Kay thought. Just about every mission of his as a SEAL would remain classified until the sun went nova.

"Just tell me this. Give me this much." His jaw muscles hardened, the skin over his temples hollowed. "Someone bothering you? Harassing you?"

She might be driven into lifelong exile, she might be tossed into the deepest dungeon in the world, she could lose everything she had worked so hard for.

Her head dropped. "Not quite in the way you mean, but...yes."

Nick was silent.

Surprised, she lifted her head.

He waited another beat. "That stops," he said. "Right now."

Actually, it did. Not because of something Nick could do, but because of what she was about to do. She was stepping into danger...but it was almost better than the last few weeks of agonizing heartache as she slowly came to the realization that someone in an institution she worshipped had sold out and had her best friend killed.

Whatever was to come, at least she wasn't tormented by doubts. Whatever was to come, she was going to face it head-on.

So, yeah. It stopped, right now.

"Thanks." Kay smiled wryly.

He cocked his head, studying her. "I can't ask and you can't tell. That's about it, right?"

She nodded, throat tight.

Oh God, how she *wished* she could unburden herself. How she wished she could open up, tell him everything, walk him through how she got here, alone and lost.

Nick was smart and, above all, Nick thought strategically and tactically. Kay was lost in this world. Her world was science, the world of truths. Eternal truths. A world of things that could be proven. Two plus two equals four had been true before humans walked the earth and would be true to the end of time. The beauty of science was its clarity. If scientists didn't understand the truth, it wasn't nature's fault, it was theirs. The universe was clear and straightforward, even down to quantum physics. It was people who were opaque and contradictory and often made no sense at all.

"Something I have to deal with myself," she said. "You can't help me." Actually, no one could help her.

"I can't help you with the science thing," Nick admitted. "But I can beat someone up for you. Easy. I'd enjoy it, too."

A laugh burst out of her, a little intense bubble of emotion that brought tears to her eyes. *Whoa.* She coughed and looked away, blinking furiously. If only it were so easy.

For a second Kay was so tempted to lay all her problems before him, put everything in his very large and very capable scarred hands. Nick would know what to do. And now that he was out of the FBI, his career couldn't be ruined.

But that would be so unfair. Kay had a heavy burden to bear, and it was hers alone. Nick was a good guy, but he'd already helped her out so much. He'd helped save her grandfather, her only family.

Nick was interested in her—he'd shown that. He'd made it clear he'd like an affair. But sex didn't mean he wanted to take all her baggage on board. It would be like lifting a thousand-ton anvil, all for a quick lay.

Though with Nick, maybe it wouldn't be so quick…

Heat blossomed through her again, a blast of it so strong it was like a hand at her back, pushing her forward.

Sex with Nick.

So.

There it was, out in the open. In the back of her mind, she'd been thinking of sex with Nick for a while now. It was, possibly, the reason she'd agreed to dinner tonight. Kay wasn't used to her subconscious tripping her up, but there it was. Her glands leading her around instead of her head.

Well, why not?

Who would it hurt? Her, actually, because it could only be a one-night stand, and Kay didn't do those. She'd never had an affair that was only sex. A night of passion then disappearing forever…ouch.

Plus, she thought Nick might like something more. A two-night stand, maybe, at a minimum. A week-long affair, perhaps. Nick wasn't known for his long-term relationships, but he wasn't a player, either. He'd want something more than slam-bam thank you, sir, which was basically all she could offer.

But one night...oh man. Payback for all the long, lonely nights wrestling with this huge, writhing *thing* at the center of her life. Nights spent staring at the ceiling, slowly coming to terms with the fact that someone in an institution she admired was fundamentally evil, way beyond anything she could ever imagine.

Nick knew about that kind of evil. Grandfather Al knew, too. They knew what humans were capable of. Their enemies were the scumbags of the earth. Terrorists, rapists, murderers, abusers, the corrupt. Men whose coin was pain and fear.

Kay's enemy her entire life had been completely different. Her enemy was nature itself. She was going to be a brick in the wall that cut mankind off from its worst enemies—cancer, heart disease, muscular dystrophy. All the illnesses the flesh was heir to.

Disease, illness, plagues—they'd always been so horrible, killing millions and millions of people throughout history. Smallpox alone was one of the most terrifying things on earth. And yet...it never failed to astonish her that people could be more dangerous than disease. More murderous, capable of much greater damage.

But Nick had known that for a long time.

She'd always thought of herself as brave. She worked in a bio-safety level 4 lab encased in body protection as strong as a space suit, but one tiny tear, one leak and she would die a horrible death. That was bravery.

Nick was braver.

She'd been so afraid these past weeks. Her heart constantly thrummed a drumbeat of terror. She'd end her day exhausted, sticky with the sweat of anxiety. Which was exactly how she woke up in the morning, too. Heartsick and terrified.

Nick wasn't afraid of anything. She knew that about him. He'd done astoundingly heroic things. She didn't know this from *him*. He never talked about it, ever. She knew it from her grandfather and from stories her friend Felicity passed on from her lover, Metal, and his guys. The guys in Nick's new company, who'd been his teammates in the SEALs. The consensus was that Nick was a really good guy, one of the rare ones. Hard-headed, yes, stubborn as they come, but brave as a lion.

Nick the Lionheart! a teammate had yelled when Nick had run across an open field of fire with a wounded soldier in a fireman's carry, bullets pounding the sand at his feet. Nick had thrown the wounded teammate over the threshold of the sandbag bunker and then tumbled over head first, bullets following him. Nick stood immediately, took up a station at a break in the wall of bags and started calmly picking off enemy targets, totally unmindful of the fact that a bullet had passed through the meaty part of his thigh.

Nothing ever rattled Nick.

What would it feel like to be like that? To be so fearless? To feel up to any possible physical challenge? She'd never know. But...maybe she could get close enough to him to borrow some of his courage. Touch that strong, tough body all over, feel him inside her...

Another bloom of fiery heat.

His eyebrows drew together in a V shape. She'd turned beet red again. He must be wondering whether she suffered from some kind of mental or hormonal disorder.

Maybe she was. Nick Lust Disorder.

"So," he said casually, leaning back. "Is that a yes? Want me to beat someone up? Whack someone for you?" His tone was light but his face was deadpan. Tough and utterly inscrutable.

She sighed. "I wish." If only this was the kind of problem you could shoot your way out of. Pity bullets couldn't kill viruses.

They'd eaten their way through dinner, though she'd left most of hers on her plate. His had disappeared and she'd yet to take a bite of hers. He took her spoon out of her hand, dipped it into the creamy panna cotta and held it in front of her lips. When she opened her mouth, he slipped the spoon inside and she nearly fainted from the sugar rush.

"Again," he insisted, heaped spoon at her lips. He watched as the spoon entered her mouth, pulling it out slowly, empty. His face was dark and hard. "Jesus." He looked like he was in pain.

It nearly made her smile. "It's just dessert, Nick."

He wasn't smiling at all. "Not the way you're eating it, sweetheart. You're making this pure sex."

Kay blew out a breath. This was so unfair. She wasn't trying to be sexy, though...well, with Nick Mancino across the table from her, staring at her with dark, narrowed eyes, it was hard to think of anything *but* sex.

"Sex," she whispered without even realizing it. The word was in her head, in the cloud of pheromones swirling around her, even in the panna cotta. It was in the molecules of the air.

Nick wasn't a fidgety man, but he froze into immobility. "What did you say?"

What? What was he talking about?

His face was a mask of tension. "What did you say?" he repeated.

What had she said? Kay ran the tape in her head back a minute and there it was. What she'd said.

Sex.

What was she thinking of?

"Sex," Nick said. His dark eyes glittered. "You said sex. I heard that. Distinctly."

Kay swallowed and nodded.

"So..." He scooted his chair closer. "Does that mean that sex is on your mind? The idea rolling around your head as a possibility? Say, in a completely theoretical and abstract way?"

"Not theoretical," she whispered through a scratchy throat. "Not abstract."

Nick's face tightened and he looked at her intensely, like looking through a screen door at something from a long distance away, uncertain of what he was seeing.

"Not theoretical," he repeated. He took the large, snowy-white linen napkin off his lap and threw it on the table. "That means practical. You're thinking sex in a totally non-abstract and non-theoretical way. With me."

She nodded.

His eyes were like lasers piercing into hers. The cords in his neck stood out, his jaw clenched.

This was crazy. She was sending out huge signals—like flares on a dark night—without thinking about the consequences. Careful, steady Kay, who always thought before she spoke, was now opening her mouth and wondering what would come out next.

Totally out of her control, as if her mouth was separate from her, run by someone else.

"Yes," she whispered.

Two

Yes!

Finally.

God, he'd waited long enough for Dr. Kay Hudson. Years, it felt. Like fucking forever.

He stood up so suddenly his chair would have fallen if he hadn't caught it. A real feat, when you considered he was having a slight out-of-body experience, as if his head was in another room while all the blood in his body rushed to his dick.

He drew in a deep breath and he felt twelve feet tall. Twelve feet tall, strong as the lion of his nickname, about to bag the biggest prey of all.

Kay.

The instant he'd seen her for the first time, back in DC, a beautiful woman worried sick about her grandfather, he'd been blown away. He'd been doing his duty by this woman, a friend of friends, not to mention that her missing grandfather was an FBI legend and he himself had recently transitioned to the

Hostage Rescue Team. He'd have put everything on the line for her anyway.

But goddamn, when he met her coming off the plane from New York, worried and anxious and so fucking beautiful he couldn't take his eyes off her, duty and loyalty to an FBI teammate faded and he knew he'd do absolutely anything to help this woman, no matter what.

And then it turned out she was not only gorgeous, but smart—smarter than him, for sure—and loyal and kind.

Her grandfather, Al Goodkind, had been kidnapped by FSB fuckers, who had tortured him for info on the whereabouts of Felicity Ward, Goodkind's protégé. But Goodkind was a tough old coot and didn't break, and Nick's guys in ASI found him and saved the day.

And Kay had kissed him.

One hell of a kiss, too. Full-body lip-lock, where their mouths stood in for their sex. Shit, that had been one hot kiss. Nick had been around the block, so one kiss shouldn't have imprinted itself on his brain and on other parts of his body, but it had.

That one incendiary kiss—then Kay disappeared, and fuck if he could get near her again. God knows he'd tried. Half the guys in ASI were laughing at him as he shot to Portland every time he got word that she was going to be there, that there was the possibility of her being there, that she was *thinking* of going there. He'd also missed her in DC and in New York.

Then he left the FBI and joined ASI. Not to catch her…well, not only for that. Because he loved the guys and the company. It was better than the FBI, more badass. Better bosses. Much, much better pay.

And with a better chance of pinning Kay down.

Because he still hadn't had a repeat of that kiss and he wanted one, badly. And the sad truth was he hadn't even been in the same room as her, much as he'd tried to.

And another sad truth—he hadn't been to bed with anyone since that kiss. Pathetic, but there it was.

Then, out of the blue, yesterday, she'd called him and said she'd be in Portland for some big scientific congress and did he want to have dinner?

Did he want to have dinner with Dr. Kay Hudson? Smart and beautiful and enticing Kay Hudson?

Fuck yes. He wanted to have dinner, then go back to his house and have sex for a couple of weeks straight.

Realistically though, he'd thought it might take the four days of the conference. Taking her out every night, seeing her at the lunch break, being with her every second he could.

ASI was cool with that. Metal O'Brien, Felicity's husband as soon as he could convince her to set the date, told him the brass had cleared the decks for him so he could pursue Kay.

There was even a pool on how long it would take, according to Metal.

They were all rooting for him because they all liked Kay.

He liked her too. That was putting it mildly.

Nick felt a massive connection to Kay that went beyond her red-gold hair, ivory skin and intense sky-blue eyes.

He liked the way she loved her grandfather. Nick came from a very large, very close, very loud family, and he understood that kind of love down to his bones.

He liked the way she talked about her work, not that he understood it. She was a virologist and geneticist—the fuck he knew about genes? Except the fact that his were irresistibly drawn to hers.

He liked that she was such a beautiful woman without being coy about it, without acting like one. Before meeting her, he'd just broken off a semi-relationship with a wannabe model who looked perfect but was empty inside, like a plaster-of-paris person. Kay was real and warm and funny and so sexy she turned him inside out without even trying.

He should be mad at her because she'd been avoiding him. But she'd called him and here he was and he wasn't letting her slip through his fingers again, no sir. No flies on him. He'd put his pride away for a chance to get his hands on all that smooth ivory skin.

Kay came around the table to stand next to him, looking at him as if for instruction. She was super smart, but this apparently baffled her. The question of sex came up, she more or less said yes, and then waited, as if uncertain of his reaction.

Well, he knew what to do, if he could only keep his hard-on from crippling him long enough to get to his house or her hotel, whichever was closest.

Kay said something. Her mouth moved and he heard her voice as if coming from a long way away. He shook his head as if he could rattle his brains into reason.

"What?"

She looked a little lost, as if unsure what came next.

Okay, he knew what came next. Though it seemed strange that she was unsure, because Nick was certain his dick was so hard it was sending signals out into space that she could pick up in her fillings.

"Nick," she said, putting her hand on his arm. "Did you—did we pay?"

"Yeah," he answered automatically, though a teensy bit of doubt clouded his already clouded mind. But yeah—he'd thrown two Ben Franklins on the table. Enough to cover the bill and leave a really nice tip in case he ever came back, because running out like they were doing was really uncool.

Though necessary.

He took her elbow hard. Not hard enough to hurt but hard enough for her to understand that she was coming with him. Only where? He steered her toward the door, hoping he could make it down to the garage where his car was. The restaurant was attached to a big hotel, which was great for parking.

But just as he reached the elaborate, big glass doors, Kay tugged. "No," she said.

No? *No?*

Nick stopped dead in his tracks, staring down at her. She didn't want this? Oh dear God. Well, he wasn't proud. He'd just fall to his knees and beg.

But it wasn't bad news, it was good news.

"I'm staying in the hotel," Kay said softly—and turned bright red.

Nick's palms broke out in a sweat. She was staying *here*? In this hotel? They were basically an elevator ride away from sex?

"Good," he said, and steered them toward the side door of the restaurant, which led into the hotel via a long slate-tiled corridor. They crossed the coolly elegant lobby that, thank God, was decorated in a spare, ultramodern style. There was absolutely nothing to stop him from walking in a straight line toward the bank of brushed-aluminum elevators, because if he'd had to navigate a series of couches and tables…

No way. Not enough bandwidth in his head.

Nick looked at her when they reached the elevator. Kay called it and they waited in silence. There was a musical ping and the doors opened onto an empty car. He ushered her in with a hand to her back. Kay pressed 9, the doors silently closed and the car lifted.

They were both staring ahead, Nick's hand still at her back. He looked at the elevator doors, not daring to look at her.

"I'm not going to kiss you," he told the doors. His voice was low and rough. "I can't. If I start kissing you, I won't be able to stop." He smoothed a hand down the jacket that hid his hard-on.

He could see them reflected in the doors, could see her looking at him. Her breath came out in a rush and she nodded shakily.

At the door to her room, Kay's hand was shaking too badly to insert the magnetic card. "Sorry," she whispered.

Nick took it from her hand, inserted it, ushered her over the threshold, inserted it into the slot that allowed the lights to turn on. A dim light in the corridor lit up. They were kissing before the door swung shut.

He held her head still for his kiss, tunneling his hands through all that soft hair. She had enough hair for six women and it was all curling around his fingers. The ceiling light in the corridor was just enough to see her when he lifted his head for air.

That pale, pale skin was pink, except for her mouth, which was red from his. Oh God, she was almost preternaturally beautiful right now, so desirable he didn't know what to do next. Kiss her again, yeah. But touch her, all over, press against her so he felt every inch of her. And he wanted to be inside her so badly his dick hurt.

He curled his hands around her skull and kissed her again, like that kiss back in DC. Only better because this was going to lead straight to sex, unless he had a heart attack first.

Her mouth was soft, wet, welcoming. He plunged, eager to taste her. She sighed into his mouth, arms folding around his neck. He slanted his head for a deeper taste. His feet moved forward and she naturally opened her legs, and oh man, his dick was right there, pressed against her. Felt so good. If not for their clothes, he could slide right in.

He pressed harder and she pressed right back with her hips and he nearly lost it.

He lifted his mouth just a little. Enough to use it for talking not kissing. "I can't wait much longer. Sorry." In his head, he'd formed the words but they came out on one breath—*Ican'twaitmuchlongersorry*.

She huffed out a little laugh, tightened her arms around his neck. Was that a yes? Did that mean she was impatient, too? He'd ask, but he couldn't lift his mouth from hers again, too much to ask of him. Her mouth felt like a sex and his tongue was a pretty good dick substitute, and he simply couldn't stop.

He lifted his mouth again, just a little. "Got to do this." *Gottadothis*.

"Hmm." She breathed into his mouth.

That was an okay, right?

Kay was wearing this amazing outfit that outlined her curves. A tight raspberry-colored dress and matching jacket. The jacket went first. Just fell to the floor with a little help from his hands and her shoulders. She held her arms out to her sides so it could slide off easily.

Jacket, check.

Dress.

Nick scrabbled for her zipper but he was pressing her against the wall too hard to wedge his hand in. He pulled her forward, took hold of the little zipper thingie and slowly pulled down. The zipper worked! All of a sudden it seemed to him that the zipper was the most magnificent technological development ever in the history of the world. Forget satellites and cell phones. You grab a tiny piece of metal, pull downward, and the most beautiful woman in the world was suddenly naked.

Almost naked.

Kay shimmied a little as Nick placed his hands on the shoulders of the sleeveless dress and slid his hands forward. The dress fell lightly to the floor and she stepped out of it. Both of them sidestepped, like a little dance.

Since Nick wasn't kissing her, he opened his eyes and ohmygod. Kay dressed was a beautiful woman. Kay in high heels, bra and a little lace thing around her hips was a sight to stop the heart of a man.

His wasn't stopping, though. Nope, it was drumming triple time.

He grunted something—not too sure what—and unhooked her bra. Luckily bra hooks were not challenging, because his hands felt like big, clumsy appendages at the end of his wrists. Anything more complex would have been beyond him.

The bra, too, fell away.

Kay's breasts were incredible—full, high, hers. He cupped her left breast and nuzzled it, feeling her heartbeat thrumming under his lips. Thank God. She was excited, too. Not as much as him, but enough.

He licked her nipple, felt a shudder go through her, then bit it lightly. She moaned.

Oh God, he wasn't going to survive this.

Nick put his face between her breasts, licking his way up to her neck. His lips rested over the artery in her neck and he felt it pulsing. Her skin was hot, releasing some kind of amazing scent. A lotion maybe. Pheromones, certainly.

"I don't think I can make it to the bed," he whispered against the skin of her neck.

"Then don't," she whispered back.

Nick placed his hands inside stretchy lace panties and slowly slid them down those long, slim legs. She stepped out of them daintily and she was naked except for high heels.

His dick was pulsing and he was very close to coming, which would be very uncool. Spurting onto her stomach, no sir. Not going to happen. Or not spurting onto her stomach but his trousers, because he was still fully dressed.

As fast as he could, Nick toed his shoes off, unbuckled, unbuttoned, unzipped and dropped. His briefs followed. In combat he went commando, but he had elected to wear underwear for his date with Kay.

Like Kay had, he stepped out of everything and moved a step to the side and she followed him, like some bizarre naked dance.

He kissed her again, and it was even better when his dick could press against her naked mound.

"You okay?" he gasped.

"Hmm," she answered. That could be yes or no. There was another way to find out if she was with him or not. His hand reached down, slid over the lips of her sex. *Yes!* She was excited. She was soft and warm and above all, wet.

Nick entered her with a finger, pressing all the way in.

Kay gasped and stood higher, arching against him. "Nick," she murmured, and the hairs of his body stood up.

She was so warm and soft, he almost envied his own finger. Moving gently, he slid slightly out then pressed back in.

And, miracle of miracles, she came. Amazing. Her sex pulsed around his finger in sharp contractions. Kay gasped in a breath, pressed her head against the wall, closed her eyes and stopped breathing. She was lost in pleasure. Nick watched her coming, felt it.

He looked down at himself, as big as a club, shiny with pre-come. There was no way he was going to last, he had to enter her or drop dead. Spreading her with two fingers, he pressed into her just as her contractions were slowing, and it set her off again.

Her legs weren't holding her up anymore. She was hanging by her arms around his neck and was held upright by his body pressing tightly against hers.

"Spread your legs more." Nick's voice was low, guttural. By some miracle, she understood and opened her legs more so he could enter deep, deep.

Her mouth found his. The kiss mimicked what they were doing with their sexes, thrusts in and out, mouths and groins making noises in the quiet of the night. Nick's hips were grinding against hers and he felt her coming again and was totally lost. With a wild cry, he emptied into her, holding himself against her, coming in spurts so intense he saw stars.

When he finally quieted, he found himself plastered against her, glued together by their juices and by his sweat, panting. It took a while for his breathing to come back under his control, for the pinwheels to stop behind his eyes.

They smelled. They smelled of sex, his sweat, a light perfume that was her skin. He gave a deep shudder and dropped his head to her shoulder. And took stock.

This was not the romantic start he'd planned. This was not romantic at all. He'd given the plaster-of-Paris wannabe model more romance than Kay. How could that be? She was a woman he wanted like he wanted his next breath and he'd jumped her. Slammed into her.

Nick pulled back a little, wincing as the skin at their bellies peeled apart. His hands had been gripping her hips. Was he hurting her? God. He lifted his fingers one by one, leaning back. One thing he found it hard to do was actually pull out of her.

A gentleman would pull out, wouldn't he? Maybe. He wasn't a gentleman, what did he know? Right now, his dick had no intention of pulling out of that warm, tight sheath.

He sighed, kissed her shoulder, opened his eyes.

Was she mad? Sad? Christ, he'd fucked it up. He'd been hoping for this, planning for this for a long time. He should have taken his time. Opened a little bottle of whatever bubbly they might have in the mini-fridge or order a nice bottle from room service. Kiss her, undress her slowly, romance his way into her body.

"How you—" His voice cracked. His head lifted and he looked into those beautiful eyes, a blue so bright they nearly blinded him in the dark. He couldn't read her expression at all. Now would be a good time to pull out, but nope. His dick refused. "How you doing?"

Her eyes—two pieces of summer sky—searched his, small movements as she studied his eyes, his face.

Suddenly, she smiled.

His heart opened up. She wasn't mad, she wasn't sad. She was smiling!

"How'm I doing?" she asked. "Wow."

Wow was right. Nick right now looked like the living embodiment of a super sexy man. Dark eyes, dark skin slightly red around the mouth and over the cheekbones. Was it possible that his hormones had made his beard grow in a few minutes? He'd been completely clean shaven in the restaurant and now it looked like he had a shadow.

He was still inside her, still semi-hard after an amazing orgasm. His and hers. She'd had several, one right after the other, if she remembered properly. It was all a little hazy. They'd walked into her hotel room and then she'd found herself plastered against the wall, somehow her clothes had come off and enough of his clothes had come off to make sex possible and the rest was a sweaty blur.

Her groin was wet. Really wet, and part of it was *her*. She remembered her last lover, a microbiologist who'd been a great scientist but a lousy lover. It had hurt when he'd penetrated, just a little. She hadn't been wet at all, even though he'd gone through foreplay a little like he was following a game plan or a protocol. Ticking off the body parts. She was sure he had a spreadsheet for sex in his head.

Nick hadn't even really done foreplay. Maybe dinner had been foreplay. He hadn't had any trouble penetrating at all.

At the memory of him entering her, so thick, so hot, her vagina contracted. His penis responded immediately, hardening a little.

Nick winced. "Oh God," he whispered.

"Sorry," she whispered back.

His eyebrows lifted. "Don't be sorry! I'm the one who should be sorry. I was going to romance you." He looked down at where they were joined. The sight was erotic but not romantic. "Didn't quite work out that way."

He kissed her neck, brushed his thumb across her nipple, and she contracted around him again.

No, it hadn't been romantic, but she'd never been desired like that before. He'd been ferocious and voracious and it had been wonderful.

He looked her in the eyes. "Do you think we can make it to the bed?"

Startled, Kay looked into the bedroom. The bed wasn't more than ten steps away. "We should make it, sure. Shouldn't we?"

Nick nodded, looked down at them. Kay looked down too as he pulled out of her. He did it so slowly, she felt like she could feel the walls of her sex contracting where he was pulling away.

His penis was very dark, still thick. When he pulled out, it glistened. Juices ran down her thighs. This was definitely the most *physical* sex she'd ever had, and it should have embarrassed her—but it didn't.

Nick sighed. "I have condoms," he said. "Brand-new, candy-colored. I think they might even be scented. And they are in my pants." Both of them looked over at his trousers on the carpet. "They might as well be on the moon. What can I say? I'm clean. We were tested constantly at the FBI and I always use condoms. Except now, apparently."

His mouth was twisted, eyes crinkled with contrition.

Well, there was an app for that.

"I, ahm, I'm clean too. And the CDC tests regularly as well. Also for tuberculosis and hepatitis. I also, um, am on the pill."

Nick's eyes shot open. He swallowed heavily. "We can fuck bareback?" he asked.

Kay winced. "If you put it like that—"

"God." Nick rolled his eyes. "I'm an idiot. Don't listen to me. Don't pay me any attention whatsoever, except for allowing me to make love to you. My brain is completely gone. Sorry." Before she could answer, he kissed her. And kissed her. So thoroughly her head swam and she lost her balance. It took a moment for her to realize that he'd picked her up and was carrying her to the bed.

She found herself lying on her back on the bed, totally boneless, arms out to her sides, legs slightly apart. She probably looked wanton. Who cared? She'd just had the best sex of her life. She'd earned wanton.

Nick stood by the side of the bed, one hand on her right ankle, looking down at her. Where he looked, she could feel her skin warm. His eyes slid up slowly, like a caressing hand, until he met her gaze and she had a jolt, as if there was a physical connection when her eyes met his.

Without removing his gaze from hers, he stripped, fast and efficiently. Tie, shirt, wife-beater. He bent briefly and she only realized then that he'd kept his socks on while they'd had sex against the wall. If anyone knew he'd had sex with his socks on, the Italian police would probably come arrest him.

On any other man, having on socks, undershirt, shirt and tie while getting it on would have looked ridiculous, but on Nick it hadn't. He'd been so ferocious, so driven by desire, he'd only taken off what was absolutely essential.

His hand returned and ran from her ankle up over her shin and thigh, to cup her there, right where she was hot and wet.

"*Sei bellissima*," he murmured.

"I took Italian in high school," she said. "I know what that means."

His eyes left hers, looking down at his hand covering her sex. "You're so beautiful you blind me."

He didn't act blinded. No, he was studying her by sight and by touch. And by smell.

Nick dropped to his knees, pulled her gently until her lower legs fell from the bed. He pressed her knees apart and kissed his way up her thigh until, oh... *Oh.*

He rose, stood like a Greek sculpture looking down at her. Oh, man, *he* was *bellissimo*. Broad-shouldered, heavily muscled but without an ounce of fat. His penis wasn't erect but it was large, full. She remembered it filling her.

Something about the way she looked at him made his penis become even fuller, start to rise...

Nick placed his hand on her thigh again. "Stay here," he said in a low, deep voice.

Well...*yeah*. She wasn't dumb. She had a PhD and two Masters'. She was smart and she wasn't going *anywhere*. Not while it appeared that more of that was on tap.

Nick came out of the bathroom with a wet towelette, which he used to wash her, wiping carefully down her thighs where his semen had flowed, between the folds of her sex. He took his time.

She closed her eyes, gave herself up to the moment. He started kissing every inch of her, along her thighs, between her thighs, long, slow licks of his tongue that made her shiver.

"Look at me," he commanded, and she opened her eyes slowly, not really wanting to connect with the real world. She'd floated into a dream world of soft sounds and soft caresses. Looking at him jolted her back into reality. His face was dark and stark, skin tight over his cheekbones, eyes almost closed. His head was between her thighs, looking up the length of her body at her.

Suddenly, she wanted to kiss him. Kiss him and feel the weight of his body anchoring hers. She cupped his head with her hands and tugged gently. There was no need to say the words. *Come to me.* He understood completely.

Nick crawled up her body using elbows and knees and he slid into her just as his mouth covered hers, laying claim to her completely. He was so hard everywhere. Her fingers dug into his shoulders but it was like clutching iron—no give. He kissed her and kissed her and stayed completely still inside her. It was a little gift. He was enormous, and though she was turned on, he'd cleaned away his juice and hers, and it took a moment to adjust.

She could *feel* herself adjusting. Each stroke of his tongue and another part of her softened. Her legs fell open because she didn't have the strength to clutch him with her legs.

His mouth left hers, kissed her ear. Goose bumps broke out on her arms. She contracted around him.

"Tell me when," he murmured low in her ear, his breath making her shiver.

"What?" His mouth now was on her neck, which she stretched to give him better access.

"Tell me when I can move."

So hot and hard inside her. It was a fine line between pain and pleasure. It was wonderful feeling him still in her, but she knew for a fact that blinding pleasure came when he moved.

Kay clutched his hard buttocks, curling her nails in.

"Now," she whispered.

Three

Kay woke up disoriented, dry-mouthed. Where was she? What happened?

Something had happened, that was for sure. She felt pounded, pummeled and yet…completely relaxed. As if someone had beaten her up and then given her a full-body massage. While kissing her.

Hmmm.

Nick.

Her body knew it before she did. She turned her head and came up against Nick's face, so close to hers that they'd be kissing if she puckered. She could feel his breath on her face. If he were awake, he'd be kissing her, that was for sure. She'd spent almost the entire night with him inside her, kissing her.

Her body flared with heat as if a bomb had gone off inside. Incendiary heat that filled her from the inside out, rushing along her veins, blossoming under her skin.

She ached in places. Her lips felt swollen, as did her breasts, the tissues between her thighs. She was marked by Nick. She brought her forearm to her nose, the memory vivid of holding those broad shoulders with her arms. Yep. She even smelled of Nick, as if his molecules had rubbed off on her.

A heavy arm lay across her belly. She was going to have to finesse things to escape from under that arm without waking him. Waking him would be...dangerous. Last night had been time out of time, a sort of going-away present to herself. It had been even more powerful and magical than she had imagined it would be.

But it was over. Real time, the real world, came rushing back. She had something dangerous to do and she had to do it alone.

Nick was incredibly single-minded. He wouldn't allow her to just disappear without saying anything and there was nothing *to* say. Nothing she *could* say to him.

Certainly not the truth.

I don't know what's going to happen in the next few hours but whatever happens, it won't be good.

No way could she say that to Nick and expect him to step back. That wasn't his way, Nick never stepped back. So last night had been a one-off.

Oh God. Kay knew she had to get going, but she allowed herself another minute or two, just looking at Nick, imagining another universe. A better one, a universe where they'd be allowed to explore this amazing chemistry they shared.

She watched his face as he slept, reaching a hand out to trace his strong features with a finger one inch from his face. What she wouldn't give to touch him. She knew his face as much by touch as by sight. She knew exactly where the rough beard ended on his cheeks and the beardless skin began—soft compared to the rasp of the whiskers. She knew the feel of the lines around his eyes, more a product of wind and sun than age. His firm jaw, the tendons in his neck, the blade of his nose—she'd traced them endlessly last night.

Her hand hovered, so close she could feel the heat emanating from him. The urge to touch him was so strong her hand trembled. If she touched him, he'd wake up. His eyes would open, those dark, fascinating eyes, and lock with hers. He'd reach out for her.

And she'd be lost.

No, she couldn't touch him. But how to get out of this bed and out of this room?

Slither out, like she was escaping. Which she was. It was hateful to think it, but she was doing an old-fashioned bunk after a one-night stand. Just like the skeeviest of guys. A female dick.

Nick was breathing deeply, regularly. *Follow the rhythm of his breathing*, she told herself, like catching a wave at sea.

She watched him carefully, pulling away just a little every time he breathed out. Each exhale, Kay shifted, breath by breath, until she was free of the heavy weight of his arm.

The second she was free, she missed it, missed being held by him. Standing by the side of the bed, she looked down at him. He was sleeping on his side, one strong arm out, the one that had curled around her. His eyes were unmoving behind the lids, he wasn't dreaming, he wasn't just about to come out of deep sleep.

In repose, his face looked relaxed, younger. Awake, he looked older than his years. He was thirty-four but sometimes he looked forty—a man who'd seen a lot of things, few of them good. A man who bore great responsibilities uncomplainingly. A man who didn't shirk his duty, no matter how heavy.

Kay was used to being around men who were responsible, at least at work. All her male colleagues at the CDC were serious men at work. Outside work, not always. Nick was always responsible, admired by everyone who knew him.

He was hers, for the moment at least. He'd made that very clear. She had a remarkable man who showed in every way there was that he liked her. And she was throwing this away, in the name of…what?

Responsibility, duty. She heaved a deep sigh, watching him sleep.

Would this be the last time she ever saw him?

Maybe, maybe not. Nothing was clear, except that after the night they'd spent together, he was going to be really pissed that she'd sneaked away. Such a generous lover he'd been. He would feel he deserved better than being abandoned without a word, and he'd be right.

She couldn't even leave a message. *Sorry I skipped out on you, but stuff is happening. Catch you at some point in the future.*

Nope.

So, in all probability, this was it. One red-hot affair that lasted one incendiary night, which was over, but which she'd never forget.

Her eyes welled with tears she tried to blink away. Oh God, no. This was no good. She was about to embark on something crazy dangerous. No time for tears, no time for any emotions at all except determination to stop something evil that had already claimed two lives and might well claim millions more. Not to mention her own.

Nick was still out, more of a coma than sleep. Good. It increased her chances of making a clean getaway.

The curtains had been drawn last night, but the rising sun gleamed in very thin stripes around the edges of the curtains, providing just enough light to see by without tripping over anything.

Kay closed the bathroom door, put a towel against the bottom and turned the lights on, the reflection off the white tiles almost blinding her. She closed her eyes against the glare for a moment and stared at herself in the mirror wondering in that first startled moment whether someone was in the bathroom with her.

She blinked. No, that wasn't a stranger. She was looking at her own reflection in the mirror.

A completely different her, transformed overnight.

Her skin wasn't that skim-milk color it had been lately, like her body had died a week ago and she hadn't noticed. No, her skin was pink and flushed and glowing. Partly due to whisker burn, though Nick had tried to be careful, and partly due to the sheer volume of hormones circulating through her body all night. Though she'd barely slept, her eyes weren't shot with red. They gleamed, the whites as clear as a baby's. Her mouth was swollen and red, as if she'd just put on lipstick. Her hair floated around her head, mussed by his hands, but the effect was like on one of those glossy women's magazine covers, where the model stood in front of a fan.

She looked...beautiful.

Kay knew she was good looking. Her parents had been genetically blessed, and she'd taken after them. Kay had inherited their skin and bone structure and the metabolism that let her eat without gaining weight.

She'd been a pretty girl, a pretty teen and was an attractive woman.

It was a fact of her life that didn't affect her that much, except there seemed to be a lot of annoying men who wouldn't take no for an answer. But in general, she'd been so busy keeping herself balanced after the death of her parents, adjusting to life with her only relative, her grandfather, who'd inherited a young girl. Then college and making her way up the career ladder. She'd chosen a hard discipline—a doctorate in virology and another degree in genetics. It required long hours of study and later, in her job, even longer hours of work and dedication and focus.

No time or place for vanity there.

But right now, she felt beautiful, because Nick had made her feel that way all night. He'd delighted in every square inch of her, and she was aware of her entire body, from her wayward hair to her toes. Which he'd kissed.

Oh God.

Kay watched herself in the mirror as she blushed down to her breasts. Remembering. Remembering how he'd started at her toes and kissed all the way to the heart of her.

The memory made her so hot that she decided to take a cold shower for the first time since she'd stayed up all night studying for Biochemistry II and needed to shock herself into wakefulness.

Now she needed to shock herself into leaving Nick behind.

The cold shower was just what she needed, reminding her that she was going to abandon something wonderful and walk straight into the unknown. It was going to be painful and she needed to be clear-headed.

Her clothes were strewn all over the floor. She picked them up and put them on an armchair. Either she would or she wouldn't be back to pick them up. Probably not. But last night's elegant raspberry outfit wouldn't do for whistleblowing and possibly running for her life. She had a stretch turquoise pantsuit that was just the ticket. Her friend Priyanka had loved it. Kay wore it because it was comfortable and light. It was perfect if she had to run and it honored her dead friend. And flats, of course. No running in heels.

Last night, she'd bought a wide-brimmed straw hat from the hotel souvenir shop and she put it on.

Right. Clean, dressed, holding the handle of her wheeled suitcase because she'd been told to pack a light carryon. Just in case. Okay. Ready to go.

But she hesitated, standing by the bed, watching Nick sleep.

She was walking out on something really, really good. The sex had been off the charts, but more than hot sex, there had been connection and affection in the bed with them. Even now, after a cold shower and dressing, with a suitcase handle in her hand, Kay could feel the connection, could almost see it shimmering in the air between the two of them.

Nick was a lot of things, but he wasn't a player. There were no stories about him loving and leaving women, using them. She knew he'd had partners but no one special. And he always treated his partners—whether for just the night or a week or a month—with respect.

She knew this because everyone at ASI, including Felicity, had made a point of telling her over and over again.

Nick was, in every sense of the word, a good man. Everyone made a point of telling her what a good guy Nick was, all but elbowing her in the side, just in case she didn't get it.

They didn't need to do that. She knew what a good guy Nick was. She hadn't known he was a god between the sheets, but…she'd suspected.

What made him so amazing in bed wasn't superhuman powers, though he did have a bit of that Superman vibe going. No, what made it so amazing was the chemistry between the two of them, exclusive to them. The joy and the heat between them.

A sob rose up from her chest, unstoppable, a searing ball of pain burning her up inside. At the last possible second, she was able to stifle it in her mouth, but it felt like a grenade went off inside her chest, shrapnel tearing up everything inside.

Goodbye, Nick, she thought. Who knew what lay at the other end of what she was about to do? It could take her away forever, she could be free within a month. She had no idea. But what she did know was that walking away from Nick, after the night they'd shared, was unforgiveable.

This was it.

Everything was blurred, but she could see the door clearly enough. The door she'd walk through to walk away from Nick.

Kay reached out one last time, her hand hovering over his. What she wouldn't give to be free. Free to touch him, free to stay with him. Free to take what was between them as far as it could go.

But she wasn't.

She turned and left before the first tear fell, texting her contact. He was somehow going to kill all the security cams in the hotel corridor, in the elevator, in the lobby.

Outside in the corridor, she wiped her eyes and quickly made her way to the elevator, small suitcase trailing.

Okay, focus.

She was supposed to be meeting with Mike Hammer, the pen name for a man who ran a website that so far had sent three senators and two CEOs to prison. www.thetangledweb.com. It published very uncomfortable truths and never backed down. Everything it published turned out to be true. Nobody knew where it was based and nobody knew Hammer's real identity.

Priyanka had first contacted him and offered to hand over very dangerous files. When Priyanka died, Kay inherited the mission. She'd contacted Hammer through channels Priyanka had given her. Hammer was amazingly proficient with computers and unusually knowledgeable about virology. He'd assured her that their email exchanges, using an email server on Tor, were private. He knew about Priyanka's death and he knew what Kay suspected.

They'd arranged to meet in Portland this morning. Kay used the excuse of her presence at the World Virology Conference, where she was scheduled to deliver a paper on the last day. She'd kept Priyanka's name on the paper.

There was almost zero chance she'd actually deliver that paper. There was almost zero chance her life would be recognizable after this morning.

It was entirely possible she'd have to leave the country with a false passport this afternoon, ending up sipping caipirinhas in Rio tonight. Mike Hammer had said he'd come prepared. He had some information for her too. Depending on what their combined info was, they'd take it from there.

One thing was for sure, though. Her life would never be the same after meeting up with Mike.

He'd provided her with a map of all the security cams in the area, with vision cones. She called it up on her cell as she walked across the hotel lobby. For a second, she looked around. This lobby was so attractive—slate floors, huge flower arrangements in beautiful enameled vases, contemporary light gray couches with pastel throw pillows. It was a policy of the hotel to offer guests tea or coffee, and many of the tables were covered in porcelain tea and coffee sets, with fruit bowls, croissants, small bowls of yogurt. People were chatting and smiling and eating and drinking. Exactly the kind of scene that always brought a smile to her face.

Now, she wondered if that was going to disappear from her life forever. If she'd be a person on the run for the rest of her life, a lighthearted cup of tea with a friend unthinkable.

No. *Stop that,* she told herself.

She couldn't deal with the future right now; the present was fraught enough. Before her lie what Nick and his teammates would call a mission. Priyanka's mission, now hers. Nick and men like him risked bullets to keep people safe. She could do this.

With a wrench, she took her mind off Nick. Last night had been her gift to herself—a night of passion with the most intriguing man she'd ever met. But it was over and danger lay ahead of her. *Be careful and focus,* she thought. There was so much at stake.

She walked out of the hotel and instantly felt the difference, leaving the past behind, facing this new, uncertain future. Outside was a pedestrian street, with pretty shops and flowering shrubs in planters.

Happy people, looking at shop windows, planning breakfast in one of the numerous elegant coffee shops. No one paid her any attention at all.

It felt like slaloming, staying out of the cone of the cameras, but Mike's map was a miracle. It moved as she moved. It was a street view, so if she watched where she stepped, she knew she couldn't be followed by cameras. Or, as he explained, if he were caught, nobody could back trace where she'd been.

The restaurant, conference venue, hotel and a big department store, Conrad's, comprised the city block. The department store continued via a skywalk to the next city block.

Mike had given precise instructions on how to get to the meeting place. Kay reached the second cross street past the department store, turned left and immediately found a narrow street with no cameras at all, and halfway down to the right, a service alleyway.

It was a sunny day but dark in the alleyway. To the right was the offshoot of the department store and to the left was a tall office building. The back of the building was windowless up to the third floor. He'd chosen well.

Kay slowed down. Mike was supposed to meet her here. She glanced at her cell phone. There were coordinates and, as if that wasn't enough, a big white X where Mike was supposed to be. This map, too, was a street view. The X was where a row of Dumpsters were lined up. She couldn't go wrong, the view exactly matched what was on her screen, but in real life there was no one where the screen X was.

Mike wasn't there.

The appointment was for 9:30 a.m. The digital time at the top of her cell went from 9:29 to 9:30.

No Mike.

Oh God, now what? The flash drive in her pocket that Priyanka had given her felt like both a thousand-pound weight and a searchlight beaming into space.

What was she going to do with it if Mike didn't show?

And if Mike didn't show, that meant—well, it wasn't good. Mike Hammer was a pen name he used for his investigative journalism, given his love of '30s noir detective novels. The Hammer of Justice, they called him. His avatar on the blog was a stylized white profile against a black backdrop. Kay had no idea who he really was, though there were rumors that he had been a big shot in either a law enforcement agency or intelligence service. Careful probing on the net showed that his identity really was a secret. But Priyanka trusted him, and that was good enough for Kay. She was risking everything for this.

But, if Hammer had changed his mind, if he had been detained, arrested or—God!—killed, she had no idea what the next step should be. None.

All she knew was she was holding information that at least two people had been killed for and she had no idea what to do with it. There was no Plan B.

She stopped, heart pounding, then walked forward slowly. They were in the heart of the city, but with no traffic and surrounded by high buildings, it was so quiet she could hear her own footsteps.

Just as she was crossing in real life the big white X on her phone, a man appeared, a tall, thin shape suddenly materializing in front of her.

"Dr. Hudson?" His voice was low, a pleasant baritone.

She stopped herself from taking a step back. She was here to meet him, after all.

"Mike? Mike…Hammer?"

He stepped forward, revealing a thin, pleasant-looking face. He looked smart and exhausted, with red-rimmed eyes and deep lines bracketing his mouth. The lines looked recent. Well, yes. If he was pursuing a story that had gotten two people killed, might unleash a worldwide pandemic, he had every reason to be stressed.

"Yes. And you are Dr. Kay Hudson."

She nodded then reached for his outstretched hand. At the last minute, she realized he was holding it palm up. Not to shake hands but to receive something. Kay handed over the flash drive. Mike's long, pale fingers closed over it, then he raised somber eyes to hers. Two people had died for that flash drive, as he well knew.

"Did you make a copy?" he asked.

Kay shook her head. "I tried. But it was so strongly encrypted I simply couldn't. I couldn't even read the data. Priyanka said to get it to you if something happened to her and that you could decrypt it."

Mike nodded solemnly. "Yeah. I can decrypt it. And if I have problems, one of the people I work with used to work at the NSA."

Kay just then realized that the hard encryption was Priyanka's way of shielding her. Priyanka didn't want Kay to be in danger, only to act as a courier.

The message had come two days after Priyanka's death, like her friend rising from the dead. They'd set up a message board in Tor under an untraceable account they both had the password to. The messages were always in draft.

Kay had logged on, simply to read some of Priyanka's old posts. Priyanka had been on someone's trail and her usual sense of humor had deserted her lately.

Kay missed her so much and wanted to read some old posts, just to feel near to her friend. But what she found was a new post, sent the day after her funeral, with a video attachment.

"Kay," her friend said solemnly on her computer screen. "If you're reading this, it means something happened to me. I'm sorry to ask this, but this is what you need to do." Suddenly her friend's face broke into an uneven smile, tears welling in her eyes. "Help me, Obi-Wan Kay-nobi. You're my only hope."

They were both *Star Wars* nerds and hearing Priyanka say that, Kay had burst into tears.

"There—there will be a lot of science data on the flash drive," Kay said hesitantly. "If you have any trouble understanding the data, you can count on me to—"

"I have a double PhD in biochemistry and computer science from Stanford," Mike said.

"Oh!" Kay's eyes widened. "I'm sorry, I—"

He waved her apology away. "No need to be sorry, you couldn't know. And I'm sure if I didn't have a strong bioscience background, I'd have needed help. I have a rough idea what's in the data. I hope I'm wrong, but I don't think I am."

Meaning—people high up in the nation's science and health establishment had gone over to the dark side of the force. It hurt Kay's heart to even think of it.

"Is there anything in the data that can be linked back to you?" he asked.

Kay shook her head. "I don't think so, but really, I have no idea. Certainly Priyanka wouldn't want to endanger me. But…" she hesitated. She didn't know Mike Hammer at all except through his articles. But Priyanka trusted him and so should she. "Some of the data probably came from my lab. Not much but some."

He nodded. "I'll anonymize as much as I can, but I can't promise that nothing will be traced back to you."

Kay took in a deep breath. "Understood."

"I think it would be a good idea for you to go underground, or away, for a while."

"A while?"

She'd expected this. Feared it, too. Whistleblowing didn't have a great tradition in terms of enhancing lifestyle. Most whistleblowers ended up fired, their reputations trashed, colleagues avoiding them. Some ended up dead, like Priyanka.

She'd put in a preemptive request for a two-month leave. It hadn't been accepted yet. If she disappeared before it came through, it would cost her at the very least her job. At first that thought had cut her like a knife, made her bleed. But now that anger had taken over, the pain was less piercing

His lips thinned. "Yeah. I don't know how long it would be. Whoever came after Priyanka and Bill Morrell will come after me, only I know how to defend myself and nobody knows my real identity. But you're different, you have a high profile, you're in the business, a lot of people know you were Priyanka's friend. At a rough guess, I would say that if your name doesn't pop up in the first ten days after publication, you could maybe consider yourself safe."

Kay nodded. "I asked for a two-month leave when I received Priyanka's message." Kay bit her lip and looked to the side for a moment. Mike said nothing. He knew that the message had come after Priyanka's death and that the pain would still be raw. "My request hasn't been accepted yet, but I think it will. Actually…" She hesitated.

"Yeah?"

"Actually, I was thinking of resigning." There. This was the first time she'd said it out loud and just like that, it became real.

Resigning from the CDC. Not an easy decision. For a scientist, a job at the CDC was top tier, a sign of scientific excellence, and you left the job only if you were planning on going into private industry for about ten times the salary. "For the moment, I can say I have health issues, ask for medical leave. And I have a place I can go to for ten days. It's—" She stopped when Hammer held up a long, thin hand.

"Don't tell me. I can't betray what I don't know."

Kay shut up. He was absolutely right.

She'd worked out a place to go. What she hadn't worked out was how sad it made her feel to abandon her job, abandon Nick, to hole up and…wait. Depending on how Mike published and what happened after that, she'd know whether she'd have to leave the country.

Felicity could get some fake documents for her. She'd done it before.

Kay cleared her throat, which had suddenly tightened. "Like I said, I might quit. I can't work in a place where I don't trust my bosses."

"There aren't many places anymore where you can do important work and can trust your bosses completely," Mike said seriously.

Kay nodded. It was true.

They were both silent. Bad things were happening everywhere, it seemed, and bad people were rising to the top. Staying clean was becoming harder and harder. One of her college friends had quit working at a biotech company and had become a baker. Said getting up at 4 a.m. was better than making drugs that made people sicker.

Okay. Kay had done what she was supposed to do. She had honored Priyanka's request from beyond the grave. It was her last link with her best friend, who'd died to get that information to her. Kay had to swallow the lump in her throat.

But, she'd done her duty. She'd handed off a problem to a very capable man who would know what to do with the flash drive and its contents. He'd know how to investigate it and publish the findings in a way that couldn't be covered up.

And Kay would be without a job, possibly without a career, and alone. She wasn't dragging anyone into her problems.

She'd always been a future-oriented person, always thinking ahead. Now a gray veil had been drawn across the world. There was no future she could see. All she could see were walls and darkness.

She'd already decided to quit in her heart. The feeling was there, she just hadn't recognized it yet because it was so painful to think about. No matter what, she was done. There was no way she could work where she wasn't sure what they were working for. Were they trying to eradicate diseases or creating new ones?

"Disappear," Mike said, new lines appearing in his face. "For a while at least. You have somewhere you can disappear to, you said?"

She nodded. An old family homestead that belonged to her maternal grandparents, and was still in their name twenty years after their deaths. Her grandfather had insisted on keeping the records murky, essentially untraceable. She remembered being amused at his paranoia when she was in college, certain that the world was rational and filled with rational and good people. She'd thought it a minor eccentricity of her grandfather's to keep what was essentially a bolt hole no one knew about.

It was entirely possible that the small country house in the woods near Denver was going to save her life. She'd rent a car with cash and drive there.

"Like I said, don't tell me where it is," Mike said. Their eyes met again in perfect understanding. "But I need a way to communicate with you. We continue with our old system?"

"Yes." He'd taken over Priyanka's password to the message board.

"If I'm being forced to send the message, if there's danger to you, I will include the word 'passage' in the message. If you read 'passage' in the message…run. Immediately."

She bowed her head. "Understood."

This was stuff she read about in thrillers. Never in a million years could she have imagined her life would take this turn, that it would be dependent upon passwords and safe houses and keeping her head low.

"Here." He held out a stiff blue and gold passport. She took it, flipped through it. It was a passport for a woman, Flora Nunes, with her photograph. She couldn't read the text. It was in Portuguese.

"What's this?"

Mike sighed. "A Brazilian passport. Don't worry, it's genuine. I had one for Priyanka, before—before—"

He stopped, swallowed.

"Before Priyanka was killed," Kay said softly.

"Yes. If this breaks unexpectedly or if you feel you are in immediate danger, buy a round-trip ticket for the first flight you can to Rio with this…" He held out a VISA card in the name of Flora Nunes. "Throw away the return ticket. I'll know if you have to run. By the time you're in Rio, check our email and I'll have arranged a safe house."

Kay held the passport and the credit card tightly. The card bit into the palm of her hand. She welcomed the little bite of pain, it helped ground her. Fleeing to Rio would make her an international criminal. She had good reasons, but if the truth never came to light, if all the good guys died, then she'd live the rest of her life in hiding.

"It's a lot to take in," she said, meeting his sad eyes.

"It is. And we're asking a lot of you. But—you know what's at stake."

She nodded. She did know. Perhaps the fate of the world. If a worldwide pandemic hit, it could take generations for mankind to come back from the brink, if it ever did.

"In the meantime," he waggled the flash drive, "it will take me some time to digest this material."

Kay gave a crooked smile. "Yeah. I think there's well over a petabyte of information."

"When Priyanka contacted me, she gave me an indication of the data and how to sort through it." His tired, serious face lost a little color. "If even half of what she suspected is true, it would be catastrophic. We'll go through every word, every chart and table. I have people and I have software. But still. It'll take a couple of days to decrypt it and go through it with my team, and it will take us a week to put together an article. Probably a series of articles. So, stay underground for at least ten days, more if you can. It's good that you asked for leave. If you need to, say you've taken ill and need treatment. Keep an eye on my site and when the articles start coming out, you can reassess. Nothing should happen to you once everything is out. You'll be the last person they'd be interested in. You should be safe." He looked suddenly fierce. "I don't want what happened to Priyanka to happen to you."

"No," she said softly. "I don't either."

"I will protect your identity no matter what. No one—" He broke off and looked around with a frown. "What's that?"

"What's what?" But she heard it too. A soft buzzing, louder by the second. The louder it got, the more she realized it was coming from above their heads. Some kind of electricity glitch?

She looked up, puzzled, when Mike suddenly shouted, "Drone!" and pushed her head down. She was initially stiff, not understanding. "Keep your head down," Mike shouted. "Don't let the drone photograph your face!"

Oh God!

Somehow the bad guys had followed Mike! Oh God! She couldn't allow the drone to photograph her! As a government employee, her face was in the CDC database. Two people had been killed for the information she'd handed over to Mike. Kay pulled the wide-brimmed hat lower, glad she had sunglasses on. "Let's get out of here."

He nodded, took her elbow, ready to run for it. He kept his head low, features in shadow from above.

Maybe it would be okay.

Holding on to the hat, Kay risked a glance up and saw with horror that the drone wasn't hovering.

It was diving. Straight at them.

Mike put one hand on her head, pushing her face down, and the other on her shoulder, rushing them to an iron service door set in the wall. He ran them toward it, taking his hand off her head—she'd gotten the message loud and clear, staring straight at the ground—reaching out for the handle. The buzzing grew louder and Mike gave her a big shove against the wall, so hard she bounced.

The drone dove down. Kay turned away, back to Mike. She heard a click and felt moisture in the air, a fine mist coming down. Swiveling her head away from the drone to peer up at the cloudless sky she saw nowhere the moisture could have come from.

The drone lifted, hovered for just a second, and then flew away, straight along to the end of the alleyway, where it lifted farther up to the rooftop and disappeared. The buzzing sound was gone and there was total silence in the alley.

"It's gone, Mike," she whispered, rubbing her shoulder. In his attempt to shield her, hurling her against the wall, he'd hurt her. "We're safe. Where do we—"

Mike collapsed. One second he was upright, the next he was sitting against the wall, legs at an unnatural angle. He'd been holding on to her arm and almost brought her down with him.

"Mike?"

Kay couldn't make sense of what was happening. Mike had been standing next to her and now he was collapsed on the ground. She kneeled, tried to pull him up. But he couldn't stand.

He was wheezing, red-faced, one hand clutching his throat. His back arched like he'd received an electric shock and his heels started drumming on the pavement. It was some kind of seizure. Kay bent his head back, looking for obstructions, getting ready for CPR.

Mike shook his head violently. "No!" he gasped.

She sat back on her heels, desperate. What to do for him?

He placed the flash drive in her hand, curling her fist around it.

"Too late for me," he wheezed. His chest expanded uselessly as he tried to draw in air.

"Wait!" Kay's shocked brain started into motion again. She scrabbled in her jacket pocket, where she remembered she'd put the cheap conference pen that had been handed out with the conference binders. She stripped the internal tube away, leaving the exterior. On a side zipper of her purse were her house keys, attached to a series of small, useful tools. Screwdriver, file and—yes!—a tiny but sharp knife. None of it was sterilized, but that was the least of her concerns right now. Right now, Mike needed to breathe.

Mentally, she went through the steps as she pulled out the knife blade. Tilt Mike's head back, trace with her finger down the Adam's apple to a point an inch below it, make a short, deep horizontal incision in the trachea, put a finger inside the cut to open it, insert the pen and blow.

She cradled the back of Mike's neck with one hand, holding the knife above his throat. She was so busy preparing for the tracheotomy that she wasn't looking at him, just at the point of his throat where the incision had to be made.

He reached up, held her hand still with surprising strength.

"No." Every muscle in his body was straining. His voice had no air behind it. She had to lip read. "It's the virus."

She froze. *The virus?*

Priyanka had been sure that Bill had been working on a weaponized form of one of the deadliest viruses on earth, the Spanish flu virus. The virus that had killed fifty million people in 1918.

This virus would be worse by a factor of a hundred.

But her face was still wet with what had been sprayed in Mike's face. She must be infected, too, though she felt nothing. How was that? Mike was the only one suffering.

Kay met Mike's dull eyes. He wasn't even struggling anymore. In his eyes, she saw the truth. He was dying. It was an animal recognition that predated civilization—the hard truth was that Mike couldn't be saved, and he knew that. He beckoned with trembling fingers. She bent down to him.

There was a knocking noise in his chest, terminal secretions collecting in his throat and upper chest. The death rattle.

His eyes were fierce, locked with hers.

"Run," he gasped, pushing the air out. "Hide."

His entire body convulsed, legs shaking, hands trembling, horrible choking sounds coming from his mouth. And then silence. And then he died. The life force simply left his body and she was holding onto a husk, a shell of a very brave man.

Kay couldn't move, couldn't breathe, couldn't think. She looked around for help for a second before admitting to herself that nothing and no one could help Mike. All she could do was safeguard the information he and Priyanka had both given their lives for.

Why wasn't she dead, too? The whole point of a weaponized form of Spanish flu was that it would be quick-acting, immediately fatal. She should be on the ground as well, just like Mike, drowned by the fluid in her lungs. She wasn't. She didn't even feel short of breath. She didn't feel anything, except terrified. If it were to act on her, she'd be dead already.

Clearly, for some reason, she was immune.

Her scientist's mind tried to figure that out, reason out by what kind of mechanism she could be fine and Mike on the ground, dead. But she couldn't think straight above the drumbeat in her head. Run run *run*!

Kay stood on shaky legs, glad she'd changed into flat shoes. She would have fallen on heels.

What to do?

Her thoughts were slow, like molasses. Shock, she knew. She even knew the hormones that coursed through the body after shock. Adrenaline. Norepinephrine. Cortisol. Hormones that were supposed to provide heat and fuel to the muscles to flee. But flee where? She was quivering with the need to run and hide, but had no idea how. And no idea where.

There was no one in the alley. All sounds were eliminated, an effect of shock. Going out onto the street would be the obvious thing to do, but there were enemies out there. There was a drone. She glanced up, then looked straight back down. The drone could be above her right now and she couldn't see it. It could be photographing her *right now*. Whatever the drone had done to Mike, it could do it to her, and all of this—the courage of two brave people who'd lost their lives—would be for nothing.

There was no way she could stay out in the open. She pushed the door open and stepped inside a storage area and stopped, unsure where to go.

What to do?

All options were bad. She couldn't stay and she didn't know where to go.

What to do?

She didn't know, but her body did. Without thinking, her cell was in her hand, dialing a number. Just thinking of the person on the other end of the line made her feel better.

"Kay?" Nick's deep, angry voice sounded like music to her ears. "Where the hell are you? Why did you—"

"Nick," she interrupted, throat raw and quivering. "Help."

Four

Nick smiled as he drifted up out of sleep. Even before waking completely, he was smiling. Oh man, yeah. Who wouldn't smile after a night like last night? And with a woman like Kay?

He drifted up, like a bird flying thermals. Usually he came awake in a rush, battle ready. It sometimes disconcerted his bed partners, but he was helpless to resist it. He and his teammates had been trained and trained hard to be ready for anything upon awakening. Ready for combat, ready to muster out, ready to face anything, you name it. The line of demarcation between the sleep state and waking state was paper thin and he could crash through it in a second.

But not right now. Even semi-awake, he realized there was no danger, there was only Kay.

It was later than he usually woke up, that was for sure. He remembered that the curtains in the room were drawn but even with his eyes closed, he could tell that the sun outlining the curtains was intense. He was usually up by dawn, but not today. God no. Today was going to be all about lingering in bed, maybe ordering room-service breakfast. Keeping his hands on Kay, kissing her, more than kissing her.

She was here for a conference, but she could miss the speeches. She probably knew more than the speakers, anyway. He wanted her in bed, with him.

The sex last night had been really intense, he should have been wrung out, but nope. He wasn't seventeen anymore but his dick was hopeful, swelling awake, already at half-mast. With any encouragement from Kay…

He frowned, eyes still closed. No source of heat, no sound of breathing. His hand reached out and encountered cold sheets. Not hot woman.

That wasn't right.

He opened his eyes, frowning. The room faced east and the curtains were framed with light, casting a soft glow over the hotel room. There was more than enough light to see by, and he could see that Kay not only wasn't in the bed, she wasn't in the room. That left one place she could be.

Nick rolled over in bed, ready to get out and go to the bathroom. Knock on the door. Suggest a shower together. But the bathroom door was completely open and he could see that there was no Kay inside.

A chill gripped his insides. He lay there, naked, a little pissed, fast becoming a lot pissed. Where the fuck was she? Had she gone downstairs without telling him? Maybe she had something to do and hadn't wanted to wake him up.

But damn it, this wasn't just any morning.

The chill became ice when he went to the closet and discovered her purse missing and no suitcase. Nobody went downstairs with their suitcase unless they were leaving.

Goddamn. He'd thought they were past the hide-and-seek stage. He'd thought last night had, well…made them a couple.

The icy cold hid genuine hurt. Nick didn't often get involved with his heart, but when he did, it was real. He'd lost his heart to her last night. Or, to be honest with himself, he'd lost his heart to her well before that, but last night confirmed she felt the same.

Or not.

Fuck.

Nick didn't play games, and he thought Kay was the kind of woman who didn't play games, either. They'd made what he thought was love all night, but maybe for her it had been hot sex and nothing more.

No! He rejected that with every fiber of his being. It had been lovemaking and the affection had been mutual and he didn't understand what the fuck was going on and it pissed him off hugely.

Goddamn.

He angrily pulled on his fine wool pants, slid into that elegant dress shirt he'd put on just for her when his natural habitat was jeans and a sweatshirt, neglecting the tie because he hated ties, thinking furiously all the while.

He was good at strategizing, planning, but Kay just...*disappearing* had him stumped. Was she expecting him to just let her go, as if nothing special had happened? Now *that* hurt. On the other hand, if last night meant so little to her, maybe his anger was misplaced. Maybe he *should* just let it go, let her go. Except it didn't make any sense.

Well, he could call her. Play it cool. *Hey babe, where'd you go?* He'd keep his voice neutral, totally down with her disappearance. *Sure, you can vanish without leaving a word, fine. How about dinner again tonight?*

He picked up his cell and it rang in his hand.

Kay.

All notions of playing it cool fled from his head.

"Kay!" he barked. "Where the hell are you? Why did you—"

"Nick." Her voice was shaky, raw, hoarse. "Help."

A bolt of electricity shot through him, crackling with desperate energy. He pulled on his shoes, grabbed his jacket, headed for the door. Of all the scenarios that had shot through his head, he hadn't considered this one. That she might be in danger.

Every thought except *Kay in danger* fled from his head. That one remained like a loosed arrow still quivering where it hit the wall.

He strode out of the hotel room, wanting to get to her—wherever she was—just as fast as humanly possible.

"Where are you, baby? What's wrong?"

"Oh, *Nick*!" Kay's voice broke. "God, he's dead, Nick. Dead! I don't know how the drone killed him, I don't know where to go, what to do…"

Nick was running down the hotel corridor, but kept his voice even and calm, though inside he was boiling. Someone dead, a drone…

"Honey, the first thing is—where are you? Take a deep breath and tell me where you are."

"Sorry." He heard a sharp intake of breath. When her voice came back, it was less shaky. "I don't know, Nick. I'm in the back of a building and there are service rooms. Wait, sorry, I'm not thinking straight…"

Ping. The elevator. Nick punched the button for the ground floor, wishing he could punch someone else, anyone else, anyone who had put Kay in danger.

"I'm in the back of a department store. Conrad's. I'm just inside the door. I walked out of the hotel, turned left, turned left at the second street, which is narrow, then right, onto the first turnoff. It's a service lane, with delivery trucks and Dumpsters. There's a dead man there now."

"There's a drone?" That raised the hairs on the back of his neck. "And it killed someone?"

"Yes. I think it—it killed him. Mike Hammer, the web journalist. But I don't know how. It sprayed him with something that was almost instantly fatal and it sprayed me, too, but I...I'm okay. It didn't kill me, even though I caught some of that spray. I can't figure out what happened! Mike said to keep my head down so the drone couldn't photograph me and I did but I don't know if I was quick enough and..."

"Okay. You can't go out again as long as that drone could still be up there." He pinged her number on his tracking app, saw her location. "I know where you are. Are you on the ground floor?"

She swallowed. "Yes. Ground floor."

Nick exited from the elevator at a brisk walk, making his strides long. He'd look normal, but he was covering ground faster. "Here's what I want you to do. Listen carefully, honey. Are you listening?"

"Yes." The panicked breaths slowed. Good girl. "I'm listening."

"Okay, then. Turn off your phone, take the battery out and don't move. I'm coming for you, but I'm also putting a plan in place where they can't follow you, follow *us*. If I'm not with you in ten minutes, put the battery back in, switch on your phone, and I'll tell you where we can meet. Is that clear? Can you repeat that back to me?" Nick knew that panic flooded the mind, eroded memory. Most people in a panic would have literally heard one word in ten. Soldiers and pilots repeated commands constantly.

But Kay had herself back under control. Her voice was steady. "Turn off my cell as soon as we stop talking, take out the battery. If you don't arrive within ten minutes, put the battery back in, switch the phone back on and we'll make plans on where to meet." Her voice shook again. "Hurry, Nick. Whoever did this is still around and the drone might have seen where I entered the building."

Nick's heart jumped inside his chest, but he kept his voice even. "Drones can be operated from great distances, honey. If there was someone nearby, he'd probably already be there." He swallowed as an image of a broken, dead Kay slumped on the ground filled his head.

Stop that. Fuck that. He was thinking like a lovesick fool.

He was an operator, a man who'd been in firefights, been to war. He tightened his focus until he was cocked like a weapon, in the zone.

Okay. Not much intel to work with, but he had something.

Kay had seen a man killed and perhaps an attempt had been made on her life, too. It was irrelevant who was after her right now. Right now, priority number one was to get Kay to safety, but a drone was in the mix and that meant trouble. It meant whoever the enemy was, he was smart and had resources and could track via the drone. However, the only way a drone could kill someone that he knew of was with a missile or an explosive. Kay hadn't mentioned anything of the kind, so they were dealing with something very high tech. Some liquid had been sprayed…a liquid that killed instantly? The only thing he knew that could do that was something like sarin. But even that wasn't instantaneous.

He was tying himself in knots when he didn't have sufficient intel. Didn't matter what the drone did. They had to get gone soon—and Nick knew where to go.

The trick was in not being tracked.

He knew exactly who could help.

She answered on the first ring. Nick sometimes thought that Felicity was connected to her phone and computer by nerves, not wires. Felicity Ward, soon to be Felicity O'Brien, engaged to one of his best friends and co-worker in the company Nick had just joined. ASI, made up of the best operators on earth. The best of the best.

"Nick, talk to me," Felicity's crisp voice said.

"Read Metal into this. And Jacko and Joe." Metal O'Brien, Jacko Jackman, Joe Harris. Former SEALs, just like him. Nick knew the entire company was at his disposal, but right now, all he needed was those two. He had a vague memory of Jack Delvaux being out of town. Didn't make any difference. Metal and Jacko and Joe were themselves an army.

He heard a couple of beeps. "Done," she said.

Stealth first. He had to get to Kay unobserved. "Felicity, I'm in the lobby of the Astoria Hotel. Kay is holed up in the back of Conrad's, the department store. A man she was with, Mike Hammer, a journalist, was somehow killed by a drone and I have every reason to believe Kay is in danger. I'm sending you her location, ground floor. I have to walk about sixty meters along Clement Street. Can you give me the position of the security cams along the way? Kay and I need to disappear, and I can't have someone pressing rewind."

She was silent. Had she heard?

"Felicity?"

"Done," she said again, and on his cell appeared a street-view map with cameras outlined in red.

"That was fast."

"While I was doing that, I checked for overhead drones," she said.

"You're the best." She was; she was amazing.

"Yes, I am." Smugly.

"And?"

"I found one." Felicity's voice turned somber, serious. "It's circling overhead, covering the entire block. It's tiny; it's a quadcopter, but it's there."

"We got your back, Nick," Jacko's deep voice chimed in. "Metal, Joe and I will drive into the underground garage of Conrad's in three identical SUVs. We'll meet on the first subbasement level and exit at timed intervals. You and Kay take one of the SUVs and head out to the Grange. No one will be able to follow you."

For the first time since waking up, Nick felt some of his tension dissipate. He didn't underestimate the danger, but he also didn't underestimate what it meant to have the ASI guys on his side.

Whatever trouble Kay was in, he was going to get her out.

"Copy that." He quickly, unobtrusively slalomed his way down Clement Street, avoiding the cameras. "Meet you in the garage, subbasement level 1 in one five mikes. Felicity, this is all secure, correct?"

He heard her huff out a breath and it sounded angry. "Please."

"Nick…" That was Metal.

"Okay, okay." Metal's official position on life was that Felicity was perfect and right every time. In this case, Nick was glad she was. "Out."

Everyone clicked off.

Nick found the narrow cross street. He checked overhead. No cameras. The buildings on either side were tall. It was like plunging into shadow. It was a beautiful day, but it might as well have been cloudy for all the sunlight that penetrated the street. It got even darker when he turned into the alleyway.

Nick slowed his stride slightly. The narrow street had been clear, he had great visuals. This alley was full of possible ambush points. Delivery trucks, Dumpsters, recessed doorways. He checked behind himself. No one.

Goddamn, he missed his weapon. Nick was always armed, always, but last night he'd decided to leave his Glock 19 at home, hoping to get lucky. Well, he'd gotten lucky, but right now he needed the weapon that was locked away in his gun safe back home.

But Metal and Jacko would make sure he was armed. Jacko, particularly, would make sure that the SUV he ended up with would have an armory of weapons.

Even though he didn't actually have his weapon with him, he made his way down the alley turned slightly sideways. If anyone was going to take a potshot, it would be of a reduced profile.

No one shot at him. But there *was* a dead body.

Nick approached slowly, all senses firing. He looked up but couldn't see a drone. That didn't mean anything. It could be stealthed, it could be so high up he couldn't see it. Height didn't make any difference. If someone had money to burn, the drone could have cameras that could see a fly's balls from a mile up.

And anyway, Felicity had her eyes on the drone, and she'd warn him. Felicity was looking down on him right now, he was sure, like some benevolent goddess, hacking into some government satellite.

He kneeled next to the body. The man Kay had watched die. To be thorough, Nick put two fingers to the carotid artery and waited for a full minute. Nothing. He swiped the heel of his hand where his fingers had touched. Forensics could pick up fingerprints from skin easily these days.

He was going to call it in, but no need to mess with the Portland PD CSU's collective head.

He pulled out a handkerchief and checked the corpse's pockets. Nothing. Absolutely nothing. Not a document, not an ID, not money. Zero, zip, zilch. Not even fucking pocket litter.

Except a cell in the man's right-hand jacket pocket. Encrypted. Hmmm. He'd probably used it to call Kay. He'd give it to ASI's friend, PPD Captain Bud Morrison, for his in-house tech person to crack and to read calls made and received, and any other info. If the tech was any good, they could geotag Hammer's movements. Felicity could probably trace his movements faster, but he didn't want to keep evidence from the police. Besides, the Portland PD's techies were good. Not Felicity good, but good enough.

Nick stared down at the body of Mike Hammer. Nick wasn't a big reader of webzines. He wasn't a big reader, period. He got his news from classified sources and scuttlebutt on the SF grapevine, the real news, not the stuff that appeared in newspapers. He read instruction manuals and military memoirs for relaxation.

But still, he knew who Mike Hammer was, and realized right now that he was one of the few people in the country who knew what Mike Hammer looked like. It was a pen name, supposedly because the guy liked his '30s noir books, and because he sometimes wrote incendiary articles accusing the mighty of robbery, corruption, malfeasance, you name it. The "Hammer of Justice".

Nick knew enough to know that Hammer wrote about powerful men and women doing terrible things. Shining sunlight in humanity's darkest corners.

Not Nick's wheelhouse. Any righting of wrongs, Nick did from the end of a barrel. But this Hammer guy had courage and never backed down. They'd had to kill him.

And in death, his identity would become known. Nick didn't know his real name but it didn't matter. What mattered was that the guy had balls.

He studied the man. Tall, lean, mid-forties. It was hard to read the features because the face was ravaged—swollen, blue tongue in mouth open in a last gasp, swollen eyelids. The man had—what? Choked to death? Some kind of anaphylactic shock? From what?

Kay had said there was a spray, and that the spray had killed him. Some kind of instant-acting poison. Somehow, thank God, Kay hadn't been affected. Otherwise right now he'd be looking down at Kay's face too—swollen and blue from oxygen deprivation.

Nick didn't shudder, but he felt a coldness rise in him, an icy determination he recognized from battle. This could have been Kay lying on the filthy pavement, dead. Whoever had done this was a dead man walking.

Nick took several photos of the dead man's face with his cell, then rose to his feet. Kay. He had to get to Kay now. The dead man was dead but Kay was alive—and she was staying that way, no question.

He'd memorized where she was. Ten feet beyond the door to the building, forty feet to the right. Now he could move fast and, in a few seconds, he was where she should be...but wasn't.

Panic hormones flooded his body. Worse, much worse than being caught in a firefight. In a firefight, he could focus like a laser beam, turn himself into a combat bot, an emotionless killer. This? This was pure pain, knives in his chest.

Was he too late? Had the spray that had killed Hammer somehow gotten to her, too, in some kind of delayed reaction?

"Kay?" He kept his voice low with effort as he spun completely around. It was a storage area, boxes neatly stacked along one wall. He gently kicked one box next to him. It shifted. Empty.

"Kay?" A little louder. Where the fuck was she? Had she moved to another location? Had someone come in and she'd been forced to move? If so, she'd have turned her cell on. He pulled his phone from his pocket. He was sweating lightly.

There was a dead guy outside. Had the people who'd killed him killed Kay, too? He couldn't even stay in the same place as that thought, and moved quickly across the big space.

He swallowed the huge lump in his throat. "Kay!"

Something bumped into him, and his arms were open before his brain had a chance to recognize her. He held her close, grip tight and fierce.

"Nick!" Kay's face burrowed into his shoulder. That was okay. He didn't want her to see his face right now. He hid his face in her hair and breathed in deeply. He smelled terror and Kay.

He'd take care of the terror as long as he had Kay.

"It's okay." He tightened his hold. It was. He had her in his arms and whatever it was that she was facing, she was facing it with him by her side. And ASI. "Everything will be okay."

She pulled back and he finally saw her face. She'd cried. She wasn't crying now, but there were tear tracks on her beautiful face. Pale and frightened and distraught, and just seeing her made his heart turn over in his chest.

He was still sort of mad at her for walking out on him and facing whatever it was she was facing on her own. But his relief overrode the anger.

Kay held on to his arms. "Nick, he's dead! That drone somehow killed him, I don't know how." She looked down at herself. The pants of her turquoise suit were dirty, like his were. They'd both kneeled next to the dead guy. He didn't care. She was alive, and so was he, and they were going to stay that way. "I think they might come after me, too. They must have the area under surveillance. What do we do?"

"We get to the garage as fast as we can. Our guys are waiting for us."

"Our guys?"

"Metal and Jacko and Joe. And Felicity's coordinating." He smiled slightly to see some of the worry drain from her face. "We're not alone, honey. We have a team at our back."

Kay let out a breath and a sob and her knees buckled slightly. He held her. He'd always hold her. "Thank God," she whispered, her voice raw. "I left. I didn't want you involved, and yet here you are. I was so afraid I'd drag you into this and bring you into danger and I was right. We're still at risk, but—"

"But with our guys on our side, we'll come out alive. We have to hurry, though, sweetheart. There's a plan but it's tight." He lifted his hands. "You okay?" Meaning—could she move? He'd felt her deep trembling, had felt her knees go. She was in shock. If she couldn't stand, he'd carry her, but it would slow them down.

She huffed out a breath, another, straightened. "Yeah. I'm okay. Good to go." She forced herself to stop trembling, looked him straight in the eyes. "But I think I'm in deep trouble."

Kay was a scientist. She lived in a world of data and research. This was not her world at all—a man had been killed before her very eyes—but she was doing her best to be brave.

Somewhere inside, he was still mad at her for leaving him to walk straight into danger. At some point in the future he was going to make sure that never happened again. At the same time, he was nearly weak in the knees from relief at finding her unharmed.

He snapped himself out of this mess of emotions back to that cold place. Emotions wouldn't help, cool mission planning would. There was still danger and he had the most important mission of his life ahead of him—getting Kay away even though enemies were probably still after her.

A mission—he could do missions, even if Kay was involved. His whole life was a mission. He forced the protector inside him into a combat mindset—a tight, narrow focus on staying alive while doing whatever needed doing.

"Put on that hat."

Her eyes widened. "What?"

He gestured to a wide-brimmed straw hat she was holding between two fingers. She looked down at it as if seeing it for the first time. She shook herself, placed the hat on her head. "I completely forgot about it."

It was possible that hat had kept her from being photographed.

"Let's go." He took off for the garage stairs, making sure she could keep up.

"There's a plan?" Kay was taking two steps to his one but she was with him.

He mentally crossed his fingers. "Yeah, there's a plan." They reached the stairwell, the elevator right beside it. No way they'd take it, elevators could be death traps.

He looked her in the eyes. "We're going to disappear. And stay disappeared until we figure this thing out."

She met his eyes, hers that beautiful sky blue, slightly bloodshot, somber. "I'm sorry, Nick," she whispered, voice raw. "So very sorry."

He shook his head sharply. Nothing to be sorry about. It was what it was. Warriors dealt in reality, not in what should be. They jogged down the stairs, Nick on full alert, until they came to the doors to level 1 of the parking area. He went first and—God yes. There they were.

The cavalry. Or rather, Jacko, Metal and Joe, standing next to three identical black Suburban SUVs. Better than the cavalry. Better than a battalion.

He could hear Kay let out a sigh of relief. Damn right.

All three men straightened, Jacko holding out a key fob. He pressed it and one of the SUVs lit up. "That's yours," he said to Nick. Good old Jacko—all business. No *hi how are you?* Or *tell me what trouble you're in.*

Jacko didn't really need a blow-by-blow explanation, though. If trouble came knocking, he answered the door. He was built for trouble.

Kay stood on tiptoe to embrace Metal, then nodded to Jacko and Joe. She held out her hand with a flash drive on her open palm.

"This is heavily encrypted," she said to Metal. "Do you think Felicity can decrypt it?"

"Sure." Metal shrugged. If Kay had said, *do you think Felicity can stop the world from spinning*, he would have said the same thing. He believed fiercely in his fiancée's powers.

"I don't know what's on it," Kay said, her lovely face frowning. She closed his hand around the flash drive, then opened her fist again. "But I do know that a man was just now killed right in front of me because of it. Because of what's on it. So, Felicity will need protection until we—" Kay's voice cracked and she looked around at them, meeting each man's eyes. "We figure out what this is and how to deal with it. There's danger not only to Felicity, but to all of us." Her eyes welled. "I am *so sorry*—"

"Wait." Metal held up a huge hand, palm out. "Just stop right there, Kay. You don't need to apologize. The fuckers who killed the guy should be the ones to apologize. No one is going to get to Felicity, guaranteed. And you have Nick by your side. You guys are going to a secure place and we'll all work on this together, okay?"

She swallowed. Her throat felt raw with unshed tears.

"Okay?" Metal insisted.

"Okay." Her voice was a thread but she smiled. Tried to smile. Metal put the flash drive in a pocket inside his jacket.

"SUVs have temporary plates on them," Jacko said to Nick. Which was a polite way of saying they were fake plates. ASI had a vast collection of them.

"That drone is still up there, we checked. They won't know where Kay is. We'll drive out at 15-minute intervals, you'll be second. We'll both drive a complicated route back to HQ and we'll make sure we're not followed. You head on out to the Grange. We have secure comms."

He handed Nick an earpiece, an encrypted satphone and took out a tablet. He switched the tablet on and swiped until he found what he was looking for. He tilted the tablet so Nick and Kay could see it. For a second, Nick couldn't figure out what he was looking at, then his mind made the necessary adjustments. Felicity had hacked into a satellite feed. He was looking at the rooftop of the building they were in, slightly out of focus, as if from a long-distance lens. "What—"

"Our drone," Joe answered. "From a Keyhole."

Nick bent over the tablet and watched for a minute. The drone above the building was slowly circling. "Shit," he breathed.

"Yeah," Joe answered. Metal and Jacko nodded grimly. That drone was looking for Kay…and it had some kind of weapon that had already killed a man.

"Luckily, you and Kay are about to disappear." Joe held out a remote control. "The keys to the kingdom. Access codes are in the phone." It was access to the Grange, a secure facility ASI was building on the foothills of Mt. Hood.

"Guys. There's a dead man outside," Kay said quietly. "We can't just leave him there."

"How did he die?" Metal asked.

Her shoulders lifted on a sigh. She looked sad and troubled. "I—I don't know. That drone came at us. It sprayed something. Mike pushed my head down, I didn't see it very well. He wouldn't let me look at it directly."

"That might have saved your life," Nick said.

"No. Whatever was in that spray affected only Mike. My life wasn't in danger." She sounded troubled.

"Mike?" Metal asked.

"Mike Hammer. You know him?" Metal and Joe had reacted to the name.

"Yeah," Metal said. "He worked on something with Jack's wife, Summer." Summer Redding had run a famous political blog, Area 8. Now she directed an environmental e-zine. "Good guy. He's the stiff?"

Kay nodded. "The drone came in close and sprayed him with something. An odorless liquid, some kind of solution. The spray caught me, too, but I suffered no effects. There was clearly some kind of agent in the liquid that compromised his breathing catastrophically, but not mine. I could actually hear his lungs filling up with fluid." She turned to Metal. "Can you get word to the medical examiner to test for cytokine levels? And do you think it might be possible to get the results of the autopsy? I have a horrible feeling we're looking at a powerful bioweapon, maybe weaponized Spanish flu. Certainly, whatever killed Mike did it in a minute, a minute and a half. Ricin and anthrax take much longer, so this is something new. We'll know once we unlock the files in that flash drive. I fear that's why Mike was killed, because word leaked to the wrong people that he was working on an article on exactly this. But I still don't understand why I didn't die, too."

Nick's heart took a wild leap in his chest as the image of a dead Kay, lying boneless on the filthy alley asphalt, blossomed in his head. He turned to his guys. "Can we read Bud Morrison into this? He'll be involved in the investigation anyway. Once we call it in."

Captain Bud Morrison was his boss's friend, and a man widely assumed to be in the running for next Chief of Police. Bud wouldn't break the law for them but he might be persuaded to bend it a little if there were national security implications. And bioweaponry definitely qualified as a national security issue.

"Yeah." Jacko checked his watch, spun his index finger in the air. "Ladies," he looked at Kay, "and lady, time to go. Metal and I exit, heading west. Nick, you exit after 15 mikes and head north, Joe will head east. We've all got secure comms. Nick, you have a lot of tactical gear in your vehicle, including a DD. Fucker's using a drone, we'll fuck with *him*." Jacko's eyes slid to Kay. "Sorry."

Her mouth thinned. "Whoever the fucker is who killed Mike deserves to be fucked. I don't know what a DD is, but if it works to bring down a drone, that's great."

Nick held open the passenger door for her. "It's sort of a ray gun, called a DroneDefender. Will bring a drone down within 400 yards." And man, was he glad to have it in the back of the vehicle.

Kay stood in the vee of the open passenger door and looked at Metal, Jacko, and Joe. "I don't know how to thank you guys," she said quietly.

Metal shrugged. "Felicity would have my head—or worse, my balls—if I didn't help you. And as far as these other guys," he indicated Jacko and Joe with a long finger, "we're a team. Where Nick goes, we go."

Joe handed out comms to Metal and Jacko. Nick put his earbud in, tapped it. "Felicity, you online?"

"Yes. And I've got the overhead drone in sight. I'll guide you. Give my love to Kay. We'll be in touch once you guys are at the Grange." Suddenly, Nick could hear a smile in her voice. "Let me know what Kay thinks of it. Watch your back, Nick. I'm holding you directly responsible for Kay's safety."

"You got it," Nick said, glancing at Kay. Scared, but standing straight, ready to face danger. He held her gaze as he added, "Nothing's going to happen to Kay on my watch."

Metal got into his vehicle, Jacko behind the wheel. They were all good drivers, had all taken combat driving courses, but Jacko was in a class of his own. He would be the first out, Felicity guiding him. If there were problems, if they were ambushed, Jacko would take care of it. All their vehicles were armored and had run-flat tires.

Jacko's vehicle headed out, up the ramp and out of sight. Three minutes later, they heard Felicity's voice over the comms. "Drone's still there, guys. High enough to keep an eye on all exits. If they are looking for her, they'll probably expect her to be on foot."

"Roger that," Nick said, and Kay looked at him sharply. She didn't have a comms unit. She wasn't part of the tactical team, Nick and the crew was. Her part would come later, up at the Grange, trying to figure the clusterfuck out. Nick's job was to get her there and keep her safe.

"The drone still there?" she asked softly.

Nick nodded. "Yeah. Buckle up."

They waited in silence until Nick heard Felicity's voice in his ear. "Nick, go. I've sent to your GPS a route out to the Grange that crosses some camera dead zones. Joe will follow you out in fifteen. Let's mess with the drone's head. We'll talk when you and Kay get to the Grange. I'll see how fast I can decrypt that flash drive. Avengers, assemble!"

Nick took the earbud out. If anyone needed to communicate, they could text him. He looked over at Kay, pale and scared but holding herself together. He leaned over to buckle her in, pressed a quick kiss to her mouth and said, "Let's roll."

She nodded.

He drove the SUV up the ramp and out into the bright sunshine. Somewhere above them, a drone was seeking out Kay. Good luck with that, Nick thought. All ASI vehicle windows were coated with a special resin that blocked anyone from seeing inside. What looked like normal windows were as impenetrable as walls.

He stopped for a second at the top of the ramp. Jacko and Metal had gone left. He took a right at the street and headed out.

Five

Oliver Baker studied the tablet resting against the steering wheel of his SUV. The screen was split, the left-hand side showing the aerial view above a city block comprising a hotel, restaurant, a conference center and a department store. The screen on the right-hand side showed a loop of video of the takedown of Jeremy Robsen, aka Mike Hammer.

He'd gotten word that Hammer was expecting intel from inside the CDC that could blow Baker's cash cow apart. That was not going to happen. It was a well-oiled machine that had earned him upwards of fifty million dollars in one year, plus earned his inside guy five million. It was clean and perfect and Baker aimed on using the system for years to come.

No skinny-ass web journalist was going to mess up his life. No way. Baker was going to defend his perfect murder delivery system with everything at his disposal.

There were others who could commit murder on command, but no one who could do so with such little risk, without using a team and without murder even being suspected. Not to mention the fact that the murderer could be miles away. It was perfect, and he wasn't letting it go.

It would take years for someone to put the clues together and by that time, even exhuming the bodies wouldn't prove anything. The virus degraded within 24 hours. All anyone could ever have was a string of unconnected sudden deaths.

Baker could continue for decades, and he had every intention of doing so.

Mike Hammer had to go.

He watched the loop again. The drone's video camera was less than perfect, damn it. He was going to have one of his techs change the camera system. Though, luckily, the virus delivery system worked perfectly.

The drone had hovered high in the air at the end of the alleyway. A camera drone had followed Hammer's taxi from the airport to near Pioneer Square, where Hammer got off and walked for an hour and a half. Hammer clearly had some training, because he'd have shaken off any human tailing him. He went into buildings at the front, exited from the rear and backtracked several times. The drone had no problems, invisible above his head. It simply circled above the buildings until he exited, then continued following him.

Finally, Hammer stopped in a back alley behind a big department store. The drone watched as he leaned over the lock of a door, picking it. He opened it slightly. That was supposed to be his exit route after meeting with the informant.

He had a flight back to Washington DC at 7 p.m., which of course he would never make.

Thank God Baker had gotten word and had been able to obtain Hammer's toothbrush, and have his inside man prepare a small batch of edited and bio-weaponized H1N1 keyed to Hammer's DNA. Splicing in Hammer's DNA to the weaponized virus meant that the virus could only affect Hammer himself and no one else. Of course, with his DNA now part of the virus, it would be lethal to Hammer and any members of his family, but he wasn't meeting with a brother or a sister. He was meeting with an informant.

If Baker had had the fucking informant's identity and his DNA, he'd have killed two birds with one stone. As it was, the informant would think Hammer had had a heart attack. You'd need medical training to understand the difference between a virulent H1N1 filling the lungs with fluid and a sudden heart attack or stroke.

Dead was dead.

Baker leaned over. Now. This was the part he'd watched ten times. He pressed a button and watched it again, in slow motion.

A woman appeared at the end of the alleyway. The drone was right overhead, so all Baker saw was a large-brimmed straw hat and slender legs in turquoise pants. The drone hovered, and as the woman advanced, more of her became visible. Wisps of reddish-gold hair, a spectacular figure, flat heels, trailing a small rolling suitcase. When she was about halfway down the alley, Hammer straightened and watched as she approached.

Baker had been surprised that it was a woman, though maybe he shouldn't have been. Was she a colleague of Priyanka Anand, that bitch? Anand had worked in a lab with ten men and two women. Baker had checked everyone in the lab. Neither of the two women fit. One was close to retirement, almost sixty years old. This woman walked with the spring of someone young and fit. The other woman in Anand's lab weighed 250 lbs. Definitely not this one.

So, no. No one from Anand's lab.

The drone started its approach. It was a quadcopter, so the footage was slightly jerky. Hammer's head suddenly rose, puzzled. The camera caught a perfect shot of his face, long, lined, frowning. It caught that moment when he realized it was a drone. It caught the moment when the viral spray was released. The spray caught the woman, too. Baker could see a high cheekbone, glistening.

Hammer put his hand on the woman's head, turning her away from the camera in the drone.

The rest was so familiar that Baker could count the beats. Hammer coughing, hands at his throat, dropping to his knees, back against the building's wall. The woman's back and hat concealed most of their movements, though Baker knew exactly what was happening.

Hammer was drowning in his own fluids.

It always surprised Baker how fast it went. A minute, two at the most, was enough.

Hammer's heels drummed against the filthy asphalt, frantically, then slowly. Then a hand fell palm up against his thigh and the legs were still.

It was over.

He couldn't tell whether anything was passed between them, but with Hammer's death, the woman would have taken back whatever it was she'd been there to give Hammer. Undoubtedly a flash drive.

She opened the door Hammer had unlocked and disappeared into the building, and was lost.

The drone kept making huge circles around the building, but it was a department store. The woman could change clothes. He had no markers. She could be walking out right now in fact.

The department store was connected via a sky bridge to another building of the complex containing menswear. Baker enlarged the radius of the drone's flight. It made a circuit every half hour instead of every ten minutes, but at least he covered more ground. It still had another six hours' flight time left, so he settled farther in the seat and watched the left-hand side of the screen carefully.

Damn, a sunny day in Portland brought out the hordes. He carefully watched everyone who exited from the hotel and the conference center and the department store. Hundreds. Mainly men exited from the conference center and mainly women exited from the department store. He didn't see anyone exiting that fit the profile he'd made of the woman.

Though…hello. He sat up straight. The drone gave him a view of garage exits. Two of them. One from the underground hotel garage and one from the underground department store garage.

His video program had an algorithm that caught repetitions, and it caught one now. Three identical SUVs, coming out of the department store garage at…Baker checked. Fifteen minute intervals, exactly.

Hmm. The kind of thing the military did when the commanding officer ordered departures at specific intervals. To the second.

He studied the video. The vehicles were exactly the same. Same color, same make, same model. The chances of three identical vehicles emerging at fifteen minute intervals exactly…hmm.

He switched to a piggyback link to a Keyhole 15 satellite that would be overhead for the next couple of hours and set the algos to follow the vehicles.

In the meantime, he ran the plates. All three were out of state, which was useful if you were hiding something. Local cops could only run in-state plates.

But Baker could tap into a national database. It would take a while.

The drone clocked seventy-four vehicles coming out in an hour. Almost two thousand vehicles in a twenty-four-hour period. Baker had a lot of crunching power but this would tax even his systems. He was going to run a plate search on every vehicle exiting the department store for the next six hours. He calculated that it would take something like twenty-four hours to tag each vehicle, run the plates and where possible follow the vehicles to their end destination.

A lot of work. But that was what computers were for and his were the best.

He was in deepest shit if the woman decided to stay in hiding until the department store closed. But that kind of patience was an operator's patience, a sniper's patience. Nothing about the way the woman moved down the alleyway made him think she was an operator. Chances were good she'd leave within the six-hour window.

While his program ran the plate-matching program, his eye was caught by the left-hand side of the screen. The killing, running on a loop. The woman had walked down the alleyway carrying a roller suitcase but he hadn't noticed that she didn't have it when she rushed through the door into the back of the department store.

He froze the video, peered closely. Zoomed in…there! Behind a Dumpster next to the door. It was the same color as the ground, but if he focused, he could see it was a handle. A suitcase handle.

The woman's suitcase had somehow been kicked behind the Dumpster and, in her agitation at Hammer's death, she'd completely forgotten about it.

Inside that suitcase would be details about the woman's life, maybe a document, an ID. That woman had witnessed Mike Hammer's death.

Baker was pretty certain that he had a fail-safe method of killing, but no one had ever been present at the death before. He had no idea how perceptive she might be. If she was a friend of Mike Hammer's, it was likely she was no dummy. And Hammer was meeting her for a reason.

Chillingly, it was also possible she was from the CDC. In that case, Baker needed to find her as quickly as possible.

Who was she? The answer might lie in that suitcase.

Baker was a mile away. Traffic was light at this time; he could make it in about a quarter of an hour. He knew which cameras to avoid and the alleyway had no cameras. In and out, easy. The area held a conference center. A professional-looking man trailing a rolling suitcase behind him would be a normal sight. In half an hour, he could be back at his safe house, going through the contents of the suitcase. Figure out who she was, go to her house and grab some DNA. Have Frank mix up the cocktail.

Spray her secretly. No witnesses. Watch from the drone's eyes as she fell to the floor, choking to death on her own fluids.

He reached out to start the engine when something on the right-hand side of the screen, from the drone video feed, attracted his attention.

Four police vehicles, pulling up outside the narrow cross street that gave off onto Clement Street. There was no audio feed but he was sure they had sirens going. They definitely used their roof lights.

A white van pulled up behind them. The CSU unit.

Damn!

Men and women piled out, walked briskly down the cross street then the alleyway, knowing exactly where to go. Baker watched them start stringing out the police tape, one tech kneeling by the body.

Well, fuck. No question of grabbing that suitcase; it would be found immediately and entered as evidence. Baker was good, but breaking into a police evidence locker was not something in his skill set. Nor should it be. He made his money by being smart. Breaking into a police station was lunacy.

But would they then find out who the woman was and bring her in for questioning? Could they find her for him? Or was she the one who called it in?

Baker waited, watching, directing the drone to fly far overhead in a pattern that kept the alleyway under direct observation. He watched the techs at work, watched as they loaded the body into a body bag and then onto a gurney that was pushed into the medical van.

In the meantime, no slim woman in a turquoise pantsuit emerged from the department store. If she'd changed clothes, he was shit out of luck.

Baker pulled out from his parking spot and headed toward the safe house, where another job awaited him and where he had further resources.

There was a job to do in DC, which he could manage from here.

If nothing happened in the next six hours, he would have to ask one of his tech people in Vladivostok to break into a Keyhole satellite after the drone had to leave and sift through petabytes of data. It would take at least another day to get the data, probably more. He commanded the drone to fly back to his HQ—an abandoned warehouse—when its energy started to run low.

Whatever problem the SUVs represented, what was in the warehouse was the answer. A fixed-wing drone that carried explosives and two machine guns.

Though Baker had never been Special Forces, he prescribed to the old SEAL motto that there were no problems that couldn't be solved by bombing the shit out of them.

Everything had happened so fast. Sneaking out of the hotel room, meeting with Mike, him collapsing to the ground, dead, the drone, Nick and his buddies to the rescue...

She hadn't had time to process everything in her head.

When Nick drove the powerful vehicle up the ramp and out into the street, she could feel the pull of the engine like something powering up in her life, pulling her into a new train of events like a raging tide. She thought she'd be giving info to a crusading journalist who would change things, change her life, take her away from the world and plunge her into danger and isolation.

Well, her life was changing, but in an entirely different way. She thought she'd have to step into a new life alone, shedding everyone. But no.

One thing was very clear—she wasn't facing this on her own. Nick had raced to her side and was staying there. And with Nick came the resources of a powerful company of powerful men and women.

She wasn't alone.

Kay stared blindly out the window at the streets of Portland rushing by. Such a pretty city. She'd never had time to explore much of it the times she'd come to visit Felicity and Metal. Last night, knowing she had an appointment the next day with Mike Hammer, it had occurred to her that she might never see the city again. It had been entirely possible that she'd have to go into hiding forever. Either in the country or in some small, isolated community, keeping her head down for the rest of her life, or somewhere abroad.

But here she was, in Portland, and not running away, not in the truest sense of the word.

Her head disconnected and Kay simply watched the streets go by, unable to think, only to see. She saw modern buildings, a few mid-20th century buildings, small parks dotted throughout the city. Portlanders out and about, enjoying the cool, sunny day. An elderly couple sitting on a park bench, faces lifted into the sun, holding hands. A skinny girl with blond dreads, being pulled on a skateboard by an enthusiastic mixed-breed dog, tongue lolling as it ran along the sidewalk. A small café, patrons sitting at tables outside, small vases of daisies on each tabletop. A pretty girl reaching across a table to cup her hands around the head of a handsome boy and kiss him. A middle-aged couple looking on, smiling.

Kay was running away from all of this, but not forever. She and Nick were regrouping, and they'd be back.

No sounds came from the outside world, not even the sound of the vehicle's engine. It was as if they were in a spaceship, shooting through time and space, alone in the universe. The windows could have been monitors.

She turned her head to watch Nick. He drove like he did most things—well and intensely. For a second she flashed on how well and intensely he'd driven *her* last night. The sure feel of his hands on her, his mouth devouring hers, his penis inside her, thrusting like a piston. Heat bloomed in her core, a line of heat from her sex to her heart. The first time she'd felt like a human being, like a woman, since she'd gotten out of bed this morning.

It was no time to be thinking of their night in bed together, but her body overwhelmed her. In some deep animal part of her, she realized that by some miracle, she wasn't dead. Right now, she could be dead meat on the pavement of an alley, lost to life.

But she wasn't. She was alive and would stay that way. Nick's grim face was testament to the fact that he was going to use every resource at his disposal to help her.

She was going to live, in the open, as a free woman. They were going to beat this. Together. Her life had been handed back to her, richer than it had been before.

She owed him so much, and she'd been such a coward, running away from him this morning. He deserved an explanation.

"Nick," she began, "I want you to know that—"

"Not now, Kay." He turned his head slightly to look at her, then turned back to the road. He was driving in hypervigilant mode, eyes on the road, flickering constantly

to the internal and external rearview mirrors in regular rotations, occasionally checking the GPS monitor. They were not driving in a straight line. He would go for about five blocks, then double back for a block or two. "We'll have plenty of time to talk when we get to the Grange."

The Grange. Felicity had mentioned this complex they were building in the wilderness. It was a business, a large server farm. Server farms had to be kept close to freezing. God, she hoped there were living quarters, and that they were heated. A shudder ran through her, the cold of delayed shock.

"Reach behind you," Nick said, eyes straight ahead. "There is usually a blanket on the back seat."

There was. Clean, thick and warm. She wrapped herself in it and felt immediately better. "Thanks. All of a sudden I felt cold." She glanced outside the window at the bright sunshine. "Don't know why."

"Adrenaline dump. Shock. You saw a man killed. Be enough to make anyone shocky."

Her seat was warming up, another layer of heat that she welcomed. Suddenly the back reclined and she glanced at Nick.

"I'm taking a long, roundabout route to make sure we're not being followed. You must be exhausted. You didn't sleep much last night and you had these shocks this morning. See if you can nap. It would do you good."

He was treating her like she'd been in an accident and in a way, he wasn't far off. But it felt wrong somehow to rest and sleep when he was vigilant. Plus, well…he hadn't slept much last night either.

A blast of heat that had nothing to do with the vehicle shot through her at the memory. Sleep had been impossible with Nick in her bed, in her.

"I'm not really sleepy," she protested, then gave a huge yawn.

"Uh huh." Nick's face was utterly expressionless. "Just close your eyes, even if you can't sleep. You'll be under a lot of pressure once we're at the Grange, and it won't be anything I can help you with. So, rest while you can."

"Not sleepy," she protested, but she closed her eyes anyway.

And fell into a sleep so deep, it could have been a coma.

Six

Georgetown
Washington, DC

Senator Catherine De Haven, member of the Senate Armed Services Committee, sat at her desk in her townhouse in Georgetown, mulling over the previous day's events. A long, long day that had tried everyone's patience, a day in which she'd had to change her blouse twice. It had been like swimming in shark-infested waters but in the end, the biggest shark of all had been bloodied.

A goodly chunk of taxpayer money was supposed to have flowed into the hands of a powerful but unethical, perhaps even criminal, man. Those contracts were no more. She'd planned her revenge for years and now she had it. And it felt good, very good.

The hearing was supposed to be a lovefest between the chairman and Stanley Offutt, CEO of Blackvale, a controversial security company. Besides the multimillion-dollar contracts for physical infrastructure, Blackvale was supposed to be given a contract for intelligence gathering worth billions.

Instead, there had been a parade of witnesses testifying to cost overruns, to unpaid debts, to gross ineptitude. All of it orchestrated by Catherine. Yesterday had been day one. By the time the three-day parade of witnesses was over, Stanley Offutt's reputation would be in tatters and no one would dream of offering him government security contract work ever again.

Catherine couldn't wait for Monday and Wednesday, day two and day three. She'd enjoy every single second of a process that wiped Stanley Offutt out.

So. Several billion dollars' worth of Blackvale contracts, gone.

There *was* justice in the world, and Stanley Offutt was on his way to being a destroyed man, just as he had destroyed her husband, Nathan De Haven. Nathan had unofficially gone into business with Offutt ten years before and had lost everything. Nothing could convince Catherine that Nathan's car plunging down a cliff side had been an accident, and not him taking his despair and bankruptcy off a cliff.

It had taken her ten years of hard work to salvage the company while retaining her Senate seat. Ten years of waiting for an opportunity to destroy the man who had destroyed her family.

Payback is a bitch, she thought, and smiled.

It wasn't supposed to be that way, she knew full well. No, when scheduled, the committee was supposed to reach a definitive finding whereby Stanley Offutt would leave the premises several billion dollars richer via a number of no-bid contracts. The chairman of the committee had gone to Annapolis with Offutt and was the type of politician who had never met a cost overrun by a corrupt contractor he didn't like. Catherine would bet her children's trust funds that some of that vast lake of money would stream right into the chairman's Panamanian bank account.

She could just picture the two of them on Offutt's superyacht, the 200-foot *Bellariva*, basking in the sun in the Caribbean, laughing at the poor suckers who weren't as smart as they were.

Think again, boys.

Catherine had only been one of the members of the subcommittee, but she'd walked in with a briefcase full of documents, which she'd handed out and carefully explained. They'd listened to the first couple of witnesses she'd called. The chairman was unmovable, of course. A vote against Offutt was a vote against another six figures in his account.

But the other members...they'd listened. Oh yes. They'd listened and taken notes and had undoubtedly had their staffs make inquiries. Monday they would come back, more aggressive and more quietly angry.

Each day was supposed to end with Offutt entertaining them with whiskey and strippers. Instead, the first day had seen three veterans testifying to the damage caused by Offutt's company, Blackvale. The corporal who'd sustained third-degree burns over forty percent of her body because the water heating system Blackvale installed didn't have a regulator. The private who'd lost both legs to a faulty steering system in a truck. The very nervous accountant who gave a list of materials that had undergone a thousand percent markup.

On and on. She had tons of this stuff.

Catherine had spent years accumulating the evidence while Stanley Offutt grew rich. She'd bided her time and worked hard to get on to the committee.

Offutt had smiled and nodded when he saw her yesterday morning. The fool.

After all, it had been years since they'd last seen each other at Nathan's funeral. He'd even—the bastard—offered her a loan because he knew she'd been left in "straitened circumstances", as he'd so gently put it.

She'd refused and thanked him for coming while vowing in her heart that however long it took, she'd get even.

In the end, it took ten years, but it was worth every second of time she'd spent, every sleepless night, every tear she'd shed for Nathan.

Watching the chairman's jaw drop, watching Offutt sweat, watching the tide of opinion in the august wood-paneled room turn against him... it was as the ad said—priceless.

The chairman was as wily and slimy as they came, and it was possible that he would adjourn "for further consideration" but as long as she was alive, Stanley Offutt would never get another penny from the US government. She had more information in her computer and her aides were following an anonymous tip that Blackvale had been involved in a sex trafficking operation in 2016.

Catherine had plenty of ammo left.

As a matter of fact, why stop with government contracts?

Catherine sipped her tea, blinking. Why indeed? She put her cup down, staring at the photos on her desk. She and Nathan grinning into the camera on their first trip together as a couple, in Hawaii all those years ago. Their wedding day, madly smiling, crazy in love, so happy it had been a thing of weight and heft in their midst that day. Happiness so intense you could almost feel it.

Aaron and Emma, blinking against the sun on a family hiking trip, grinning because Nathan had forgotten to take the lens cap off for the first pictures. Catherine had reached over and gently removed it and they had all laughed their heads off, Nathan more than anyone. It was the year Nathan died, and it would be two years before she and the kids could laugh again.

Stanley had done that. He had taken Nathan out of their lives with his greed and corruption.

She'd schemed and worked to cut off government contracts, but Stanley had connections everywhere.

Why should he prosper? Why should he be allowed to live like the Sun King while Nathan's bleached bones lay in the cold ground?

Her heart cried for revenge.

Oh God, yes. Catherine had ruined government for Offutt, but maybe she could do more than that. One dossier, the one where four Blackvale employees were accused of sex trafficking, was ready to go. *The Washington Post* had a section dedicated to anonymous whistleblowers. She could send the dossier to them. To The Intercept. To WikiLeaks. Send it wide. He would go to jail. She would sit front row center every single fucking day of his trial. And when he was sentenced to a long jail term, she would—

What was that annoying sound? She frowned, cocking her head. A faint buzzing, like a faraway insect, only a big faraway insect. Coming from the window.

Catherine got up and pushed away the curtains fluttering in the warm breeze. The old-fashioned window was open to the wind, something she loved in warm weather. So unlike the sealed-tight windows with constant recycled air she worked in all day.

The sound was louder and it took her a couple of seconds to trace it to a big insect floating in front of the window about two feet above her head. She was about to pull back when something strange about the insect caught her notice. It didn't move, was stock still in the air, and it had a funny shape. Like a wasp, only not a wasp. Bigger. A central body with eight...legs. Not legs, really.

What *was* it?

With a shocking suddenness, the...thing dropped until it was right in front of her face. She recoiled, stepped back, but the thing followed her, so close to her face she had trouble focusing her eyes.

Suddenly, her face was wet. Something wet had come out of nowhere.

Had the thing *spat* at her? How could that even be possible? Ewww.

Disgusted, Catherine walked to her desk for a handkerchief. She sniffed. Whatever was on her face didn't have an odor. She touched it. Drops. Drops of something on her face.

Ack.

She went to grab a Kleenex to wipe herself with but grabbed the edge of her desk instead. Her knees couldn't hold her up. She fell into her chair more than sat in it, opening her mouth to call her assistant.

No breath. No breath to call, no breath to pull into her lungs. No breath at all. She brought a hand to her throat, not understanding what was happening to her. It wasn't a heart attack. Nothing hurt in her chest, it wasn't a stroke, she didn't feel anything in her brain.

But she couldn't breathe. Her chest expanded but no air came in, it was like being choked but there was no one there to choke her.

Every muscle in her body trembled, spasmed. She fell out of her chair, sprawling on the carpet, putting a palm on the floor to push herself back up, but nothing happened. Her chest was burning as she tried to draw in air and failed. Heat and pain seared her chest up to her throat as she gasped for air that wouldn't come.

Spots appeared before her eyes, growing larger and larger, the chair, the desk disappearing from view into the blackness.

One last futile kick of her legs, and she was gone.

The insect-like thing buzzed into her study, dropped down and hovered in front of her bright red frozen face, waiting for further instructions.

Portland, Oregon

Back in the warehouse serving as HQ, Baker froze the video on the senator's old face, mottled hand clutching her throat. Her brown eyes were still, her body limp in the unmistakable stillness of death.

"*I want her deader'n shit*," is how Offutt had described the service.

Baker picked up his encrypted satphone and called.

"Yes." How glad Baker was that this was the last time he would have to hear Offutt's nasal voice.

"It's done," Baker said.

"How do I know it's done?" Offutt whined. "I haven't heard anything in the media."

Because she died minutes ago, you dipshit, Baker wanted to say but didn't. The hit had been an absolute scramble to get some DNA, get it down to Atlanta and have it spliced to the engineered virus. It had been so fast there had been the risk of violating opsec. Baker had made Offutt pay through the nose.

Instead of answering, he sent four stills to Offutt's secure phone. From the spray to when she fell to the floor.

"For all I know this could be staged. How do I know she's *dead?*"

Again Baker didn't answer, but switched on the video feed and patched it through to Offutt. Minute after minute went by in silence, the time elapse scrolling by on the bottom of the screen. In case Offutt might think the time elapse was fake, De Haven had been kind enough to keep a big desk clock in the line of sight of the video camera. The clock showed five full minutes elapsing while her chest didn't move and her open eyes didn't blink.

Most people blinked 20 times a minute. Five minutes without blinking was almost beyond human capability.

"She's dead," Offutt finally said. "Good."

"Yes." Baker always said as little as possible over the phone. In his head, this conversation was already over.

"In a way that will not raise suspicion."

"A natural death. Yes." The red would fade soon. She would look like any heart attack victim or stroke victim when a member of her staff found her. The longer she lay undetected, the better.

"Check your account," Offutt said.

Seven and a half million had already been deposited in an account Baker had in Panama. He checked now. Another seven and a half million had just been deposited. It had been made very clear to Offutt that De Haven would die an untraceable death that would come for Offutt without fail if he didn't make that second deposit.

Baker hadn't thought Offutt would try to cheat him out of the second payment. First, he'd be looking over his shoulder the rest of his life, as well he should. Baker's drones could reach him anywhere, anytime. And second, seven and a half million dollars was, after all, a drop in the ocean for Offutt. The running costs for his yacht for a year.

"Got it," Baker said and disconnected.

He switched back to the video feed of the police swarming over the site here in Portland, having already forgotten Offutt.

The CSU was wrapping it up. The handle was gone—they'd recovered the suitcase. They could study that crime scene site until the galaxy died and they would never be able to pin it on him.

Time to find the woman.

Seven

Mount Hood

A gentle hand shook her shoulder. "Honey, wake up."

Startled, Kay bolted up, heart pounding. *Danger!* Danger all around her! Someone had died, Mike had died…

"Whoa." That big hand curled around the back of her head, cupped her neck, shook it lightly. "It's okay. You're safe now. We're here."

Kay looked over at Nick, ashamed of her reaction. Her heart had nearly burst out of her chest but now it was slowing down. "Sorry," she whispered.

Nick released his seat belt and hers and bent over to kiss her cheek. His beard already had a little bite to it. It felt good, grounding. She remembered how smooth his cheeks had been against the sensitive skin of her inner thighs. There hadn't been any whisker bite then, oh no. Just smooth skin and smooth tongue…she'd been laid out on the bed like a human sacrifice, only lashed by pleasure not pain. Writhing, holding tightly to his head between her thighs as the one solid point of stability in a hot, restless sea.

Heat filled her down to her fingertips and toes and it felt so good. It washed away the cramped chill of fear and anguish.

"Nothing to be sorry about," he answered, moving away from her, big hands hanging over the top of the wheel. He was giving her time to come back into herself. "You needed the rest. I'm glad you had some."

Spears of lambent light shot through a thick copse of pine trees, the kind of light only late afternoon could provide. "Where are we? Have we been driving all day?"

If it was late afternoon, they'd been driving for at least five or six hours. One could cover a lot of ground in that time. They could arguably be in Idaho or California or Washington. She'd thought they were going to Mount Hood, but clearly, she'd been wrong.

"On Mount Hood," Nick said, and exited the vehicle.

Mount Hood? They'd driven hours to get to Mount Hood?

He was at her door, big hands up to help her down. Ordinarily Kay didn't like or need help getting in and out of vehicles, but her muscles were stiff and unwieldly, as if she'd been hurt. Looking down, the ground seemed a long way away, like through the wrong end of the telescope. She leaned forward and Nick lifted her down with no effort at all.

It was embarrassing to feel so weak. She was a strong and healthy woman. She practiced yoga, ran over lunch hours and hiked on weekends. She barely recognized her own body. Her skin felt like a stiff hazmat suit she'd had to don. "How'd it take us hours to get here? Mount Hood is about an hour from Portland, isn't it?"

Nick gave a half smile. "We took, um, the scenic route. One guaranteed to ensure that no one was following us. So, welcome to the Grange. Where we'll be spending the next while until we figure out what's going on." He swept his arm as if presenting the castle of a fairy tale kingdom.

Hmmm. Pretty shabby as castles went. A tiny, dilapidated shack with moldy wooden siding that had turned gray with age, fronted by a rickety porch that sat forlornly on a concrete foundation that had cracks in it. There wasn't a lawn or a garden, just this gravel apron where Nick had parked.

The idea of spending "the next while" here was daunting. Still, she was grateful for the shelter and for the thought. And for Nick standing by her side, not so tall but so very broad and so very reassuring.

They'd get through this. They'd camp out here and as soon as Felicity decrypted the flash drive, she'd go to work and figure the whole thing out. Nick had gotten her to safety and she'd take it from here. In that rundown shack. She shivered and hoped there was heat in the shack. Maybe a wood-fired stove? God knew there were enough trees around for kindling.

She pulled in a deep, pine-scented breath. The air was cool and super clean and smelled of trees for miles and miles, with no pollutants at all. It was pleasant and bracing, clearing her head. It wouldn't be so bad. The shack looked desolate and uncomfortable, but they'd manage.

She smiled at Nick, who was watching her closely.

"Well, what do you think?" he asked. "This was Midnight's place that he bought when he first arrived in Portland. A little hideaway."

"Midnight", she knew, was John Huntington, one of the owners of ASI, and Nick's new boss. She knew Nick really liked both his bosses, John, and Douglas Kowalski.

But…John had had a couple of years to fix the shack up. Why hadn't he? Their headquarters, which she'd visited once on a quick trip to Portland, were spectacular. Cool and elegant and very high tech. The exact opposite of this ramshackle hut. Maybe he'd been too busy building one of the biggest security companies in the country to restructure here.

"It looks, um, cozy," she said. About the only thing she could say that wouldn't sound whiny.

There was something wrong, and she couldn't figure it out. Something about changing beds. Hopefully, there'd be sheets and blankets. Why was she thinking this? Because she'd had a flash where two thoughts bounced together. Nick. And bed. And…

Her eyes rounded and she brought her hand to her mouth. "Oh my gosh, Nick!"

He lifted a black eyebrow.

"My wheelie! I took it with me when I left the hotel!"

He rolled his eyes and looked pained. "Tell me about it. When I saw you'd packed your bag and took it with you, I nearly had a heart attack."

"I left it there! Where Mike died!" She closed her eyes a second, spinning the movie in her head backward. She'd had it in the alleyway. The wheels had made a little grinding noise. But she hadn't had it in the department store, certainly not when she'd made her way down the stairs to the garage level. Absolutely certain of that. "They'll find my suitcase with a dead body! I mean I don't think I have a document in it, but I definitely have a conference folder and—"

"Stop right there." Nick shook his head. "You did, honey. You did leave your suitcase. The police have it, and they know it's yours."

She staggered. The blood left her head suddenly, plummeting downward. Her suitcase in the hands of the police! Was she running now from the *law?* Her knees trembled.

Nick flashed out a hand, steadied her.

"Easy now. Yes, they have your suitcase, yes they know it's yours, no it's not a problem. I talked to a good friend, Captain Bud Morrison of the Portland PD. They know everything."

Kay couldn't move, could barely breathe. She was shaken to her core. "They know it's mine. Then they know I was there. They must be looking for me."

A cold expression crossed Nick's tough face. "They'd like to talk to you, that's true. But I am not letting you go where you are expected. I told them you were targeted and that you'll be in for interrogation when the danger is over. Bud said that if Felicity can establish a secure link, he'd like to talk via Skype. Felicity refrained from mentioning that there's a secure link already. She can hold him off for a while."

"I don't know—"

"Exactly. We don't know anything and we don't know who was after Mike. It will take as long as we want for a secure link to be established. Let's not think about that now."

Kay nodded slowly. Nick had bought her time, time to process what had happened and what she'd seen. Time to study Priyanka's files. "I'm going to want to see the autopsy results."

"That can happen." He nodded. "Either legally or illegally, if you need those results, you'll get them."

"Okay. I'll do my part. When I do go in to talk to the police, I hope to have some data other than me watching him being sprayed and then watching him die." She shuddered.

"Come on, then. Let's get settled in." He slanted a look at her, put one hand around her arm, walked forward up the porch. The front porch steps creaked, Kay noted with alarm. Nick was a heavy guy. It was all lean muscle but he was dense. Each step made the porch shiver.

Kay glanced down, hoping to catch the wood cracking in time so they could hop out of the way before they plunged through the porch to the ground. Watching her feet, she missed what Nick did. It wasn't as easy as putting a key in the lock—though why anyone would lock the door to this place was beyond her. He'd used something she hadn't quite seen, like maybe a remote control? At any rate, he was slipping something long and slender in his pocket when the door clicked and opened. Very smoothly.

Huh.

They walked into the one-room shack, Kay a little warily. The place smelled of abandonment, and where there was abandonment there could be rats, or worse. Spiders. She hated spiders.

Nick stopped her by simply tightening his hold on her arm. Okay. She stood still, taking in the sad shack. A hot plate on a counter where there was also a sink, which meant there must be some form of electricity, probably an outdoor generator. A single light bulb hanging from a wire in the middle of the ceiling. Two sagging armchairs, a rickety table with four mismatched wooden chairs, which looked like they'd barely support *her* weight, let alone Nick's.

Oh, and a steel frame cot in a corner with a bare mattress that looked stained.

The flooring was splintered hardwood, except for just inside the entrance. They were standing on a steel plate.

The whole place reeked of mold and looked so desolate it hurt the heart.

She could do this. She could. So what if the place gave her the creeps? It sure beat being dead.

Nick was still holding her arm. Well, she'd seen what was here. Not much. So—what were they waiting for?

He pulled something out of his jacket pocket. A weird-looking pair of goggles. He handed them over. "Put them on," he said quietly.

She did—and recoiled. "Whoa."

The entire shack was crisscrossed with laser beams, invisible to the eye and visible only through the goggles, which must have been IR-enabled. The beams covered almost the entire area, from the floor up to a height of about six feet.

Suddenly, she realized what she was looking at. A very effective security measure. No one could enter without triggering the beams. An interruption in the light would doubtless be signaled to some control area.

Kay lifted her foot and put it back down. That steel plate felt very solid.

"This is a trigger plate, am I right?"

"Bingo. Give the lady a brass ring." Nick slanted a glance at her, one corner of his mouth lifted in a half smile.

"So I guess this place isn't quite as desolate as it looks?"

"Hmm. Yeah." Nick reached to the side and pressed something and the laser lights blinked out. "There are a few surprises."

Kay handed him back the goggles and they walked across the shabby, dusty floorboards to the opposite wall, where an unpainted wooden door led to another room.

Or so she thought.

When Nick opened the door, there was a stainless-steel panel behind it. A beeping sound came from his jacket pocket and the panel slid open to reveal a space the size of a small bathroom. They walked in, the panel slid shut and the ground fell beneath her feet.

An elevator.

They fell fast, but came to a surprisingly gentle halt. Kay estimated that they had fallen perhaps four or five stories. The panel slid back open and she walked out into…wow.

Nick dropped his arm as Kay turned in a full circle, trying to take everything in. It was one of the most amazing spaces she'd ever seen.

She met Nick's amused eyes. He winked at her. "Like the Time Lord says, it's bigger on the inside than on the outside."

"A Mount Hood Tardis." Kay smiled. "I see Felicity's rubbing off on you."

He gave a mock frown. "I liked Dr. Who before I met Felicity. I just wasn't a nerd about it the way she is. So—what do you think about the Grange?"

"It's—it's amazing."

And it was. They were in a huge open-air plaza with circular balconies connected by four transparent external elevators. The ground floor—the floor they were on—was paved with slabs of limestone, interspersed with rectangles of earth filled with thriving plants. Kay had no idea how it worked because outside it had seemed that the shack was surrounded by dense forest, but down here, there was a huge circular space seemingly open to the sky, flooding the space with light. Looking closely, she could faintly see a covering over the open area. Nothing material, more like a shimmer.

The materials were rustic-chic, in earth-tone colors. Limestone, wood, brass. Plexiglas benches everywhere giving a feeling of lightness. Across the plaza, she could see other areas clearly designated as areas for social groupings, work spaces, eating spaces. They were under the ring of balconies but somehow the place was very well lit.

"Suzanne designed the look of the place. She said she refused to have a bolt hole that technically was designed to help us survive a nuclear holocaust and have it be ugly."

"Quite right." Kay nodded. Suzanne Huntington's ability to infuse beauty into everything she touched was amazing. "If you're going to survive, you should survive in style."

"What she said, more or less. This is also a server farm. ASI has opened a new business, keeping corporate data secure for companies. We can barely keep up with demand. I think it represents about a quarter of our revenue now."

She smiled. Nick talked easily of "our" company, after working only a short time there. It was something she'd noted in the others, that they identified with their company. John and Douglas were excellent employers who treated everyone who worked at the company as a partner. Everyone who worked there was very well paid, very well treated and very well respected. Everyone who worked there loved it.

Her heart gave a hard, painful pulse in her chest, breaking a little. She'd loved her job, too. Going to work at the CDC every morning, she'd felt a burst of energy and, yes, even love. Everyone there was a good guy. A white hat. Everyone there had one goal—to stop disease. To heal, to cure. To make life better. To help mankind break the terrible chains that had held it in its iron grip since the dawn of time. People crippled, blinded, brought low by devastating pain, children dying young before their potential could be realized—all of these things the researchers at the CDC fought against with every ounce of energy in their bodies.

Like the FBI and CIA fought terrorists, the CDC fought disease. With no quarter and no rest. They fought the good fight.

Or so she'd thought.

Such pride she'd felt, entering the building, making the world a better place, striking a blow against evil, every single day. It hadn't even occurred to her that evil might be right there.

She missed her job, missed it fiercely, wondered if she'd ever be able to go back. Probably not.

Nick was watching her with a frown. For such a tough guy, a guy's guy, he was disconcertingly sensitive to moods. Damn him. "Is something wrong?" he asked. "You look—"

"Tired," she replied quickly. Her sorrow at losing a big chunk of herself and of her reason for living wasn't really helpful right now. Pointless burdening Nick with it. She said something that would make sense to him. "Tired and hungry."

Nick was Italian. Italians hated the thought of someone going hungry.

"Oh yeah." His face smoothed out. *There we go.* He had something concrete he could do for her. "Wait till you see the food stocks. Let's get you settled and you can take a shower while I prepare lunch." He checked his watch. "Early dinner."

"I like that division of labor," Kay replied. "Food stocks? Are you guys preparing for the zombie apocalypse up here?"

They were crossing that big open-air plaza. The air smelled glorious, as it had on the gravel apron outside the deceptively forlorn shack. Outside it had smelled of pine, but in here it smelled of exotic flowers and plants. Looking up again, she could barely see whatever it was that covered the roof. Whatever it was, it let in sunshine and fresh air but wasn't cold. It was definitely warm inside.

Nick guided her around various plantings on a zigzagging route across the plaza. He kept a hand on her at all times and it felt wonderful. He kept her close enough so that his broad shoulders brushed hers as they walked and it almost felt like a transfer of strength and energy with each touch.

He looked up at the strange sky then over at her. "I personally believe the zombie apocalypse is coming, though sadly I seem to be alone in that. But a lot of us feel that if things ever go south, they'll go south fast, and it'll take time for things to get back to normal. Maybe even a generation. The place is organized to shelter at least two hundred people for a long time. It is almost completely self-sufficient in terms of energy and there are plans for growing food. Right now, it's a useful profit center with the server farm and it's a place where we can all celebrate holidays together. And at the moment," he said, with a sweep of his arm, "it's your new home."

Her new home.

They were in an area that was meant to be communal. Various beautiful sofa and armchair groupings, cozy and inviting. A huge sofa in front of a massive horizontal gas fireplace at least fifty feet long. A billiard table, a grand piano, a bank of foosball tables. Against one wall, a 100-inch plasma curved TV that looked almost large enough for a commercial movie theater.

They might have to stay a generation but they wouldn't be bored. If Felicity was in any way involved, there'd be ebooks, streaming movies, TV series and, above all, video games on tap, and as much music as anyone could want.

To the right was a huge kitchen and a long table that could sit the entire staff of ASI. Or the court of Henry VIII. But smaller tables were scattered around and the kitchen had a cozy breakfast nook.

They entered a long, wide corridor with pretty wrought metal sconces and plants in huge enameled pots. Even here, in the bowels of the earth, the air smelled fresh and clean.

Halfway down the corridor, Nick stopped and placed his palm against the wall to the side of a door. "My room," he said. There was a metallic click and he pushed the door open for her, gesturing with his hand. *Go on in.*

Kay walked through a corridor and into a large living room area. She turned around, taking it all in. This space, too, was beautiful. Flagstone tiles, a dusky eggplant-colored couch with light gray armchairs, a fully equipped kitchenette, framed black-and-white photographs along the way. The impression was of comfort and elegance.

"Wow." She turned back to Nick with one eyebrow raised. "I didn't know you had a hidden talent for interior decorating."

He lifted his hands. "Hey, I'm not responsible for the décor. My apartment in Portland was decorated in one very painful afternoon at Ikea and looks it. This is all Suzanne's doing. Don't ask me how but she decorated every single person's room in a different way and we're all delighted with what we got. I couldn't have done this in a million years."

She smiled. She didn't know Suzanne Huntington well, but what she knew of her she liked. A lot. One of the country's top decorators, she was totally unpretentious and down to earth, with a wild sense of humor. Word had it that she had her husband—a true badass tough guy, a former SEAL like Nick—totally wrapped around her little finger.

Nick's cell pinged. "Yeah," he answered. "She's right here." He held the phone out to her, switching to speakerphone. "It's Felicity."

Kay snatched the cell. The video function was on and she stared at her friend's face, tears coming to her eyes. "Felicity! Oh, it's so good to see you!"

Felicity looked tired. "Hey, Kay." Felicity ran a finger down her screen as if touching Kay's face. "I wish these were better circumstances."

A deadly bio-weapon in play. Her best friend, dead. Priyanka's colleague, dead. Mike Hammer, dead. "Yeah. I think some very bad things are happening, Felicity. I hate to say it, but I'm really scared."

"You're right to be scared, girlfriend, just not right now. Right this minute, you're super secure at the Grange, or the Batcave, as the girls call it. And you have Nick. He's not going to let anything happen to you."

Nick gave out a low guttural sound.

"Was that a *growl*, Nick?" Felicity's tinny voice asked from the speaker. "Being in the Batcave doesn't mean you get to revert to a primitive state."

Kay sat down, the cell cradled in her hand. "Did you get the flash drive?" she asked.

Felicity bit her lips and looked worried, which blew Kay's mind. Felicity never looked worried. She was always serenely confident in her own abilities, and rightly so.

"Yeah, Metal got it to me right away, and I've been working on it ever since. It's got some serious encryption, Kay. And a couple of traps. I'm making my way through the firewalls slowly, so I don't accidentally trigger data destruction. Someone who knows what they're doing encrypted this."

Kay nodded.

"By the way, if you come across a password-based hurdle, try 'naanisbetterthanwonderbread'. All lower case. It was our password for our secret email system."

Felicity smiled. "Will do, great password. So…" She disappeared from the small screen for a second. She lived in her wheeled ergonomic chair, zipping from screen to screen. Her pretty face popped back up. "I'm back. My systems tell me it will be another four hours. I'll send you the files as soon as they're decrypted."

"I hate to ask, honey, but are the communications systems here secure?"

Felicity cocked her head. "I really like you, Kay, and I know your head's on the line here, so I'll forgive you. Yes, everything is very secure there. As a matter of fact, security there is a 10-million-dollar business at the moment. Growing as we speak."

That's right, she'd forgotten. This place was not just a coolly elegant zombie apocalypse bug-out place, it was a cyber security business. God only knew how many Fortune 500 companies had their files backed up here. Probably billions of dollars' worth of info. So yeah, it should be secure.

"I'll contact you the second the files are available. Rest a little bit, though, because the data files are enormous and you have a lot of work to do. And none of us can help you, since no one here has a PhD in biochemistry or virology or genetics. You'll have your hands full."

Kay nodded. "I think I'll know what to look for. But you're right. I'll rest. What—what happened to the drone?"

Felicity blinked. "Pass that over to the master. Metal?"

A jumble of images, and then Metal's solid Irish face showed on the small screen. "Let's go to the big screen," he said, and the cell connection closed.

Nick helped her out of the armchair and they walked over to a work desk set up with a huge screen. Nick touched the top corners of the screen and two other screens popped out laterally, making for one continuous two-foot screen. He switched the system on and Metal's face appeared, so clear she forgot for a second he was miles away. Felicity's face appeared in a small square screen on the lower right-hand side. The screen was so wide she could see the great room at ASI behind them. One of the most impressive tech offices she'd ever seen. There too, elegance was married to efficiency.

Her own face was in a little square on the lower left-hand side. Nick appeared behind her, one big hand on her shoulder.

"Kay. Nick." Metal nodded at them. It felt so much like he was in the room.

"Where's the drone?" Nick asked.

"Disappeared an hour ago." Metal's mouth tightened. "Dipped under a covered passageway and must have had a pre-mapped route of covered exits. Or maybe went to ground. We don't know. We were going to take it down just after nightfall, in about half an hour. Jacko was going to go up on a rooftop in stealth clothing and aim a DroneDefender. He wouldn't have shown up on FLIR."

"God, it could have fallen on someone's head," Kay said, alarmed.

"No, Jacko would have made sure it was right over Conrad's rooftop and he'd have been able to see if anyone was there. But now that's not gonna happen."

Kay shuddered. She remembered all too well the mechanical creature swooping down with a faint buzzing sound, Mike collapsing to the ground, the insectoid camera lenses. She shook her head. "The drone might have photos of me. I can't guarantee that it doesn't. Mike tried to shield my face but it all happened so fast…" She stopped and bit her lips.

Nick's hand tightened on her shoulder and she looked up at him in gratitude.

"The drone would have been sending intel constantly." Felicity frowned. "We'll look at the drone if we ever catch it, but any photos would have been sent at the time."

"Do drones have IDs?" Kay knew next to nothing about the things. They had never caught her attention except for the large ones that sent missiles into deserts and small ones that took amazing landscape photos. "If we had caught it could we have figured out who sent the drone by looking at its innards? Like that Roman priest…"

For a second, she flashed on a book of Roman history she'd read as a child. It had been lavishly illustrated. One of the illustrations had been of a group of men in togas carefully watching one man pulling out the entrails of a sheep. The divination centered on the lobes of the liver. She'd been creeped out by liver ever since. What was the name of the guy who'd carried out the divination? Something beginning with an "h"...

"Like a haruspex," Felicity said with a slight smile. "No liver in the drone and I suspect any identifying marks would have been eliminated." She looked around. "What?"

"We're all really impressed that you knew the word," Kay answered. Metal, Jacko and the other boss, Douglas, were all looking at her.

Felicity sighed and rolled her eyes. "I guess no one here has played *The Ancient Gods Return*. Listen, Kay. You get some rest and I promise to send the files as soon as they're ready. I think Metal's got something to say."

Metal's sober face took center screen. "Mike Hammer's body was autopsied. Bud said the autopsy results could not be disseminated but that he knew Felicity would just hack the coroner's office and leave no trace, so he gave us the results anyway. He said that Hammer died of suffocation."

Poor Mike. Kay still had the wheezing sounds he made as he'd tried to drag oxygen into his lungs in her ears. "His lungs were filled with fluid," she said.

Metal nodded. "Yeah."

"And the cytokine levels?"

"Through the roof, the coroner said. By the way, they don't usually test for cytokine levels. The coroner wants to know how we knew to ask for it."

"A hunch. But it doesn't mean anything good. As a matter of fact, this could be devastating news." She felt overwhelming sadness and exhaustion. And fear. "I'll know more when I can look through the files."

Nick had both hands on her shoulders now. It felt so good—the heat, the strong weight of his hands anchoring her. Metal in front of her on the screen; by his side, Felicity and the entire ASI crew. Nick behind her, touching her. She was surrounded by support.

She reached up and clasped Nick's hand. He tightened his grip then loosened it.

She looked at Nick, then at the screen. "I don't know how to thank you guys for all of this. If it weren't for you—"

"Whoa." Metal's eyes widened in alarm. She knew how tough guys thought. Was she getting sentimental on him? God forbid. He'd want to cut that off *stat*. "We don't need thanks. Of course we're on your side, of course we're going to help you. We won't stand by with a threat like this looming. And you're Felicity's friend and Al's granddaughter and Nick's—"

He stopped suddenly, bit his lips, looked frantically to the side to Felicity to rescue him. His hand reached out, switched the camera so his face disappeared and Felicity's face filled the screen. She rolled her eyes. "Don't mind Metal. He suffers from foot-in-mouth disease. I'll be in touch as soon as I can."

The monitor winked off.

Nick massaged her shoulders for a moment and her head hung forward, giving him access. His strong fingers dug into stiff muscles expertly.

"What do you want?" he asked.

"Shower and food." She cracked her neck to the left then the right. "In that order."

"Coming right up. You shower and I'll prepare dinner, okay?"

Kay craned her neck to look up at him, so broad, so steady. He'd saved her life and he was still looking after her. "Thank you," she whispered.

"Don't thank me yet." He bent and brushed his mouth across hers, the contact soft but almost electric. "Not until after you've had dinner."

Kay smiled. "I'm told there are food stocks."

"Oh, the food is fabulous, but I've been known to ruin food in the microwave. Nuke it to death. Lucky there's plenty of it. Oh, wait."

He disappeared from the room and came back with folded fabric between his hands. "Women think of everything. There's a huge stockpile of clothes, including casual wear that can double as pajamas. You'll be comfortable in these." He held out soft yoga pants in a light lavender jersey and a matching long-sleeved tee shirt. All of the Grange seemed to be temperature-controlled. Goldilocks climate. Not too hot, not too cold.

The outfit was pretty, casual, and looked amazingly comfortable.

"Next question. So, shower. Or bath?"

Kay thought about it. A bath sounded wonderful. She was sore and tired and a hot bath would definitely relax her muscles. But there would be work tonight, hard work, and she'd have to be alert.

"Shower," she said on a sigh.

"Shower it is. Follow me."

"Oh man." The bathroom was bigger than her first apartment. It was glorious. Tiny golden-bronze tiles created a mosaic effect that looked super modern and byzantine at the same time. One wall held a huge bathtub so deep you needed to climb up three steps to get in. It was ringed with waterjets.

"At some point, I'm going to want that bath."

"Anytime, honey." There was a slight dent in his cheek as he sketched a smile. Those dark eyes watching her carefully were full of heat. At one point, she was going to want that, too. "You can have whatever you want."

She met those dark eyes. "Careful what you say, Nick. What if I want something impossible?"

"Then I'll just have to work hard to give it to you. I know how to work hard." He did. And he knew how to say the exact perfect thing at the perfect time.

"Well lucky for you, right now all I want is a shower and some food."

He opened the etched opaque-glass shower door and she peeked inside. It was a huge space, marble-slabbed, with multiple showerheads and a seating bench.

"Hot or cold?" he asked.

"As hot as possible."

He reached inside the shower door and punched a few buttons. Hot water streamed from the huge rainfall showerhead. Steam rose, immediately filling the room.

Nick kissed her forehead. "Enjoy the shower. There's soap and shampoo inside. Towels are here." He indicated a white lacquered cabinet. The yoga outfit was on a bench near the cabinet. "Take your time."

She smiled at him, holding the smile until he closed the bathroom door behind him. She was on her last reserves, shaking with fatigue while still charged with adrenaline.

This morning's events popped up before her, as clear as if she were living them again. Her trek to meet up with Mike Hammer, fully expecting to disappear from her life for an unknown period of time. The drone, the spray, Mike's sudden collapse, him drumming his heels against the ground, turning red then blue. Watching him die a terrible death.

Wondering if she was next.

Kay slowly took off her clothes. They smelled used, unclean. She wondered if evil had a stench and if this was it. Whatever had reached out to smash Mike was definitely evil.

She was so glad to have a change of clothes because she knew she could never put this outfit back on. Maybe she'd burn it. The pantsuit was pretty—a light turquoise that the saleslady said brought out the color of her eyes. She'd enjoyed buying it and she'd liked wearing it, and now it had an association that hurt her heart.

Kay had other clothes in the suitcase that was now with the police, but she was happy with the casual yoga outfit that evoked no memories. She'd thought when she'd crept out of the hotel room this morning—was it only this morning? God! It felt like days, weeks had gone by—that her life was changing forever in one direction. Well, it had changed profoundly and forever, only in an entirely different direction.

Though Mike hadn't given specifics while they were arranging the meet-up, she knew that she'd be going underground, at least for a time. Some whistleblowers stayed underground all their lives, and she'd been prepared for that.

Mike had warned her not to pack a suitcase so large it would raise suspicions. Just what she'd normally pack for a four-day conference in another city. That had made it almost easier. No special mementos, no family heirlooms. Just outfits for four business days plus casual travel wear. Her one indulgence had been a small hard drive with all her family photos scanned and stored. That was it, what she'd be carrying into an unimaginable future.

This morning, she thought that she'd be spending the night in some kind of safe house Mike and his magazine would have arranged. No idea where.

Instead, here she was in some kind of deluxe hideout with every comfort known to man, built to survive the end of the world.

This was to be her place for the next little while, with Nick.

But first, oh man, first she needed to wash all of this off her.

Kay winced as she shrugged off her jacket. What had been a dull ache down her right side turned into sharp pain when she lifted her arms. Her entire body hurt but the pain was most focused on her right arm and shoulder.

Kay flashed again on that horrible moment this morning. The drone with its soft buzz, so alien-looking, swooping down on them. So far from anything she could recognize that for a frightening moment, she'd thought it was a huge mutant insect. It was coming so fast her lizard brain knew it would crash into them. Mike, pushing her out of the way so hard she bounced off the wall. She hadn't even felt the pain at the time, she'd been so terrified.

It had all been in the slow motion of adrenaline overload—the hormone speeding up the frames the eye saw so that it felt as if it were happening slowly. That big black...*thing* swooping down, the light of recognition in Mike's eyes, his body swiveling to push her away hard. Falling against the concrete wall, bouncing off it with her shoulder.

Her body felt every ache and pain, but there was no serious damage. She'd dislocated her shoulder once as a kid so she knew what something like that felt like. That wasn't this. It was painful but without the deep hurt of serious bodily harm.

Still, taking off her pants hurt, bending down to slip off her flats, take off her socks—pure pain. Thank God her bra had a front clasp.

She stepped into the shower, face up to the huge showerhead, and closed her eyes, basking in the hot stream of water. Oh God, that felt so good. Turning slowly around, arms out, giving herself up to the moment.

The hot water and steam penetrated her muscles down to the bone. She emptied her mind of all thought, drifted up and away from her body like when she did her meditation practice. Time floated, carrying her on waves. She bent her head forward now, to feel the heavy stream at the base of her neck and the tops of her shoulders.

Without thinking, she reached for the shampoo, groaning as her hand grabbed the bottle. Pain shot through her, a lightning bolt from hell. Her right arm was useless; she'd have to do this one-handed with her off hand. Even opening the bottle was hard. In trying to unscrew the cap, it fell to the tile floor.

"Here," a deep voice said in her ear, "let me help."

Nick stepped forward against her back, taking the shampoo bottle from her hand. His hard, naked body against her increased the heat. A cold dribble on the top of her head from the shampoo, then the feel of his strong hands washing her hair. Her head fell back against his shoulder as he massaged her scalp. Amazing. Those strong fingers were scrubbing the day away.

He angled her under the showerhead, rinsed her hair and poured more shampoo on. This time the massage was long, so long she drifted in space for a little, feeling but not thinking, her body utterly happy from the top of her head down to the bottom of her feet.

That dense hot body behind her disappeared and she opened her eyes, blinking. She turned and saw him, washcloth in one hand, soap in the other. He smiled at her and she smiled back. He bowed his head. "Your valet awaits instructions, milady."

Kay rolled her eyes, opened her hands by her sides. "You may proceed."

"God, yeah." Nick wasn't able to hold that subservient expression for more than a minute. He stepped forward, cupping her neck with one hand, gliding the washcloth over her shoulder with the other. His hand was so sure, she allowed herself to relax into it, knowing he'd hold her up, knowing he wouldn't hurt her.

He kissed her, one of those ferocious Nick kisses that were another form of sex. Tongues and lips and teeth, and when she opened her eyes, all she could see was Nick. His face and broad shoulders in the periphery of her vision. Water was pouring down over both of them. They could have been under a waterfall, like in the movies. Well, since they were both naked, probably an X-rated one.

Who cared?

Nick's mouth moved to her neck, which last night she had discovered was a major erogenous zone, something she hadn't known before. All it took was Nick's mouth, his teeth nipping lightly, and she turned on like a light bulb whose switch had been thrown.

He took another step back and looked at her, really looked, head to toe. With any other man, Kay would have felt uncomfortable with that kind of scrutiny of her naked body, but it felt warm. And definitely approving. His dark eyes gleamed, a half smile on his face. He hadn't shaved and there was a definite five o'clock shadow—or whatever time it was—thing going on. It made him look slightly scruffy, dangerous.

The washcloth slid over her shoulders, down the center of her torso, down to the center of her. She made a sound that galvanized him. He tensed, watching her closely, gaze going from her eyes to her mouth and back again.

He slid the washcloth between her legs and waggled his hand. She obeyed the unspoken order and slid her legs apart.

The washcloth slid to the floor and it was now his hand that was stroking her, right...*there*.

"Milady likes?" he murmured, voice so low it barely carried over the sound of the falling water. She felt it in her belly more than heard it.

Softly, gently stroking, one finger barely inside her. He reached deeper. "You like that?" he repeated.

Kay breathed out slowly as her legs started shaking. He was fully erect now. Her hand closed over his penis and she pumped once, hard, base to tip and back. Nick's head went back and he gave a sound of pain. "I like it as much as you like this," she said, leaning forward to lightly bite his nipple.

"Oh Jesus. I wanted to play for a while." He picked her up with one arm and with the other hand, did something to the shower jet as he sat down on the bench with her straddled on his lap. The water continued streaming down, hot but not as hot as she felt.

"Closer," Nick murmured. His arms brought her closer, so her breasts were crushed against his chest and her sex was open against his erect penis. "That's it."

That *was* it. Kay locked her arms around his neck, loving the feeling of touching him all along her front. He bit her ear, lifted his lips, bit her neck, rubbing his penis against her open sex. God, it was almost as good as penetration. Every nerve ending was stimulated, the slow movement like honey.

She put her mouth to his ear. "Nick."

"Hmm?"

Another long, liquid stroke against her outer sex. Her thighs were trembling. She was close and he knew it.

"Come inside me," she whispered directly in his ear, and felt him shudder.

"A minute, I have to do something first."

She opened her mouth to protest and he kissed, hard and deep. If he thought he was going to win arguments by kissing her...he was probably right.

Another long, slow glide against her and she felt his finger, touching her exactly where he should be touching her, and it all coalesced. The fragrant steam, the falling water, Nick's mouth on hers, his careful touch where she was so sensitive.

Kay gasped in his mouth as the climax rolled over her and she contracted sharply against his hand. He lifted her high, positioned himself, and let her slowly slide down him, the effect electric while she was climaxing, so deep inside her that he felt like a part of her, the best part of her, holding her hard as he kissed her and kissed her. She felt utterly possessed.

The contractions slowed, stopped. She was sprawled on his lap, legs wide over his, so close she felt his crinkly pubic hairs brush against her.

There was no more strength as she slumped against him, held up by his arms and mouth and sex.

"That," Nick said. "That's what I had to do first."

And he started moving inside her.

Eight

Portland

There were always bumps in the road. Oliver Baker understood that. But this was a major hurdle, and potentially very dangerous. So far no one had noticed the engineered H1N1. No one. The absolutely perfect murder weapon, like in that story where the wife killed her husband with the frozen leg of lamb she roasted and served to the police inspector.

A weaponized super-fast version of the Spanish flu linked to the victim's DNA. You could be right next to the victim, dying fast and dirty, and not get so much as a cold. And you could extend the range of the DNA. You could kill the person, the person's kids or parents. You could wipe out a family or even a tribe. At least in theory.

That theory was going to be tested in four weeks' time. A tiny inbred tribe in the heart of the Congo was sitting on one of the world's largest deposits of coltan, essential to the manufacture of computers. The tribe would be made to disappear. A gallon of the liquefied DNA-edited virus would be sprayed over their hunting area. Baker had thousands of hours of footage of the tribe's movements and had mapped out their territory exactly. Half an hour after spraying, the tribe would be no more. Give it a week for the jungle to reclaim the dead, and Collux Mining could move right in and start extracting.

Superdeath, Frank Winstone called it. He should know. As head of the CDC, he dealt with death daily, only he was famous for defeating it. As a young researcher, he'd developed a vaccine for a rare hemorrhagic fever disease and had saved hundreds of thousands of lives. And would save millions over the years to come.

And hadn't earned a dime from it.

It was why he'd come to Oliver last year, because he knew—everyone knew—that Oliver was King Midas. Whatever he touched turned to gold. Though Oliver had never actually quite something so…remunerative, so *golden* in his hands before. He'd started life as a lawyer and had done well. Knowing the law helped you navigate its outer reaches. He became the go-to guy. If you had a problem, Baker would get you out of it. Whatever you needed, Baker could get it for you.

He'd done a stint at the CIA and had an ad hoc team of former Clandestine Service agents who liked earning money. A roster of fifty kickass operatives on retainer ready to go at any time. It was perfect. He made them enough money to earn their loyalty but they weren't employees and weren't on the payroll. What they did in their downtime was their business. He didn't pay salaries. He paid fees.

Baker had made his first twenty million before Frank approached him with the most perfect weapon ever, guaranteed to solve any problem that was human. Just eliminate it.

Frank had developed it, but didn't know how to use it. But Baker did. Oh yeah.

Baker made his second twenty million in the first six months he had access to Superdeath. And this year, he was going to double that. There was, almost literally, no limit to what he could earn, to what he could do, as long as no one understood what had been created.

Sometimes he had to take a little risk, like the De Haven bitch. Normally Oliver let a little time go by between a threat to a client and the elimination of the threat. But Offutt had been adamant. He wanted her dead yesterday, and so Oliver had been forced to act right in the middle of a congressional investigation, with the spotlight turned on De Haven.

So far no one had shown any interest in the sudden death of a woman in late middle age. The newspapers universally spoke of a heart attack.

Baker understood Offutt completely, even though he despised the man. De Haven was trying to take Offutt's very lucrative business away from him. And it was De Haven's own fault she was targeted. She wasn't happy with damaging just some of Offutt's business, oh no. She wanted Blackvale's total destruction, and the only response to that was total war. Why couldn't she have been susceptible to a bribe? Even a big one, like a million dollars? Would have saved everyone a lot of trouble and would have saved Offutt fifteen million. But no.

She had signed her own death warrant.

There would be no fallout, no investigation. De Haven died a natural death. There probably would not even be an autopsy. And if there was, nothing would emerge. And if by some stroke of terrible luck, the ME wasn't happy, Baker had an envelope full of unmarked bills to give to the medical examiner. Shocking what they paid MEs these days for doing a nasty job. And if the ME wasn't amenable to a little persuasion, well, Baker's operatives could arrange a car accident, a mugging gone wrong, a dog attack while he was out running, electrocution at the building site of his new home. All sorts of things could happen.

Not Superdeath, though. He was careful not to shit in the same place twice. So far, use of Superdeath had been spread out geographically and over time. There wasn't even a hint about it. He should know, he kept his ear close to the ground.

He hadn't used the virus either for Bill Morrell or that Indian bitch. Morrell was the man who'd created the weaponized Spanish flu that Frank bonded to the particular DNA of an individual. He'd been very well paid, but he had been starting to make waves, so he'd had to go. That Indian bitch Priyanka Anand had definitely had to go.

And now another woman was a threat. Baker had informants everywhere, and one had told him that Priyanka Anand had been in touch with Mike Hammer. Mike Hammer was the pen name of a muckraker called Jeremy Robsen. Just finding out who the hell Hammer really was had cost two hundred grand. But he had a complete file, including his address. The instant he found out that Anand had been in touch with Hammer, he had two of his guys break into Hammer's house and gather DNA. As a precaution.

Baker thought ahead.

The fucker had quite a following. Baker had kept a close eye on Hammer. He had to, because Hammer's cell and computer security were top rate. Nobody on Baker's team had been able to penetrate anything. As far as they knew, Hammer didn't communicate by phone or by computer, though of course that was crazy.

In the end, it was a member of Hammer's team that betrayed him. A junior member of the editorial team who received an anonymous email promising information on a weaponized virus created at the CDC, information from a very dead Priyanka Anand. The anonymous emailer asked for a meeting in Portland, Oregon.

Baker had had to get himself and a team to Portland via private jet before Hammer, and get a drone locked onto him.

He'd sent a plane to get the DNA to Frank, who edited it. Frank got the DNA-bonded virus out fast and loaded into the drone, so they were ready. Because Hammer was meeting someone, someone with information, and he had to be stopped.

Baker turned back to his computer monitor, where he stared at the footage for what seemed the thousandth time. The camera followed Hammer to a small hotel in a seedy part of town. He entered and didn't leave until the next morning, when he made his way downtown. Ducking into an alleyway and stopping. Then, out of nowhere, the woman appeared. Slender, dressed in a blue pantsuit with a wide-brimmed straw hat. At the first iteration, the hat seemed like a coincidence, but checking the footage of the big avenue where she must have come from, there was no recording of a slender woman in a blue pantsuit with a big hat. She'd been careful. Which meant that she was either trained or had been well-advised.

Baker watched, switching to slow motion as she walked down the filthy alleyway, trailing the wheelie. So—she was a visitor to Portland? Planning on flying out immediately afterward? What?

Baker slowed the video down even more, inching his face closer to the monitor, watching carefully. Hammer's face could clearly be seen. For all his tight cybersecurity, he hadn't counted on a drone. The alleyway itself was without security cameras. Hammer had had every reason to believe that this meeting would go unrecorded.

Baker studied the face. Hammer never appeared in public. He operated under anonymity and under a pen name. It wasn't clear from the drone footage how tall he was but he was thin, with a narrow, clever face. A thinker's face. Not a doer.

Hammer straightened when he saw the woman walking down the alleyway, expecting her. The woman walked right up to him, parked the wheelie against the wall, turned to him. Damn! With her back to the drone and its lens.

Hammer and the woman talked briefly as they increased in size. The drone coming closer. The woman placed something in Hammer's hands. Something tiny, something Baker was sure was a flash drive.

This was the point of the meeting. Hammer's fist closed around it and he closed his eyes briefly. Triumph. The exchange had gone off without a hitch.

Suddenly Hammer looked up and Baker saw him frown, his eyes opening wide in recognition and fear as he saw the drone. The drone sprayed him, the woman's face almost completely turned away. Hammer shot out his hand and shoved the woman against the wall, hard. She bounced, went down on one knee, turned her head toward Hammer.

By now, Hammer's terrified face filled the camera. Drops falling off his cheeks and nose. The virus in a solution.

Both Hammer and the woman were frozen, uncomprehending. Hammer lifted his hand and wiped his face, puzzled. He'd probably been expecting a bullet. A liquid spray didn't seem dangerous to him.

The woman started to turn her head up, but Hammer pushed it down before the camera could capture it. The camera showed him speaking to her, unfortunately at an angle that didn't allow for lip reading. Baker vowed that next time he'd capture sound, too.

Then Hammer brought a hand to his throat and started turning red. He swayed, his head bobbing. The woman stood still for a moment, then tried to catch Hammer as he fell to the ground.

Fuck fuck fuck! The drone had been programmed to follow Hammer's face and it focused on him exclusively. It could have swooped around Hammer, taken footage of the woman's face, identified her, but no. Smart as the drone was, it wasn't smart enough to change the mission parameters mid-mission. And the mission had been to follow Hammer and take him out.

Which the drone had done.

It was supposed to be a smooth, clean taking out of a potential enemy, a flawless operation that would leave no traces. Instead it had turned out to be messy, and with a witness.

Hudson watched for the tenth time as Hammer died, gasping for a breath that never came. Baker watched again and again as the woman reached with a visibly shaking hand to get the flash drive from Hammer's hand, then disappeared through the door into the building.

Not even on the tenth attempt did Hudson manage to glimpse more than a fraction of the face of the woman. Definitely not enough for facial recognition.

Well, if ten iterations didn't work, the eleventh wouldn't either. There had to be another way. He sat back, drumming his fingers.

Baker could have sent the problem to his cybersecurity team in Vladivostok. A group of ten highly gifted and larcenously expensive hackers who seemed to be awake 24/7. If this were a normal mission, he would have, and then charged his client ten times what the hacker collective, known as Badboyzz, charged him. In this case, he was his own client and this was the motherlode. His most lucrative business, what in a few years would make him ludicrously rich. The Boyzzz were wicked smart and dedicated, but didn't understand boundaries, and they were amoral. They were perfectly capable of adding two plus two to make a billion, and they were also perfectly capable of blackmail.

And they were ten thousand miles away, which was awkward if he needed to eliminate them. Not to mention, he had no idea where their base was in the city of over four million inhabitants.

No. Try to deal with this in-house, he told himself. Keep the circle small. So far, the operational circle was him, Frank Winstone, who could cook a fatal viral cocktail in two hours as long as he had viable DNA, and two drone operators who were paid so much money they would never talk. Baker was making them very rich, very fast. There wasn't that huge a market for ex-military drone operators, and they knew they'd lucked out with him and weren't going to endanger that.

So. The drone footage was useless with regard to the identity of the woman who had incriminating information. Who, indeed, was the origin of the incriminating information via the Indian woman. That flash drive had gone from Anand to her to Hammer, not the other way around. The woman had very dangerous knowledge.

Who the hell was she?

She had to have come from somewhere.

Baker's hacking skills weren't bad. The CIA trained its operatives well and he'd been taught a lot of tricks by the best. It was probable she'd come from Clement Street, down the alleyway, then turned left. Clement was lousy with video cameras and she was wearing a distinctive turquoise color.

The last the drone had seen of her had been at 10:02. Hudson hacked into the citywide security-cam system and carefully checked the tapes of security cams on Clement starting at 9:30 a.m., fast forward and reverse and slow motion. Over and over again.

He bolted upright when he saw what he hadn't seen before. Nine twenty-one a.m. A tiny stripe of turquoise blue at the outer reaches of the security cam at the corner of Clement and Drummond.

Mystery Woman had somehow known to avoid the cameras. Hmmm. Had she been trained? Was she an operative? Was there someone in the security apparatus—CIA, Homeland Security, FBI, NSA, any of the other alphabet soup agencies—who was on to him? That upped the stakes considerably.

What was on the street? He checked an internet map. Four restaurants, eight boutiques, two jewelry stores, a big department store connected to an even bigger office building, a hotel. The Astoria. Where had he heard that name?

Oh God. His blood ran cold. The Astoria Hotel was where the World Virology Conference was being held, right now. As a matter of fact, Frank was going fly in to deliver the concluding speech. She couldn't be staying there, could she? If she was...

Hotel security video was amazingly easy to hack into. Unlike city footage, a commercial entity like a hotel, with no known security issues, wouldn't keep footage for more than 48 hours, so he had to be thorough. Luckily, if she was there, it would be footage of this morning.

He accessed hotel security and put in a time frame: 7 a.m. to 9:15 a.m. The color resolution was crap but it would show turquoise. He checked the breakfast room, putting it on fast forward. A lot of fat tourists and dandruffy scientists scarfed down an amazing quantity of coffee, croissants and yogurt. No slender lady in a turquoise pantsuit. He ran it back and forth, as they comically rushed from the tables to the buffet and back in quadruple time, like ants.

She hadn't eaten in the breakfast room. Maybe she'd had room service, but since he didn't know the name, it would be pointless to check room-service orders.

That left the lobby.

And the lobby's cameras were blank from 9:15 to 10 a.m. The same for the cameras in the hotel corridors.

Christ.

Where had she disappeared to? He needed to find her and eliminate her, *now*. Not via the virus. No way could he have two choking deaths in one small city. And there'd be a connection between her and Hammer. Using Superdeath would be insane. But there were plenty of other ways.

Now it was a question of finding where she'd gone.

His drone had picked up on the three identical black SUVs. The woman hadn't left the building complex all day. Not on foot. Every instinct said she was in one of those SUVs. Or definitely in one of the many vehicles that had exited the department store.

This went way beyond his skills and his crunching power.

Okay, now it was time to spend some money.

He contacted the Badboyzz, patiently waiting for the call to be bounced from the US to Europe then back to the US, through Singapore, and on to Vladivostok via Riga.

"'Allo?" Fuck. It was the joker who tried to pass himself off as French. Baker didn't have time for this.

"Cut the crap. I'm sending footage of three SUVs in Portland, Oregon. I need you to follow them, find out where they went. Inspect who comes out. Give me shots if a woman dressed in turquoise pants steps out from one of those vehicles. And follow all the vehicles exiting a department store in a specific time frame. I'm sending coordinates and as much intel as I have."

"Duuude." Oh shit. Now it was the one who pretended to be a California dope dealer. "That would have to be off Keyhole 15. That's going to take time and monn-ayy."

"Find her. A million."

Even over the bounced line he could hear his interest. "Yeah, dude? A mill? You got it."

"How long will it take you?"

"Mmm."

The mercenary shit was going to bargain. Not going to happen. Baker put command into his voice. "Get me footage of the inhabitants of as many of those vehicles as you can, and particularly those SUVs. It has to be inside twenty-four hours or forget it." He hung up. There. That was a challenge. He knew the hackers would turn themselves inside out, both for the money and to show that they could.

Kay slumped into Nick's arms and they sat there, under the shower, for a long time. The sex had kept the bad memories at bay, but as she nestled her head against his neck, tears joined the water falling on him from the shower.

Finally, he turned the shower off and started drying them.

She was physically and mentally depleted but above all, he understood, shocked. Though she'd been raised by an FBI grandfather, Nick knew Al Goodkind enough to know that he'd have shielded Kay from the dirtier side of the job.

She'd talked about her relationship with her grandfather while they'd waited in Goodkind's house, his blood on the floor, for news of him. Goodkind had been kidnapped by monsters and Kay had been out of her mind with frantic worry. She idolized her grandfather. She saw him as a knight in shining armor, and goddammit, he was.

So was Nick.

But Goodkind had never told her that he'd killed seven men in the line of duty, four of them in one raid when he was a rookie. Nick couldn't count the men he'd killed.

Goodkind had shielded her from the nature of the world, which was raw and predatory. He knew she'd been dedicated to her studies, had lived in a lab coat since she was eighteen and was a world-renowned expert on things no one could see or hear or taste. She lived in a world where knowledge was precious and people were smart and dedicated to the common good.

She'd just found out that she'd been living a lie her entire life.

People were stupid and greedy, capable of vast cruelty. There were people who would kill for pennies, let alone for wealth. And there were people willing to kill for the knowledge she and her colleagues worked so selflessly to produce.

It was a real fucked-up world.

Nick had known this all his life. His dad had been a cop and his brother and two sisters were in law enforcement. The youngest, Roberto—Bobby—had inexplicably decided to become a spook, but was forgiven this transgression, because he was a kickass spook.

The entire Mancino family fought the bad guys and protected the innocent.

Nick had always had backup in school. Nobody, *nobody* bullied a Mancino because you'd have your ass handed to you, broken and bloody. In turn, he'd provided backup to the younger members of the extended family—which was three brothers, two sisters, twelve cousins and twenty-two second cousins. All of them lived in Philly and they all got together often. He'd grown up in a huge clan and though he knew the world was big and bad, he had a lot of tough guys—even the girls in the Mancino clan were tough guys—on his side.

Kay had only had a loving grandfather on her side, and understandably, he'd shielded her from the shitty fuckup that was the world.

But one thing Kay had to understand. She had *him* on her side now. He had her back. She no longer had only a retired, ailing 80-year-old, she had Nick Mancino and the entire ASI team, who were all smart and tough. And, for that matter, all the Mancinos.

She wasn't alone.

"Arms up," he said quietly, and she obediently put her arms up. He slipped on the yoga top without bothering about a bra. Because it would be fussy having to put a bra on her and because, well…because he was a horn dog. Her breasts were so incredibly beautiful and they would be showcased with only that silky top on. Just like he slid the pants on without panties, because the thought of that warm, wet, soft little sex just a second away from his hands and his dick…

Fuck.

Good thing he'd put on jeans and a tee, and that the jeans were new and stiff, because his dick was stiff, too. Hard as rock.

After last night and in the shower, he shouldn't be hard as a rock. He wasn't twenty and perpetually horny anymore. He knew how to control himself. A hard-on—a *painful* hard-on—wasn't appropriate or even politically correct right now. His dick didn't give a fuck, unfortunately. It felt ready for sex anytime Kay Hudson was available, and having had her only made him want more, soon. She wasn't out of his system.

At all.

He sighed when she looked up at him. Goddamn, she was beautiful. But right now, she looked so lost and sad, his heart warred with his dick and his heart won.

There was a first time for everything.

"Food's waiting," he said, as he moved around behind her. "You hungry?"

She waited a beat. "You know," she said, sounding surprised. "I am. I am hungry. There's food here, right? That's what you said. Those military rations? What do they call them?"

Nick picked up a wide-toothed comb and lifted her damp hair out of the back of her top. "MREs?" he asked, amused. MREs were the most disgusting meals available and they gummed you up like nobody's business. He'd lived off MREs for ten days once and had only taken a dump twice. Awful. "No, we have something better than MREs. Isabel set up the provisions."

"Devereaux?" Kay twisted her head to look up at him. She had a slight smile on her face. Yeah, Isabel's cooking would do that. He gently ran the comb through her tangles until they smoothed out.

"Yeah. Isabel Devereaux. Soon to be Isabel Harris. Joe's been champing at the bit to marry her for a while now. So yes, Isabel set up the food stores and is getting ready to start up a big hydroponics farm for fresh vegetables. Okay, there you go. All done."

He'd untangled her beautiful hair, braided it, and tied the braid off with a piece of gauze.

Kay looked at herself in the mirror, turning this way and that to see the braid. Nick was really happy with his policy of not having her wear underwear because the material stretched over her breasts lovingly. He made a manful effort to keep his eyes on hers and not look down.

"That's a good job you did, and you didn't hurt me combing it out. How do you have experience braiding women's hair?"

"Two little sisters who had to get ready to go to school every morning and my mom had to be at school before them. She was a teacher. So my brothers and I were on Braid Patrol. We had records. We could get our sisters up, washed, dressed, feed them breakfast and get them out the door to the school bus in 28 minutes. I timed it."

Kay smiled. "You come from a big family."

"The biggest," he said. "And the best."

She gave a small sigh. "For almost as long as I can remember, it's only been Grandpa and me."

"Yeah. Good old Al."

Kay smiled. "He did a good job, though. He was always around and was always good to me. It was only a few years ago that someone told me that he was being groomed for the directorship when he…inherited me, I guess would be a good word. When I asked him, he just smiled and shrugged and said it was water under the bridge."

True. Goodkind had refused all postings, even if they meant promotion, to stay in the DC area. He'd have made a kickass director, but instead he'd opted to be a kickass substitute parent.

"It's true, isn't it?" Kay asked, looking directly into his eyes.

She was way too smart to lie to. Nick nodded.

She sighed. "And to think he was so encouraging about my career, even when it took me away from him."

Goodkind hadn't traveled after becoming Kay's caregiver, but she had. She'd studied in Cambridge and Paris and had worked for the WHO, where she'd been posted to Singapore and Gambia. Nick had done his homework and had quietly grilled Goodkind, who'd answered all of his questions with a sardonic smile.

"He loves you," Nick said quietly. "And he loves Felicity."

Goodkind hadn't broken under torture to deliver Felicity to Borodin, a Russian mobster in a good suit. Felicity had something Borodin badly wanted and he'd used Goodkind to get to her. It hadn't worked.

Kay nodded. "He was like a father to her, too. Her own was cold and remote. Grandpa is really good at being an anchor for lost girls." She gave a shake, as if to cast off bad thoughts. "I heard you talk about food, was that just you blowing smoke?"

"No, ma'am." Nick put a hand to her back and ushered her out of the room. "I wasn't blowing smoke at all. I'd never joke about food."

They walked along a corridor of doors, which were all bedrooms/living quarters for the various ASI people, until they came to the end of the corridor and walked across another huge living area into a small kitchen.

"Wow." Kay's head was on a swivel.

Well, the place was pretty fantastic. Half the guys at ASI *hoped* the zombie apocalypse came so they could hang out here forever.

"That's the third kitchen I've seen. How many are there?"

"Four. All fully functional but different sizes. The biggest one has three ovens, one you could roast an ox in. That kitchen's for when we all get together. This one's for a small party." Nick touched a button on the remote in his pocket and a microwave started up. Another button and a cascade of ice fell into an ice bucket.

"So we get the magic kitchen, do we?" she teased.

"Yep. So, milady, your chair awaits."

Nick pulled out a chair that was shaped like a Louis Whatever—Suzanne had explained the whole thing to him but there was nowhere in his brain the intel could stick to—only almost invisible Plexiglas. There was a round table and he'd set two table mats out and two plates and two wine glasses. It wasn't an evening for water.

He knew where everything was because, well, after an ASI agent had asked permission to bring his girlfriend for a weekend, he'd fumbled and opened every cabinet before he'd found the essentials. His girlfriend—now his wife—had made a sarcastic comment and Suzanne had sighed.

The next weekend, all kitchen cabinets in all four kitchens were glass-fronted, and Nick could see clearly where everything was.

"Ma'am. Sit please."

Just as Kay was seated, the microwave pinged and he placed a trivet—a word Suzanne had taught him—on the table and pulled out a deep ceramic dish from the microwave, placing it on the trivet while inhaling deeply. Man, that smelled good.

Kay leaned forward, too, taking a deep breath of the glorious smell. "Wow. Lasagna. Did you whip that up while I was taking a shower?"

Nick wrestled briefly with the temptation to lie but decided against it. She'd never believe him anyway. "No, sadly, I didn't. But Isabel did. She and four of her interns came up for a few days and made about a billion servings of lasagna and other stuff and froze them. She said they had a great time."

Isabel's interns had all been good cooks but more to the point, hot babes. Several of the newer recruits to ASI had spent those days going up to the Grange and volunteering for slave labor and KP.

At another time, Nick would have volunteered, too. But by that time, he'd had Kay in his head and she wasn't leaving it. Hadn't left it. And now he knew would never leave it.

Another ping and Nick opened the bread maker, and a small loaf of five-grain bread came out, adding to the delicious aromas. The magic freezer had small doughs of the bread and the bread maker defrosted and baked. All he'd done was pop the dough in. He shook some salt and poured some olive oil over a sliced tomato salad—his only contribution to the dinner—popped a cork on a bottle of merlot and sat down.

Kay watched him. "What?" he asked as he spread the napkin over his lap.

"Really? Freshly made bread and a fresh tomato salad? In a country hideaway?"

He poured their glasses and lifted his philosophically. "Well, a really, really well-equipped country hideaway." It wasn't the moment to tell her about the massive security measures, the armory that had enough weaponry to go to war with a small country—say, Aruba—the fact that the entire complex was encased in a Faraday cage built to withstand an EMP...

"That it is. Mm." Kay closed her eyes as she put a bite of lasagna in her mouth. "Oh my God. I hope those interns got a lot of really good sex in return."

Nick's hand stopped halfway to his mouth. *What?* What did she just say?

Kay laughed. It felt good to hear her laugh. "Oh, Nick, if you could only see your face. You think a company filled to the rafters with testosterone and single guys wouldn't latch on to a cooking session with interns? In a beautiful mountain hideaway? Isabel is out of the running of course, since she's totally devoted to Joe, but I'll bet there were a bunch of guys running up and down the mountain. You included."

"Nope." He put his fork down. That was the old Nick. He leaned forward and Kay put her own fork down at the serious expression on his face. Time to give her the new Nick. "That weekend had a lot of ASI guys—the single ones—going up and down the mountain, just like you said, and a few got laid, but I wasn't one of them. I met you for the first time two months before the lasagna weekend. Since I laid eyes on you I haven't fu—messed around."

There. It was out in the open now. He'd nailed his colors to the table. Ball in her court.

Kay folded her arms and leaned forward, keeping her eyes on his. "I've been avoiding you," she said.

He nodded. "I know. The whole company knows."

She winced slightly. "It wasn't like that."

"No?" Nick held her gaze. "So, how was it?"

Her chin firmed. "There's a reason I was avoiding you. I was trying to protect you."

Nick's jaw dropped, then he clenched his teeth. "Protect me? What the hell? I don't need protecting."

Kay reached out with one hand, letting it hover over his, then drop to cover it. Her hand was slim, pale, soft. A scholar's hand. His was larger, darker, tougher. A fighter's hand. He waited to hear how she thought she was going to protect him.

"The weekend we were supposed to meet up in Washington, remember?"

God yeah, he remembered. He'd switched training cycles with a teammate when he heard Kay would be in town for a full weekend, bought tickets to something high-minded at the Kennedy Center. And then sat around steaming when she canceled her visit at the last minute.

Kay dicking him around. More of those to come.

She tightened her grip on his hand. Met his eyes. "The day before our meeting, Priyanka asked me to meet her in Grant Park in Atlanta."

"Priyanka?"

A sad smile that didn't reach her eyes. "Priyanka Anand. A biochemist at the CDC and my best friend. *Was* my best friend. She died. In a car accident where she drove herself off the road while drunk, so they said. But that was impossible—because Priyanka never drank, ever. She was allergic to alcohol, something very few people knew."

Oh God. Nick put his other hand on top of hers, sandwiching it. Her hand was chilled.

"She hadn't been much in touch lately and when she asked me to meet her on our lunch hour at a park far away from the CDC, I thought maybe she was going to tell me she had a new boyfriend or had accepted that job teaching at Stanford. She was being headhunted ferociously. Priyanka is—was—a genius. Not to mention funny and kind."

Kay's eyes welled and she dropped her head between her shoulder blades. A tear plopped on the table. She took a napkin and wiped her eyes with her free hand. Her head lifted.

Nick's gaze didn't waver. "Go on."

Kay cleared her throat. "So, I thought it was a casual meeting between friends. Instead, Priyanka was agitated, worried, anxious. She said she wanted to meet in Grant Park because there were no security cameras. That was my first clue that something serious was going on."

"What was Priyanka's job?" Nick asked.

"She was trained as a biochemist, but she was an expert in bio-warfare."

Fuck. Nick opened his mouth to say something, then closed it again.

"Yeah." Kay shook her head. "If Priyanka was worried, I was worried too. It turns out that a colleague, a man, had been acting strange. I know the colleague in question, Bill Morrell, and honestly, I don't know how she could tell strange from normal with that guy. He was a high-functioning sociopath, definitely on the autism spectrum."

"Was?"

"Mm. Alive when we met, though. At first, I didn't take her too seriously. Bill had a thing about Priyanka. Somewhere in the recesses of his brilliant but sick mind, they were meant to be together. Two people who knew so much about the genetics of viruses were destined to be a couple. And of course, to fall straight into bed together. No matter that Priyanka was blindingly beautiful and Bill's eyebrows had dandruff, and his eyebrows were the most attractive thing about him. He'd have needed about a year of plastic surgery and dentistry and serious gym time to even think of asking Priyanka out on a date. And he had bad hygiene. Horrible personality, awful looks coupled with amazing arrogance. A male trifecta. Priyanka couldn't stand him and had complained several times to management about him."

"They should have gotten rid of him. Any guy in the FBI whose female colleagues complains about him to management would be gone."

"Unfortunately, Bill was also brilliant at his job. Even Priyanka conceded that. When she told me he became rich all of a sudden, though, things changed."

"Rich?"

"Yup."

"Let me guess," Nick said dryly. "New car, snazzy wardrobe, vacations in St. Lucia."

She nodded. "And let's not forget the new penthouse in Chapel Tower. A luxury condo skyscraper in the heart of Atlanta. Expensive and flashy and terminally stupid for someone on a researcher's salary to buy."

"That's major league new wealth. Someone die and he inherited?"

"That's what he said. But Priyanka is—damn! *was*—cynical and untrusting. I just loved that about her. She looked his family up and there was no one within a thousand miles who could die and leave him that kind of money. His mother lived off social security and his only brother was in jail for drugs. Bill was brilliant at science, but really dumb at life. He didn't even manage to make up a good excuse for his sudden money. And he was also bad at social relations—wasn't discreet. Everyone on the research floor knew he suddenly had access to a lot of money, big time. Priyanka was really worried because of his current research project. If he'd sold out to someone, his field was dangerous."

A rogue scientist who was an expert on bio-warfare, showing clear signs of corruption. What could possibly be wrong with that picture?

"What was his specialty?" Nick asked, dreading the answer. As both a SEAL and an FBI special agent, he'd had extensive training on bio-weapons, though thank God he'd never encountered any.

Mainly he'd encountered bullets and bombs, which were fine. All you needed was bigger bullets and bigger bombs.

But he remembered briefings on sarin, ricin, anthrax. So scary his balls tried to crawl up into his body. There was one mission where they'd had to don MOPP suits because they hadn't known if there would be a bio-weapon.

There hadn't been a bio-weapon, but he remembered vividly the sweaty confines of the awkward and fiercely uncomfortable suit. A teammate had reminded everyone that if their fears were true, they were in suits in which a mere pinprick or slight invisible tear would be enough to guarantee them a horrendous death. He'd added that the suits had been delivered by manufacturers who'd been the lowest bidders.

Not a couple of hours he'd care to replicate.

Bombs and bullets were fine. Tiny particles he couldn't see that would make him puke his lungs and stomach out—not so much.

"He was studying the Spanish Flu."

Nick blanked. The flu? Next to what he'd read of the other diseases—Ebola, Lassa, smallpox—the flu didn't sound so bad.

Kay saw his expression. "We're not talking sniffles and a touch of fever here, Nick. The Spanish flu was a never-before-seen strain of flu that in 1918 wiped out half a billion people worldwide. More people died in one year than in four years of the plague in the 14th century. More people died than in

World War I. Life expectancy dropped by twelve years. Bill was studying the virus taken from the lungs of a body frozen in the Antarctic. We still don't understand the mechanisms of the strain. But Priyanka thought that he'd figured it out, replicated it, and made it even more swift and deadly. A fast-acting and deadlier form of Spanish flu..." She shuddered.

"Hell, if Spanish flu 1.0 killed half a billion people..."

"Exactly."

He thought about that. It wasn't pretty. "Though—1918. That was before antibiotics, right?"

"There's no antibiotic on earth that can combat H1N1. And most antibiotics are unfortunately becoming ineffective. Anyway, that's why I called off that weekend. Priyanka was supposed to come over to my place and we were going to go over the information she'd gathered."

"You're a bad liar," Nick said. "I thought you were having an affair."

She was a *terrible* liar. She'd stammered and stuttered and made up three stories, each more ridiculous than the next. They'd Skyped and she might as well have grown a Pinocchio nose in front of his very eyes. You didn't need to be an FBI behavioral analyst to tell she was lying. She'd turned beet red in the face and her eyes had constantly shifted to the left.

He'd have said that was that, except for the fact that just before signing off, she'd said she was going to be in Portland the next weekend to see Felicity.

And fuck, he'd said, wasn't that a coincidence, he was going to be there too. Except *Nick* knew how to lie. There wasn't one tell on his face, he knew. After Joe Harris, who was The Man at poker, he was second best at bluffing. And it sort of wasn't a lie. If you squinted.

He'd been thinking more and more about joining ASI. First, because they were all buddies of his from way back. Second, he'd worked for the government all his adult life. He'd had good men commanding him and bad. His last two bosses at the FBI had been cover-your-ass types. What in military-speak had been known as REMFs. Rear echelon motherfuckers. Men who rode desks. More intent on snaking their way up the career ladder than on doing their job putting away fuckheads.

ASI was run by exactly the opposite type of man. John Huntington, aka the Midnight Man, and Douglas Kowalski, aka the Senior, were righteous dudes, great bosses who never asked anyone to do something they wouldn't do themselves. They were building a truly great company, employing the best of the best. The starting pay was double his income as an FBI Special Agent. And Portland, Oregon, was a nicer place to live than Washington, DC.

Because then and there, he'd made up his mind to join ASI. He'd had a standing invitation and decided to take John and Senior up on it. He'd scheduled a meeting for the next weekend and damned if she hadn't left the city while his plane was touching down. She'd come early and left early.

"I know I'm a terrible liar," Kay said, rolling her eyes. "Of course I am. It's a professional deformation. Scientists can't lie. We can't distort the truth, because digging for the truth is what we do. Unlike you slick superspy undercover dudes."

Nick blew out a breath of air. "Well, you were *really* lousy at it."

Kay looked him straight in the eyes. God, her eyes were beautiful. This amazing bright blue color, like the sky over the sea. So bright they almost glowed.

She was saying something and he didn't catch it. "What?"

"I was protecting you. Because the further Priyanka dug, the more it appeared that Bill was working on, or had perfected, a deadly bio-weapon. Someone tried to hack Priyanka's computer, but her brother made sure that they hacked into these fake files, perfectly innocuous. Her real files were behind a wall. Then Bill was killed."

"Wait." Nick frowned. "He was killed? When?"

She sighed. "The Wednesday after. A mugging. But of course, it wasn't a mugging, he was either threatening to talk or, even worse, his usefulness was over. By the time Priyanka found out, his office had been cleared out, his computer gone, his condo and all its contents gone. Someone did some serious cleaning up after him; it was almost like he didn't exist."

Nick frowned. He didn't like this, any of it. Three people killed. And she thought she had to protect *him?* What was that shit?

"Luckily, as I told you, Priyanka was sneaky, and she had had her brother copy all of Bill's files and put them in the cloud. It was a ton of data. She'd gone through some and on the basis of that, she contacted Mike Hammer."

"I can't believe you ran away from me while this was happening. You should have come to me."

She looked to one side, then back to him. "You're FBI," she said simply. "Or were," she added when he opened his mouth. "It was clear that Priyanka was going to blow the whistle on the CDC, and I was going to back her up. Do what I could. But…we all know what happens to whistleblowers. Then Priyanka…died."

She swallowed heavily, cleared her throat. Pain flashed on her beautiful face. "Car accident. I couldn't believe it when I heard the news. She was so beautiful, so full of life. And then—then they were saying that they'd found a high blood-alcohol level, that she'd been drunk. I read the autopsy report." That long white neck bobbed as she swallowed heavily. "Nobody would give it to me, so I emailed Felicity and she just hacked into the coroner's office and copied it for me. She'd met Priyanka and was as horrified as I was. The coroner must have been bought off, because Priyanka definitely did not drink any alcohol. If she did have a high level of alcohol, it could only be because she was infused. So there must have been a pinprick in her elbow or subclavian. You can infuse alcohol into the system via an IV line. It's the only way she'd have alcohol in her system. Whatever it was, Priyanka was…gone. She was thirty-two years old, brilliant and beautiful and the best friend anyone could ask for. And she was gone."

Nick watched as she bowed her head, another crystal tear dropping off that smooth white cheek. She was mourning her friend while holding on to him. Damn right. She could hold on to him for as long as she wanted and needed. Beyond.

Her head lifted. "Then I got a message from her."

That surprised him. "From beyond the grave?"

"Yeah." She gave a strangled laugh. "Just like Priyanka to do something like that, nothing stops her. She decided at the age of seven to become a researcher because she thought lab coats were cool. I've never seen anyone more determined and more organized. She knew she had moved into the danger zone, and had taken precautions. She put together a file that was to go to me if two days passed without her entering a specific code. She was a planner."

A planner. Nick kept his tongue. Priyanka might have been a friend, might have been desperate, but she had painted a huge bullseye on Kay's back. Kay wouldn't want to hear it, but that's what had happened.

He was a little mad about that, but didn't—couldn't—show it. And to Kay's credit, it never even occurred to her that her dear and good friend had dumped a bomb primed to go off right into her lap.

Kay watched her finger run around the rim of the wine glass. "And then it became clear that I was going to have to be the whistleblower. The best I could hope for was that my career would be ruined. Whistleblowers are subjected to legal harassment; their contacts are scrutinized. Their friends come under scrutiny. You had a good career going that I could ruin for you, Nick. I wasn't going to do that. No way."

Nick ground his teeth so hard he was surprised he didn't crack a tooth. "I can't believe you were thinking that." She was terrified, in danger, and she was thinking of his career? That it might suffer? Fuck that.

Her hand in his was shaking.

"I went over it and over it in my head. Looked at it from every angle, and there wasn't any angle where I didn't ruin your life for you."

He felt like someone had punched him in the chest. With his free hand, he rubbed the spot over his heart. "Kay, there's no way you could ruin my life. I wanted you. *Want* you."

"I know." The slight sheen in her eyes only made them glow more brightly, made them more beautiful. "You don't think I know? I wanted you, too. But I wasn't going to destroy you. Then—" With her free hand, she swiped away another tear.

Jesus, even tears looked good on her. Nick had never seen a woman grow more beautiful with tears, but Kay managed it. She looked so fragile he was afraid she'd break.

But she wasn't fragile, that was the point. She'd taken up the flag when her friend had fallen, perfectly aware that she could be trashing the career she'd worked so hard for, perfectly aware that there was danger, and still she'd thought of him. Of his fucking *career*!

No, this woman wasn't fragile. She was just exhausted and terrified.

"Then?"

"I asked Felicity to contact Mike Hammer through the dark web and she did. Mike knew a lot of the background. I told him I was coming to Portland. He told me to meet him and give him the flash drive. But he also said to be prepared to go underground. He said maybe I could surface a week or two after Priyanka's findings were published, maybe longer. He said I had to be prepared to go to a safe house for a while. But of course, the subtext was that staying in a safe house might become…permanent."

She looked at him, heart in her eyes. "By that time, you'd quit the FBI and joined ASI. And I knew that something like this could never compromise your position at ASI, they don't think like that."

"No," Nick said, voice steady. "They don't. But I want you to know that even if I'd still been a Special Agent, I wouldn't have been scared of the association with you. They could have come after me all they wanted."

"Nick," she said softly. "Don't forget that people have ended up dead over this. It wasn't just a question of your career taking a hit. The blowback could have ended up costing you your life."

Nick didn't scoff. He'd known of too many people who'd lost their lives to bad guys. Not only to terrorists abroad, but to greedy bastards at home. A potential vice president had killed hundreds of people at a Washington hotel in what was known as the Washington Massacre. Countless men and women dead for his greed and power hunger. Still... "I know how to handle myself."

Kay pinched the bridge of her nose. "I know you do. Anyway, once you were ASI and I was planning on disappearing anyway, I—I thought...I thought maybe I could allow myself one meeting with you." She pursed her lips. "I wasn't planning on sleeping with you, though."

"You were thinking about it." Nick was certain of it.

She cocked her head, studying him. "Yes." A slight smile. "I was thinking about it. I thought—if I'm going to throw my career away, maybe I can give myself a little treat."

He faked indignation. "A *little* treat?"

The smile was still small but genuine. "Okay. A big treat."

"*Very big* treat."

"The biggest."

They grinned at each other. Nick's heart lifted. Whatever was in the cards for them, whatever was going to happen, they would face it together. And he had all of ASI at his back. He would never say it out loud, and could barely think it to himself, but he'd rather have ASI at his back than the FBI.

"It'll be all right, Kay," he said softly. "We'll figure it out. It's big and it's scary but we'll figure it out."

She slid her hand out from between his and he immediately missed it. Picking up her fork, she finished the last of the lasagna and sat back. "I sure hope so. I hate this. I hate knowing Priyanka's and Mike Hammer's deaths were in vain. I'm even sorry that jerk Bill is dead. I'm sorry you've been roped into something that isn't any concern of yours, I'm sorry—"

Nick put a finger across her mouth. Her lips were soft and full against his finger and he remembered with a flash of intensely uncomfortable heat how those lips had felt kissing his stomach, moving lower, taking him in her mouth…

Blood shot straight to his dick.

Kay must have felt the sex vibes suddenly clouding the air because her eyes widened and her lips moved under his finger. "Nick," she said.

Oh man, there was no response. He couldn't talk, could barely breathe, with a hard-on he could hammer a nail with.

From touching her mouth.

Oh shit, he was in deep, deep trouble. This was not the time and the place. She needed reassurance, a plan. She didn't need to be fucked half to death.

They sat there like that, a little tableau of imminent sex, angled toward each other, eyes locked, the remains of an excellent meal between them.

God yes. Food and then sex. Guaranteed to help overcome trauma. Best thing in the world.

Nick started rising to usher them straight back into the bedroom when his cell rang. His satphone's ring was unmistakable. From ASI.

His gaze never wavered from Kay's. "It's probably Felicity."

She straightened. His sex vibes pulsing at her had given her a slight blush, but she paled again.

Nick was ashamed of himself. Since when did he have problems focusing on the mission? Never. He was intensely mission-oriented. You didn't become a SEAL or join the FBI's HRT without being maniacally focused.

The thing was, Kay just overwhelmed him. He had to start getting his priorities straight, starting right now. Some very bad guys who had already killed and who might be wielding a bio-weapon were after Kay. His job was to keep her safe while she ran them to ground.

He felt his head clear, his heart settle. Yes, that was the mission. Keeping Kay safe. That was what he was good at. He was always picked for protection detail. He was picked because he knew what to do and how to do it.

Kay was not going to be harmed, not on his watch. Not ever.

He could protect her best by keeping her close. Yeah, man. Very close. He wrapped an arm around her shoulders as his satphone rang again. He answered without taking his eyes from hers. "Yo. Going to the ops center."

Nine

They moved quickly to one of the rooms in that immense corridor. Nick entered a code in the keypad next to the door and it slid open as lights turned on. He put his hand to her back and walked her in.

Kay blinked. It was a command center, and it looked like the White House war room in *Doctor Strangelove*, only from the 22nd century instead of the 20th. Huge monitors covered the walls and there were keyboards, wireless headsets, and speakers everywhere.

"Here." Nick was holding out an expensive mesh office chair, the kind that supported your back and was easy on the thighs and made coffee for you. She sat down and it was like sitting on a cloud. Whatever make it was, she wanted one for her office.

Then, like cold water dashed in her face, she realized she would probably never work in her office again.

"Okay. I've got Felicity on the line." Nick thumbed his cell phone screen and Felicity's pretty face popped up on a huge wall screen.

"Hey," Felicity said, and it was like her being in the room. She smiled at Kay, whose face was on-screen in a small box in the lower right-hand side, just like before. Behind Felicity stood her boyfriend, Metal, as large as a bridge support. He had a big hand on her shoulder.

Nick appeared behind her on the small screen. She saw him and then felt his hand on her shoulder, as well.

"Hey." Kay smiled at Felicity. "Did you—"

"Decrypt the flash drive? I did. Hell of a job, too. Gave even me some trouble. And it's a lot of stuff. Part of what was encrypted was a link to more files in the cloud."

Oh God, it was so good to see Felicity. She wasn't an operator like Nick, or Metal, or any of the guys at ASI but she was whip-smart and Kay felt better just seeing her.

"Yeah, part of the encrypting was done by Priyanka's brother. Sorry to have to ask for your help."

Felicity waved a long, slender hand. "Don't even mention it, are you kidding? I had fun. Lately all I've done is boring stuff for ASI. What?" She turned around to look at Metal when he made a noise. "Not that much fun in devising data algorithms, don't try to tell me otherwise. Kay's stuff was a real challenge."

Behind her, Metal looked amused and resigned in equal measure. He bent down and whispered something in her ear and her fair skin turned pink. Kay sympathized. She had the exact same kind of skin. It showed all your emotions, good and bad. Judging from the sexy sideways glance she shot Metal, it was good.

"What was in it?" Kay leaned forward. "Did you go over it?"

"Oh God, honey." Felicity cocked her head, straightened it, as if listening to a secret internal voice. "I have no idea what's in it. There was almost a terabyte of info and it's all biochemistry and virology and genetics. Most of it anyway. I did isolate a video made by Priyanka, and some emails between her and Mike Hammer. Also, she did some research on him, so there's about ten of his environmental articles and a couple of documentaries he made for his webzine. He doesn't appear, only as a slightly modified voiceover. He's good. He manipulated the recordings and there would be no way to obtain a voice match without sacrificing too much quality on the recording itself. I didn't have time to watch all the docs—meatspace time is different from digital time—but I gathered they were all hot topics where big companies are polluting. One was about a flu vaccine scam."

Kay nodded. She knew what that was about. A pharmaceutical company that invested ten million dollars in drumming up a flu scare and then delivered thirty million doses on the market of a vaccine that didn't work. There had been 150 deaths and the company had made seven billion dollars, which it promptly deposited in Panama.

Scam was too mild a word. It had been criminal.

"Can you please send over the information?" Kay asked.

Felicity looked blank for an instant. "Uh, Kay…"

"She sent it immediately," Metal pitched in. "And it was sent securely, you don't need to worry about that. We have an internal system. Check the log. It's along the top of the image."

Kay looked and found it. She clicked on the log and immediately Felicity and Metal were reduced to a small box next to the image of herself and Nick. Data started scrolling down the screen.

"Whoa," Nick said behind her. "Looks like the Matrix. What a mess."

Kay was studying the screen intently. "No, not a mess. There's a lot of data from Bill's drive, and it's standard research, going back years. But here," she tapped the screen with a stylus, "and here, and here and here," she looked up reassuringly at Nick, "those are the formerly encrypted files, where we'll find what he was secretly working on. It shouldn't be too hard to sort them out. And Priyanka will have already arranged the files in an easy-to-follow order. It's just a question of time, now. We have the yellow bricks and they're laid out on a road. I just have to walk it."

"Hm. If you say so." Nick's voice was full of doubt. "Hell of a lot of info there."

"It's what I do—what we do at the CDC." *Did at the CDC*, Kay thought with a pang of pain. What they *did* at the CDC. Studied all of nature, in its unfathomably huge details, to find what could harm humans, and fix it.

Until someone inside the CDC—and that never failed to astonish her—used data to harm humans.

"Okay. This is your thing, Kay." Felicity was scowling on the screen. "If anyone can figure this out, it's you. You go, girl."

"Oh, I will," Kay promised softly. Priyanka and Mike Hammer, good people, had died for what was in those files. She'd find out what it was and ASI would go after them. Of that she had no doubt. Maybe call in the FBI, too. Nick trusted the FBI. At this point, Kay herself didn't trust any institution.

"Good. I think that—" She frowned.

"Felicity?"

Felicity had turned sheet white. Like flipping a switch. From its usual pale rose, her complexion had turned to dirty ice, dead white with a gray undertone. Felicity slapped her hand over her mouth and disappeared from the screen. She could be seen in the background, running.

"Good God!" Kay leaned forward. "Metal! Is Felicity okay? Is something wrong? Is she sick?"

"Is it official?" Nick asked behind her.

She swiveled. "What?"

"Yeah." Metal's super-broad chest lifted on a sigh. "We told everyone."

"So...you know what it is?" Nick asked.

What *what* is? What were they talking about?

"Twins." Metal flashed a quick grin, then it disappeared from his face. "Boys, we think. The next sonogram should be definitive. But she's been sicker than a dog. I hate it."

Kay, who had a master's degree in biology, finally got it. Her jaw dropped. "She's pregnant? Felicity's pregnant?"

"Oh yeah. Super pregnant. Double pregnant." A corner of Metal's mouth lifted. "We've been trying and trying and finally it caught."

"Tough job," Nick said. "But someone's got to do it."

"Well." Kay smiled at the thought of Felicity expecting kids. She'd had a very lonely existence, much lonelier than Kay's own, though she'd had both parents until she was in her late teens. Her parents had been Russians, undercover, and they had lived in the Witness Protection Program all her life. Kay had Gramps to love her. Felicity had had no one who loved her, truly loved her.

But now she had a future husband—Kay heard from everyone that Metal asked Felicity to marry him daily, and she'd accepted without setting a date—and she was expecting twins. A full, happy household. "At least you know your kids will be gorgeous and have IQs off the charts."

Felicity's father had been a Nobel Prize winner in physics and she herself had been tested at genius level.

"Yeah." Metal tried to smile, but his big plain face was creased with worry.

"She's got morning sickness," Nick said.

"Morning, noon, afternoon, evening and night sickness," Metal answered. "It's awful."

"Oh my God." Kay was horrified. "I asked her to decrypt those files while she was *sick*? I didn't know! I had no idea, I would never have asked her if I'd known—"

"Nah." Metal held up a huge hand. "There was no way to stop her. As a matter of fact, she was so engrossed in your files that she wasn't sick for hours. A first. So thanks for that. And Felicity would have kicked me in the balls if I'd tried to stop her. You did her, and me, a big favor."

He was half turned toward the back of the vast room, his hand clutching the back of the chair so tightly his knuckles were white. He was champing at the bit to get to Felicity.

"Go see how she's doing, Metal," Kay said gently. "It's up to me now. As soon as I know anything, I'll let you know." He blew out a breath of relief and was already on his way to Felicity when she called him back. "Metal!"

He stopped himself with difficulty—he was practically vibrating with impatience.

"Send me John, if you can."

He nodded and nearly ran across the room.

A minute later, John Huntington popped up on the screen. He was in his private office, which was amazingly elegant and as silent as a church.

He was…intimidating. That was the only word for it. Sharply handsome, he always looked grim and cold. The people who worked for him worshipped him, but Kay was just a little—a teensy bit—frightened of him.

He was one of the good guys. He'd founded one of the best security companies in the world. He'd managed to make a beautiful, gentle, highly creative woman fall in love with him and he had two little girls he hadn't eaten like the big bad wolf. Yet.

But still she was a little scared.

"Dr. Hudson." That cold, handsome face looked, as usual, as if he'd just received news that World War III had broken out.

"Mr. Huntington."

He dipped his head, lifted it. She swore his eyes could see inside her head though he was in the heart of Portland and she was on the slopes of Mount Hood. "Good to see you alive and well, Dr. Hudson." His dark eyes shifted to the man behind her. "I am counting on you to keep her that way, Nick."

"Yeah. You can count on me." Nick respected John Huntington a lot, but he wasn't intimidated like she was.

"This feels like bad business, Nick." Huntington scowled.

"It is bad business, sir."

Kay lifted her hand and Nick grabbed it, held it. He might have thought it was her way of showing John Huntington that they were together, but that wasn't it. John unnerved her.

"Mike Hammer's body was recovered and autopsied. The ME said that if he hadn't been ordered to carry out the autopsy, he wouldn't have bothered. He said it looked like a natural death." Huntington's eyes narrowed.

"Except that he drowned in a back alley."

Huntington dipped his head again. "Exactly. His lungs were full of fluid."

"Not water." Kay shook her head. "Transudates."

He briefly consulted a sheet in front of him. "Exactly."

This was safer ground; this was her field. "I understand Captain Morrison asked for the blood panel to be tested for cytokines."

He dipped his head again. "As you asked. And again, he said he wouldn't have tested for cytokines if there hadn't been a special request.

"And the count was high."

"Off the charts. I assume that is significant."

Time to share what she knew. The time for secrecy was gone. "Very significant. I need to study Dr. Anand's files, but I suspect that someone—probably a biochemist called Bill Morrell—perfected a bioweaponized form of the Spanish flu."

Huntington winced. "Didn't that kill off more people in 1918 than World War I?"

"It did. This one will be worse." She nodded, while keeping eye contact. "This version is highly aggressive, fast-acting and airborne. From what I observed, the weaponized virus is in aerosol form, in this case delivered by drone."

His mouth tightened. "Insane. We could have a pandemic on our hands."

"We could, yes. But I think something else is happening, something less devastating to society but highly dangerous all the same."

He leaned forward a little. "Something else?"

She put it in words for the first time. "I suspect that the virus has been encoded with specific DNA."

He just stared, looking blank.

"In other words, the weaponized virus is being tailored to specific people. That virus was encoded to Mike Hammer's DNA and not mine, which is why he died and I walked away. They didn't know I was going to be there, so they only prepared the virus for him. They could have gotten his DNA from anywhere. Hair from a hairbrush, a glass he'd drunk out of, a plate, a tiny bit of blood from a cut."

He looked stunned. "How is that possible? Something that is lethal for one person and not another? Wouldn't it take a vast scientific apparatus?"

"Well, the CDC is a vast scientific apparatus in itself. It can be done using a machine called a CRISPR-Cas9. CRISPR stands for clustered regularly interspaced short palindromic repeats. It's a machine for editing genes."

"But that's—"

"A perfect murder weapon. A virus tailored to someone's DNA, delivered by drone. Essentially a natural death, put down to a sudden allergic attack, a stroke or a heart attack. The murderer can be far away, guiding the drone by a tablet, waiting for the right moment. Who knows how many people have been killed so far."

"My God." His jaw tightened. "Shouldn't we—"

"Shouldn't we what, Mr. Huntington? Look for sudden deaths with high cytokine counts? Most of the bodies won't have been autopsied. The cytokines dissipate quickly. And it would be the job of the CDC to note this kind of pattern. I think—"

Her throat seized up. Just saying the words hurt, like knives slicing her inside. She swallowed and when she spoke, her voice was a raw whisper. "I think the CDC is involved. We can't go to them. Do you think your police captain friend can inquire discreetly about any sudden unexplained deaths nationwide?"

His eyes narrowed and he looked more dangerous than ever. "Count on it."

"A deadly virus tailored to a specific person's DNA is incredibly dangerous. You can widen the scope. You could target an individual, a family, a tribe. Without endangering anyone who might be physically close who doesn't share DNA with the victim. It's the perfect weapon, surgically precise. We have to stop this. Imagine being able to target a people in the Middle East, a family in Washington, one specific person in a crowd."

"Someone's going to pay for this," he said in a deep, low voice.

Kay repressed a shudder. Huntington was scary in a way Nick, Metal, Joe and Jacko weren't. His partner, too, was frightening. Former SEAL Senior Chief Douglas Kowalski, who was not only terrifying but spectacularly ugly.

Both of them were worshipped by the men under them.

And loved fiercely by two gentle, elegant, artistic women.

Go figure.

Whatever her personal feelings, though, this man and his partner had made the entire resources of their company—and they were considerable—available to her. They were making a real effort to keep her safe and to help her unravel the mystery. She was nothing to him. A friend of one of his employees. However important to the company Felicity was, Kay wasn't a sister or a cousin. Was he doing this for Nick? Nick had made it clear that his first priority was Kay, and they seemed to be okay with that.

She owed them. She owed them her best efforts to finish this quickly and well.

They'd done their share. More than their share. Now it was up to her. Well, this was what she did.

She wasn't a warrior, she wasn't a computer genius. But this?

"Okay, Mr. Huntington—"

"John," he said. His lips moved in what for normal people would be a smile.

"What?"

"You must call me John."

Her own smile froze. "Of—of course." God. It would be like calling the Pope "Frank". There was only one thing to say. "And you must call me Kay. Remember, John. This is pure conjecture. I think I'm right, but I'll know for sure only after studying the data on the flash drive."

"You guys stay out of sight for the moment. I'm liaising with Captain Morrison and I'll let you know what emerges from the investigation."

She leaned closer to the screen. "Hammer was killed by a drone."

"Yeah. We got that. Felicity traced the frequency back to a spot on the road. It was being piloted by someone in a vehicle who then left. We're working on that. Soon we'll know who was piloting it. One way or another, we're hoping to wrap this thing up soon."

Soon. They were in a hurry. Kay nodded. "I imagine you need Nick back in the office."

A veil of coldness dropped across his face. Just amazing. She realized that he had been warm and fuzzy before in contrast to now. Now he looked like he was about to kill someone. "No. That's not it.

Yeah, we'd like Nick to come back when he can, but he's doing good work right where he is. This company doesn't stand for murder, for threats to good people. And I've heard enough to understand that there's the possibility of a dangerous bio-weapon in play that could go wide. We were born to fight things like this. And we will. We'll talk soon."

The monitor winked off.

It was like a powerful source of energy had just been switched off and Kay slumped in her chair.

"He's something, isn't he?" Nick asked, amused.

It was very cool in what she thought of as the command module. All those electronics. The chill in the air was the only thing that stopped her from sweating like a pig. John Huntington was a force of nature.

"I'll say." She switched gears, turning to face Nick. "So—Felicity's pregnant. How long have you known?"

"Couple of days now."

"Do you think she's freaked?" During Kay's visits and when they Skyped, she and Felicity had talked about this. Metal was eager, really impatient to start a family. Felicity wanted to start one too but, unlike Metal, she'd never really been part of a happy family. She doubted herself, not Metal.

Kay didn't doubt for a second that Metal would make a great father. Metal's father had been an incredible role model and his uncles were all really good family men. Felicity's parents had been cold and secretive, shutting her out. She said she wasn't too sure she was cut out to be a good mom.

"Yeah. Metal's *more* freaked, though."

"He is? Felicity said he was really ready, raring to go."

"Mm." Nick smiled grimly. "He didn't calculate that in order to have kids, Felicity would have to be pregnant. Apparently, she's having problems and it's making his head explode. He wants kids with Felicity but he doesn't want her to have to be pregnant."

"Little cognitive dissonance there. Hard to have the one without the other."

"Well, they'll work it out. Eventually, Felicity will give birth. To two kids at once. That's really super-efficient, just like her. Now." Nick leaned forward, grasping the arms of her chair. His face was sober and serious. "There's not much I can do to help you go through the files, but I can fetch and carry and make sure you're comfortable." His hand lifted, moved over her hair in a caress. "I suggest you stay here, it's the place where there's the most computing power. You can have music if you want. Any kind except heavy metal. Drives me crazy."

Okay, so cool dude Nick Mancino didn't do heavy metal. Interesting. Kay usually worked to new age music or Mozart. But when she had heavy-duty focusing to do, she needed silence.

"No, no heavy metal, promise. As a matter of fact, I think I'd prefer silence."

He dropped a kiss on the top of her head. "You got it. Anything else?"

"I understand that the room needs to remain cool because of all the electronics but it's too cold if I'm going to be sitting in a chair. I'll need a sweater and socks. And while you're at it, some water, fruit and hot tea at hand. A Thermos would be great. Any kind of herbal tea. If Isabel stocked up, there's bound to be plenty of herbal tea."

"Dunno, I'm a coffee guy myself, but I'll look around. Be back in a second."

Okay, she thought, as she brought the contents of the flash drive up on the monitor in front of her. She also threw the data up on one of the big screens.

She scrolled, tapped on the screen, scrolled some more. The material was organized into several subsets. One was Bill's normal work files, going back two years. That data had had normal CDC encryption, the same encryption all of them followed. His files were similar to her own, except of course he'd been working on different projects. But the structure was similar, and familiar.

She selected that data out, and threw it up on a second wall screen.

He had an extensive database of ongoing research throughout the world on Spanish flu and flu viruses. She recognized most of the papers. These were selected and put up on another monitor.

Basic research on viruses and gene manipulation. Selected and thrown up on a fourth monitor.

His work emails—up on a fifth.

Hello. There was a section that had been subjected only to his own heavy-duty encryption, not the CDC's. Which meant it had never been on the CDC servers. This was his private email.

She opened the files, scrolling through the headings. *Bingo.* Goose pimples rose on her arms and neck.

Nick appeared by her side holding a tray. He placed a pitcher of water, a Thermos, a glass and a cup on the desk. A platter with grapes and peeled orange sections. A pile of sandwiches on whole wheat bread.

He placed a heavy sweater on her shoulders. Kay bent her nose toward her shoulder and smelled clean wool and fabric softener.

Nick smiled at her and dropped a knee to the ground.

She blinked at him. What on earth… Oh.

He slid her slippers off her feet and put on soft, thick socks, then put the slippers back on. She'd been so engrossed in separating out Bill's files, she'd forgotten she was cold.

"Better?" he smiled up at her, still kneeling.

It should have been a ridiculous position, on one knee at her feet, but he made it super macho and super sexy. There was absolutely nothing submissive about him. With Nick kneeling at her feet, she could see how incredibly broad his shoulders were, how thickly muscled his thighs. He could have been a knight awaiting orders, but a knight who could slay dragons.

His mouth was tipped in a half smile, dark eyes gleaming behind half-closed eyelids.

A flash of heat that had nothing whatsoever to do with the sweater and socks shot through her and damn, he could tell. Like Felicity's, her skin was like a sensor for her emotions. She might as well have had a sign flashing on her forehead. *Hormonal female in heat.*

"Down boy," she said.

"Ah, but darling, I *am* down," Nick answered, and grinned. "Down for the count. Completely at your mercy and at your feet."

Yeah, right.

Kay spread her hand over his jaw, feeling the scruff of his five o'clock shadow even though in these antiseptic surroundings, she had no idea if it was five o'clock or not. None of the monitors showed the time, either. They would show time if she pressed the right button. They would show the time of any time zone on earth, since ASI operated around the globe.

His skin felt warm beneath her palm. Their eyes locked. He still had her foot on his knee, big hand loosely holding her ankle. His hand tightened, his eyes tightened. If she dropped her gaze, she would undoubtedly see something else tighten and grow.

She didn't even dare give a sigh because they were both on hair triggers. Nick's hand around her ankle loosened a little and he began sliding it up.

She closed her eyes, savoring the feeling. His calloused skin against the tender flesh of her calf felt so exciting. He'd done the exact same thing in the hotel room, only his hand had continued the journey up her shaking thigh until he'd reached the apex. She'd been warm and wet and aching.

Like now.

Only they weren't in a hotel room. They were on the run.

"Nick…" She barely had the breath to get the word out.

His hand froze. His dark, glittering eyes never wavered from her face.

"Not now?" His voice was low, rough.

She couldn't talk, could barely breathe. Her heart drummed in her chest. She shook her head.

Slowly, as if it hurt, Nick lifted his hand from her leg. Shockingly, her skin felt chilled at the loss of his touch.

"Okay, okay." Nick winced as he rose to his feet. It was easy to see why he was wincing. Under the jeans his erection was visible.

"Ouch?" She sketched a smile.

"Ouch," he confirmed. He leaned forward, kissed her on the forehead. "I'm going to hobble away now and nurse my dashed hopes. You drink that tea and eat those sandwiches. You're not going to starve on my watch."

She smiled. "No, sir, I guess I'm not."

Nick put a slick rectangle of dark Gorilla Glass on the desk. "If you need anything, yell. If I don't come right away…" He swiped at the dark glass, which lit up at his touch. The screen had a big red button on it. "Press this."

Kay picked it up, turned it. "Is this a cell phone?"

"Nope." Nick grinned. "Its only function is to summon your humble servant. And now, I'll leave you to your work." His grin disappeared. "I don't know how long you'll need to go through those files, but I expect a long time. It's a hell of a lot of data. But you're not going to kill yourself doing it. You need to eat and rest. I'll make sure you do that. You're no good to anyone dead on your feet, Kay."

It was her weak point—working until she dropped. And no, it wouldn't help anyone.

"Okay, Nick. I'll try to be smart about it."

He stood and stared into her eyes, all playfulness gone. "Yeah. You will. I'll leave you to it. I'll check in with you from time to time. In the meantime, I'm going to monitor our perimeter and contact ASI. Find out if there's any more intel."

"Find out about Felicity, if you can."

"Will do." He leveled his index finger at her as if pointing a gun. "I'll be checking in on you." And he walked quietly out the door.

He did check in on her from time to time. She'd sit up to stretch her aching back muscles to find that the water pitcher had been refilled, fresh fruit on the plate, new sandwiches. Kay barely noticed. She sank into the job like you sink into quicksand, pulled ever deeper.

It was impossible to tell whether it was day or night. Didn't matter, she was digging deep into the files and trying to figure out what was going on that had cost Priyanka and Mike Hammer and Bill their lives—and figure out who was behind it.

She dove into Bill's work files, opening each and reading enough to discard it. There were thousands of files, each one interesting. She had to tug herself away from most of them because however fascinating they were, they didn't pertain to the issue at hand.

It was an overwhelming job. Not all the files were his—some were research papers from around the world. The Infectious Diseases Data Observatory and the Epidemic Diseases Research Group in Oxford. The French Institute of Health and the Pasteur Institute in Paris, the Nagasaki School of Global Health, various agencies within the World Health Organization…the list was endless.

His root directory wasn't organized according to author or source, but according to material. He was a well-known expert on influenza, which was one of the most-studied viruses on earth. The printed information on the influenza virus could fill an entire university library—and in some universities, did.

She sighed and resigned herself to manually examining all the files. It was intense, eye-straining labor, and after a while, the words began to blur on the screen.

She stopped, rubbed her eyes.

She'd scrolled though about a thousand files and had barely scratched the surface. She couldn't even outsource it because you needed to be an expert to understand what to look for. Mere keywords wouldn't do it. All the files were about the influenza virus and would contain those hundred or so keywords pertaining to it. It would take her days to train someone even as bright as Felicity to search the files, and even then she could easily miss something significant.

It was as if someone had opened up a firehose of knowledge of the influenza virus and was flooding her with it.

In fact, it was almost as if…as if Bill was blinding her with science. From beyond the grave.

Damn! She straightened, widened her eyes to knock the sleep out of them. So far she hadn't found out anything, not after hours and hours of work.

Were all these files essentially smoke?

Because…because he had been working on something illegal, something that transgressed the Biological Weapons Convention, the convention that prohibited research into bio-weaponry. So he'd have done it in secret, wouldn't he?

Could there be a hidden section with the information she was seeking?

Kay went right back to the root directory and searched harder for something that would indicate secret files within secret files behind firewalls and fire-breathing dragons. She went over the lists carefully but as much as she tried to find a secret or separate section of files, she couldn't.

And yet, he'd encrypted his entire computer with another layer of encryption. No one did that if there wasn't something to hide. CDC encryption was very good. But you weren't supposed to be working on non-CDC research.

Maybe…maybe that was it. Maybe he carried out his secret research after hours, when the day staff left and a skeleton staff remained for the evening and overnight.

She'd done that sometimes, with a time-sensitive research project. Her office had an armchair that became a very uncomfortable cot. More nights than she cared to think about, she'd worked until morning, stretching out on the cot for short breaks.

The building grew quiet after six p.m. and there were no interruptions. Just silence and almost unfettered access to the computing power of the institution and all its high-tech equipment.

If Bill had been working on something illegal, surely he'd have done it after hours? And maybe—maybe he'd finessed access to the BSL-4 lab? Mostly only governments ran bio-safety level 4 labs and there were only 9 government labs in the country, including the CDC. And a few private ones.

Though obtaining unauthorized after-hours access to the BSL-4 labs would be incredibly difficult, it was feasible that Bill had done the basic research at work and then tested the virus in one of the handful of privately owned BSL-4 labs with no cumbersome reporting protocols.

Or he could have done the theoretical work and then handed off the testing to a private lab. This kind of project, in the wrong hands, would have almost unlimited funding, unlike the CDC's funding, which was squeezed harder and harder each year.

But then, Kay and her colleagues were trying to save lives, not a top priority these days. If you were trying to take as many lives as possible, create the most suffering possible, well then…money would flow to you. A weaponized Spanish flu virus would, really, be worth billions. Using bio-weapons was crazy reckless, but if you knew what you were doing, and if you could design a flu that degraded quickly and you were far from the borders of the country being attacked, you could depopulate a country in a few weeks and take over the infrastructure.

You'd have to be as mad as Hitler, but theoretically, it could be done.

No!

Her entire body rebelled at the thought.

Kay went back to the root directory and selected files from no more than a year ago and files time-stamped past 1800 hours.

Priyanka said she'd started observing odd behavior eight months ago. A year would probably cover it all.

The files appeared on her screen, but there were 20 files per screen and—she peered at the numbers at the bottom of the screen—50 pages each. A thousand files. Doable, certainly. And better than the hundreds of thousands of files that had at first appeared.

By the fourth file, Kay knew she had hit gold.

Bill had put together all the latest research on the Spanish flu, including Russian research on a patient buried in the Russian permafrost for a hundred years. It took her several hours, but she read it all and saw that he was interested in a fast-acting, fast-degrading flu.

Made sense. The virus was like tossing nuclear bombs around. No one wanted a worldwide pandemic, not in these days of mass air travel, of mass movements of people. At any given moment, there were 40 million refugees awash in the system, more than at any other time in the history of the world. A locus of infection in a group of refugees who were not monitored and the spark could turn into a conflagration that would burn the world down.

This original weaponized influenza virus had been genetically engineered to kill select individuals or groups with shared DNA.

Kay stopped for a moment, rubbing her eyes.

All of this was so freaking *hard*. It felt like she was twisting her brain so much it hurt. This was the opposite way of thinking of a medical researcher, who was trained—and trained intensely—to look for ways to mute the effects of disease. If possible, to eradicate it. The brass ring for every researcher was to do to all infectious diseases what had been done to smallpox—eliminate it from the earth.

Humankind's most ancient and relentless enemy made powerless.

And now she had to follow the thought processes of someone who wanted to make our mortal enemy *stronger*. More virulent, more dangerous, more lethal.

It went against absolutely everything she believed in. It went against everything she'd ever done with her life. It went against everything science stood for.

Kay had grown up with an FBI Special Agent and she knew the men of ASI. They trained hard to serve and protect. It was their instinct. Her grandfather, as a young special agent, had run into a burning building to save two children who had been held hostage. The hostage taker had set fire to the building, preferring death to capture. The two children survived, thanks to her grandfather.

She'd asked him how he'd had the courage to run into a fire and he'd looked at her blankly.

Because that was what he did.

What Nick did. What Metal and Joe and Jacko and the other men at ASI did.

What she was doing was the equivalent of asking them to cower and hide if terrorists attacked. They couldn't do it. She couldn't do this.

But she had to.

She leaned forward again, holding another sandwich that had magically appeared at her elbow.

Hour after hour went by as she began to pick up on what Bill had been doing.

The first thing he'd done was increase the morbidity of the virus. She deleted out for the moment everything but the effect of the virus. In one file, she found a 3-D rendering of the virus, the elements in yellow where the virus attacked the human system. That was on one half of the screen. On the other half was the original virus, the yellow smaller, more scattered.

The new gene had been *designed* to attack the immune system immediately, like an RPG. The effect was immediate and devastating. The incubation period was reduced to almost zero.

He—and whoever was working with him—had created a virus that blew the immune system up and flooded the lungs with fluid.

God, the image flashed in her mind of Mike Hammer clutching his throat, drowning before her very eyes in a back alley. How he'd clutched his throat, chest heaving to bring in air that couldn't fill the lungs, which were already filling with fluid. His face going from shock to fear to death in a minute and a half.

Someone had created that. Someone had *wanted* that.

She rested her forehead on her palm, exhausted and demoralized. Such horrors, things she and her colleagues had fought against all their adult life, being *planned*. The thought of the virus rotating in front of her on the screen being let loose to choke hundreds of thousands—millions!—of men, women and children…it hurt her to even think of it.

This virus for the moment was being used selectively, but it was there, engine idling, waiting to escape and become a worldwide pandemic, threatening humanity itself.

How could people *do* this?

Heavy hands on her shoulders. "Okay, princess. Time for a rest."

Nick turned her office chair around until she sat facing him, inside the vee of his legs. Nick frowned, framed her face with his hands. "What's wrong, honey?"

She must look as stricken as she felt.

Kay curled her hands around his wrists, trying to anchor herself. Tears were welling in her eyes, but it was mostly rage that she felt.

"Let me tell you what we're up against, Nick. Like I said, in 1918, the Spanish flu killed more people than World War I. The most deadly war in history couldn't compete with the Spanish flu. This particular flu attacked the immune system, making it go haywire. So, the stronger the immune system, the higher the death rate. Most flus kill children and the elderly, but this one affected strong young adults most of all. People couldn't shop or meet up or even attend funerals. For a while, there was speculation that it would kill most of humanity. Even now, we don't fully understand it. And someone, someone in the institution where I work, has taken that and made it *worse*. Made it faster-acting, even more deadly. I've studied these files and I keep backing away from that, because it's too insane for words, but I can't. Someone has taken this knowledge—which is the upshot of the work of thousands and thousands of the best minds humanity has—and turned it against us. I...I can't wrap my head around it."

There was still rage, but a tear fell down her cheek.

Nick wiped it away with his thumb, and sighed. "I know, honey."

"I am just so...so *angry*."

He nodded. "I know exactly how you feel, believe me."

Kay blinked. "You do?"

"Oh yeah." He hooked another rolling chair with a foot, pulled it toward him, sat down. He took her hands in his. The warm fleece sweater and socks had helped in the chilly room, but her hands had been cold. She'd been so focused on the files she'd barely noticed. But his big, calloused hands chased the chill away, filled her with heat. Those hands infused her with warmth and strength.

She cocked her head. "There's a story there."

"Damn straight. A terrible one, too." He leaned forward, kissed her cheek. "So. You and I are alone here, but in a week, we wouldn't have been. A new ASI recruit will be starting work soon. Matt Walker. Former Lieutenant Matt Walker. A very good man whose path crossed a very bad man's."

Kay was listening with every sense she had, not just her ears. Nick's expression was serious, almost grim, his voice flat, as if intent on not betraying emotion. He didn't realize it, but he was holding on to her hands so tightly it almost hurt. He'd gone continuously out of his way not to hurt her. If he was holding her hands too tightly, it was because of the emotions he was trying so hard to repress.

This was important to him, and therefore to her, too.

Discovering what Bill had been trying to do had been like an abyss opening up at her feet, the earth breaking itself apart. What had before been solid terrain was now dangerously cracked. But this was the world Nick operated in, where bad people did bad things.

She needed some insight into this world to remain sane, this new insane world of black hearts and sick minds, where bastards work really hard to kill as many people as possible.

It made no sense to her, but it made sense to Nick.

"A SEAL like you?"

"Yeah." His jaw flexed, and his hands tightened even more. "Lieutenant Matt Walker was a legend. Three tours in Afghanistan and Iraq. Spoke decent Arabic and Pashto. He led from the front, always, the bravest of the brave."

The way he was speaking… "Is he—is he dead?"

"No. No thanks to the US Navy, though."

"What happened?"

"He and his men were stationed at an FOB in Helmand. An FOB is a—"

"Forward operating base," she said. At his look, she shrugged. "I listen when people talk. You'd be surprised what I've picked up from the guys."

"I hope just military slang."

"Mm. And some other stuff. Jacko's very inventive. I've got a PhD and I've never heard that stuff before." Jacko, who was a very gifted mechanic, had once had a piece of engine bite him and she'd learned a lot of interesting expressions before he discovered she was there, listening to him with a grin. He'd shut up immediately.

Nick winced.

"Never mind that." Kay leaned forward. "What happened at the FOB?"

It was as if she'd waved a wand. It wiped the slightly amused wince from his face and replaced it with an expression she couldn't quite pin down.

"Matt and his team were on endless patrols. We're not even at war anymore in Afghanistan but goddamn if fine men aren't still being killed. So anyway, in prances this CIA prick. Not gonna say his name because it's still classified, but his middle name was mother—" His eyes glanced to the side, then back. His jaw clenched as he bit back the word motherfucker. "He briefed Matt on the new mission. Turns out the new mission was sort of the old one, except for one thing. They were supposed to keep the local warlord happy at all costs. Give him the total whiteglove treatment."

Now it was her turn to wince. "I've heard that some warlords were—are—nasty people."

"Scumbags, most of them," Nick nodded. "This particular scumbag was the worst of the lot. Ignorant and brutal. Matt said he took an extra-long shower whenever he had to visit the warlord, keep him pacified. Then one day he arrived unexpectedly, had some patrol schedules to share with the fuckhead." Another sideways glance away. "Sorry."

Kay nodded. "I'm a scientist. I know how to recognize correct technical terminology. Fuckhead sounds about right. So, your friend Matt arrives unexpectedly…"

"Yeah." Nick drew in a deep breath. "He entered the compound, went to what passed for the warlord's office, which was crumbling stucco walls and a beaten earth floor with some flea-laden rugs over it. Matt heard screaming and broke into the warlord's room. The warlord, he had," Nick swallowed, his Adam's apple bobbing up then down, "he had a little boy bent over a table and was raping him brutally. The boy was screaming and crying. Warlord looks up, frowning, says the Pashto equivalent of 'the fuck you want?' Totally ignoring the little kid who's screaming under him. There's a charming practice in that part of the world called 'Bacha Bazi'—boy toys. They use underage boys for sex. It was supposed to have been wiped out, but that's wishful thinking."

"What did Matt do?" Kay could almost see the scene, feel a good man's pain at watching a little boy being brutalized.

"Broke the sick fuck's jaw is what he did. He freed the little boy, helped him clean up, then the little boy led him to a basement where," Nick swallowed heavily again, "there were twenty-two little boys, ages six to ten, more or less, *chained*. They were too cowed even to cry. Some had scars from being beaten with sticks. Matt freed them, loaded them onto the Humvees, then went back into the warlord's office and kicked him in the balls."

Kay was theoretically against violence, had heard the slogan *violence is never the answer* a thousand times, but she was fast coming to understand that sometimes violence was indeed the answer.

"Good for him," she said.

"It doesn't end there and it doesn't end well." Nick's mouth pursed into a thin line. "Back at the FOB, he was busy arranging for placing the little boys in the care of an international aid agency when the CIA prick came storming in with Matt's commanding officer, screaming at Matt that he'd fucked with *our* son of a bitch and that Matt had to hand back the warlord's property."

Shock chased the air from her lungs. *"Property?"*

"Yeah." Nick nodded grimly. "Property. Little boys as property. At which point, Matt pointed out that this country fought a fucking war a hundred and fifty years ago so that the US government never again thought of human beings as property."

"I hate that CIA guy already."

"According to the CIA fucker—who had the audacity to introduce himself as John Smith—there was a deep game being played and Matt had stuck himself right in the middle and messed it up. So not only was Matt supposed to deliver those poor terrified and abused boys back to the monster who was torturing them, he was expected to apologize to the warlord, too."

Oh God. "Was that a direct order? From his commanding officer?" Kay knew enough about the military to know that disobeying a direct order was the worst crime a soldier could commit, besides treason.

"Gets a little tricky, because the direct order was verbally given by CIA Fuckface. Who then told Matt's XO to confirm. The officer nodded, but didn't give the verbal order. By which point Matt was getting back into his Humvee to head for Kabul. CIA Fuckface said if he left the FOB, he'd pay for it with his career, but at that point Matt was so pissed, he left anyway. By the time he got to Kabul, the shit had hit the fan."

"They blamed Matt?" Kay asked, appalled.

"No, all the SEALs were on his side, but the CIA guy, *John Smith*, had accused him of 'causing bodily harm to a crucial ally', making it sound like Matt had lost control. No mention of the kids, of the Bacha Bazi. A lot of US military personnel are tempted to break a lot of warlord jaws, so they decided to turn Matt into an object lesson. Smith was foaming at the mouth for a court martial but Matt is a hero. Has medals coming out his ass. No one would dare court martial him. And there was resistance to giving him a dishonorable discharge. So, he got an OTH discharge. Effective immediately."

"OTH?"

"Other Than Honorable."

"Oh my God, that is terrible!" A loyal Navy officer, a SEAL, a man who risked his life daily for his country, being discharged under a cloud…Kay could barely believe it.

Nick lifted Kay by her shoulders, kissed her gently on the mouth.

"Yes, it's terrible, honey. But ASI and anyone who knows Matt is standing by his side. And we're working to get the OTH discharge overruled. We're fighting back. Just like you're fighting back. Either you stand for something or you don't. You and I and our friends—my teammates, Priyanka, Mike Hammer—will live or die by what we stand for. We will never give up and we will never back down. But right now, to continue the fight, you need to rest, otherwise you'll collapse. Am I right?"

He was looking deep into her eyes, so deeply she couldn't lie. Kay wanted to continue tracking down the criminals who had infested her world of science. Not rest until she found the bastards. But she was exhausted. Her knees were trembling; she could barely stand. She needed to rest or she'd collapse, just as Nick said.

"You're right." No use in lying. Another half hour of work and she'd fall asleep with her face on the keyboard. She'd worked this hard before and there came a point when her body simply shut down. She was at that point now. "What time is it?"

"Four."

"Four what?"

He looked at her curiously. "Four in the afternoon. You've been working nonstop for almost 24 hours. Time to rest."

She nodded.

"Good girl. How long do you need?"

She looked up at him, strong and steady, waiting for her answer. He was clearly willing to roll with whatever she said. She knew enough of Nick to know he was protective, maybe even overprotective, like her grandfather. He'd want her to sleep around the clock, but he wasn't pushing for that. He trusted her to know herself, know how much rest she'd need to be functional. He wasn't pushing in any direction, just waiting for her to tell him.

They crossed the room, walked into the big corridor. She was a little turned around and wouldn't have been able to find their room without his help.

"I think if I could rest for about four hours, I'll be okay."

His glance was piercing, but he didn't say anything. "Four hours it is. I'll have coffee and some dinner waiting."

"A sex god and he cooks dinner."

"Let's not go overboard. A sex god, yes. Dinner, no. That would be thanks to Isabel and her minions."

They were in the huge bedroom. Kay turned around, linked her arms around his neck and lifted to kiss him, breaking away when the kiss got interesting. Sex would be wonderful, but it would wipe her out.

He held up the covers. "Get in, honey."

All the fatigue, all the horror and terror of the past day came down on her like an anvil. With barely the energy to move, she crawled into bed and felt him get in behind her, curling around her like a strong, warm wall.

Nick reached up, did something, and the light dimmed almost completely. He held her, one thick arm around her stomach, knees tucked in behind hers, a living blanket. He had a huge erection against the small of her back.

"Nick, I—" An enormous yawn overtook her.

"Shh." His lips moved against her ear, his deep voice sounding like it came from the pit of his stomach, vibrating against her back. "You're too tired. I just want you to sleep in my arms. I almost lost you yesterday, Kay. I need to hold you."

She sighed. It felt so good to be held. Desire was there but it was far away, beyond the fatigue. It could wait. She was falling, falling into sleep, but she knew if she fell too far he would catch her.

"Sleep, darling," he said in that dark dark voice, and she plunged straight down.

"Help, Kay. You've got to help."

"Priyanka!"

Kay looked greedily at her friend. She was back! So beautiful, so smart. Priyanka. "I've missed you so much."

Priyanka smiled for an instant. "Yes, I know. I know everything."

"If you know everything, then help me, Priyanka. Help me stop this craziness. I watched Mike Hammer die."

"I died, too, Kay."

"God, I know. Killed. No way were you drunk behind the wheel."

Her face was sad, her skin ashen instead of that beautiful bronze color. "No, I wasn't drunk. Is that what they're saying? But I am dead."

Grief shot through Kay all over again, as piercing as the first time she'd heard Priyanka was dead. "But you're here now. Stay. Stay with me," she begged. "Let's work this out together. I need you, Priyanka. I can't do this alone."

Priyanka looked down then back up. Kay gasped. There were holes where Priyanka's eyes had been. No longer that warm chocolate brown, full of amusement and life and intelligence. Now there was nothing. Emptiness.

"Can't help you, Kay." Her voice was low, barely a whisper. Priyanka turned and started walking away. A freezing cold wind blew up out of nowhere and her long dark hair whirled around her head.

No! Kay couldn't let her go! She missed her, needed her. Priyanka knew how to tease out the mystery from the thousands and thousands of files. Ahead of Priyanka were endless doorways, fading into infinity. Door after door after door...

Priyanka was walking through them, one after the other, becoming smaller and smaller.

Kay ran after her, but her feet weren't working. She couldn't move, her body simply wouldn't work. She struggled but it was useless, it was as if she were tied down, encased in something hard and unyielding.

Priyanka was barely a dot on the horizon, walking through the doors stretching into infinity.

Kay leaned forward, trying to move her feet. She put everything into her scream, but it came out soundless. She couldn't move, couldn't speak!

Priyanka was at the edge of infinity. She turned and spoke softly, her voice directly in Kay's ear, though she was so far away.

"So many dead, Kay. Such a horrible death, though you were spared. You know why. The dead will tell you why. The dead will become crisper."

"What?"

"Crisper, they will become crisper." And the voice disappeared and the faint dot on the horizon that was Priyanka winked out.

The wind was freezing, the cold bitterness of a world where Priyanka was gone.

"Crisper!" Suddenly Priyanka was screaming, right in her ear, anger and fear in the voice. She gave a howl that Kay felt down to her toes.

Kay bolted up in bed, heart pounding, the sound of a scream echoing in the room. Nick held her tightly with one arm, the other holding a heavy black gun, which he pointed where his eyes looked.

She was sweating, heart pounding. Nick's muscles were rigid, tight.

He relented first, relaxing, putting the gun down on the night table. She hadn't even known it was there.

"Sorry," she whispered through a tight voice. "Nightmare."

"That's okay, honey," Nick said, kissing the top of her head. "You scared the shit out of me, though. Must have been a hell of a nightmare."

She eased up against the headboard. A bottle of water and a glass had been placed on her side of the bed, which she thought was better than a gun. She poured herself a glass with shaking hands. Nick's steady hand cupped hers as she brought the glass to her lips and drank deeply.

"It was." She leaned into him, into that strong body, steady as a rock. The nightmare had chilled her but his body heat was starting to warm her back up. "Not so much a nightmare, just sad and cold. Priyanka leaving."

That was it. Priyanka's spirit had left the world. It was as if she'd been hanging around, maybe trying to help Kay, but now her time was up. Priyanka had walked through that endless corridor of endless doors and had departed this earth. Kay shivered, feeling bereft all over again. With hindsight, she realized she'd still somehow *felt* Priyanka, guiding her, helping her, but now—now there was only emptiness.

She was gone. Forever.

"She's gone." Nick echoed her thoughts. His voice was so low, she perceived the words through the vibration in his chest rather than from his lips.

"Yeah," she whispered, throat tight. "I know." The words hurt.

Words. She remembered the fun times with Priyanka, who had been a chatterbox when she relaxed. All business at work, such a complex and fascinating woman outside of work. How odd that her last word to Kay had been *crisper*.

Priyanka was so embedded in Kay's heart that she thought she could still hear her voice. *Crisper*.

Kay stiffened.

"Honey?" Nick pulled away a little, frowning down at her.

"Crisper," she whispered.

"What?"

Kay looked at him but she didn't see him. She saw through him, to a point a million miles away.

"Kay?"

"Crisper." The word bounced around inside her head. Bless her, Priyanka had given her the key from beyond the grave.

CRISPR.

Because Bill Morrell hadn't been a geneticist. He wouldn't necessarily have known how to edit genes using a CRISPR. But she knew someone who was a geneticist and would have known how to splice DNA into a gene.

Oh God.

Kay gave Nick a little push and rolled out of bed, pulling on the soft yoga outfit. She ran toward the room where she'd worked, but only got as far as the huge plaza. She was almost jumping with anxiety.

Nick was right behind her, frowning. "Kay, what's crisper?"

"Clustered regularly interspaced short palindromic repeats. I told John that. Where's the office, Nick? Priyanka just gave me the key!"

"Come with me." He led her back, without once mentioning that a dead woman had talked to her. If Kay's head weren't whirling, she'd have kissed him for that. Down one hall and then another and he opened a door and there it was—her workspace, just as she'd left it.

Kay made a beeline, sitting down, opening the root directory.

"CRISPR is the gene engineering and editing system. It can target specific areas of genetic code and can edit DNA at specific locations. If the H1N1 was engineered with specific DNA, they had to use a CRISPR. It wasn't Bill Morrell. He wouldn't know how to splice and edit DNA at that level. Someone else did it, did the genetic engineering. I need to check usage of the CDC CRISPR-Cas9 machines. Someone used those machines, and I think I know who—"

The rest was lost in the explosion that rocked the Grange.

Ten

"Kay!" Nick shouted. He threw himself over her, mantling as much of her as he could. The force of the explosion had to be huge to make the floor shake. The Grange was built as solidly as technology would allow.

The floor stopped shaking, nothing falling from the above. Was another explosion coming?

He jumped up, pulling Kay with him. He grabbed her hand and ran while thumbing in the first number on his ASI cell. Each ASI operative had the bosses on speed dial. No matter what John "Midnight" Huntington or Douglas "Senior" Kowalski were doing, they'd answer, day or night. The Senior was away, so Nick called Midnight.

Midnight answered on the first ring. It wasn't a number you called to say *hey, howzzit hangin'?*

"Nick. Talk to me."

"The Grange is under fire. I don't know who or what is out there. I'm taking Kay to the safe room then I'm going up."

"Get back to you in a minute," Midnight said, and the line went dead.

Nick pulled Kay back for a second at an unmarked stretch of wall. "Here, honey."

"Here?" Her eyes were wide as she looked at the unbroken wall. She wasn't panicking and she wasn't out of breath. Good girl. He felt a surge of pride in his smart princess.

Nick put his hand on a section of the wall and a door slid open. As it did, a light went on inside. He knew what was there. A large, comfortable space with a separate electricity system, separate air system and food and water supplies. There was also a separate weapons locker.

Figuring this thing out was her business. Protecting her while she did it was his.

He urged her into the room but stopped at the door. "This is a safe room, honey. Nothing can get to you here. To get out, punch 2001 on the keypad by the door, but don't go out unless I'm on the other side of that door. I need to get topside."

"Can I help you in any way?"

Nick repressed a shudder at the idea of Kay in the line of fire. "No, no way. You need to stay safe here. We need you, I'm just the muscle."

"Okay." She was watching his eyes, taking her cue from him. "I don't want to get in your way. I'll stay here, don't worry about me."

God yeah, this was a woman in a million. Her world was upended, best friend dead, a man had died in her arms, and she didn't want him to worry about her. He kissed her, waited for the vault-like door to close, and turned to run for the main weapons locker.

His ASI phone buzzed. "Yeah?"

It was Felicity, only on speaker, not on vid. "Nick, you've got an overhead drone. Not a quadcopter like the one that came after Kay. We don't have a perfect visual, I'm piggybacking on a communications satellite, but it's got missiles. It just shot one at you—"

With anyone but Felicity, Nick would have said, *no shit Sherlock*, but Felicity didn't deserve it. She was working hard for him, she worked hard for everyone.

He was passing the entrance elevator. Smoke was drifting down from the top.

"It wiped out John's shack and your vehicle. I don't know how, but someone followed your vehicle up to the Grange. The guy's good, Nick."

"Yeah." He didn't want to think too closely about someone good at being bad targeting Kay. "Can you tell how many more missiles the drone has?"

"Negative," Felicity said sadly. Metal's bass tones rumbled in the background. "We can't see the belly. However, my guy—who is usually right—guesses the drone only has one other missile to shoot, given the size. But this is outside my wheelhouse, Nick, and Metal doesn't like the thought of you paying the price if he's wrong."

"I trust Metal. Do you think the drone has FLIR?" Meaning, would it have infrared and could its cameras see him if he hid in the trees.

Metal's voice came on. "It's a drone model I've never seen before, a little smaller than a Watchkeeper. Act as if it has FLIR, that way you're safe. Anti IR blankets in the armory."

"Altitude?"

The keyboard clickety-clacked. "He's in a circular flight path, counterclockwise, at about a thousand meters."

Nick did the calculations in his head. Hard, but doable. "Speed?"

Another moment of clacking. "About 80 mph."

He hit the armory and came out with comms, an IR cloaking blanket, Kevlar-plated body armor and a MacMillan TAC-50. Jacko was in charge of gear, always, and Nick had no doubt at all that the rifle would be in perfect working order.

It was a damn pity that he'd left the DD in the SUV. Nick would have kicked his own ass if he could have reached it. He'd been so keen to get Kay into the Grange that he hadn't unloaded the vehicle.

Fuck.

Nick grabbed a few grenades and ran to an auxiliary exit.

"I'm headed to the north exit since the main exit is destroyed. When the drone is facing away from me, give me a heads-up." The photographic equipment would be in the nose.

"Roger that," Metal said.

Nick rode up to the ground but held back on opening the elevator doors until Metal gave the okay. "Hundred meters north-northwest," Metal said. "I estimate you have about four minutes." Nick punched the buttons. The doors opened silently and he stepped out. A lot of work had gone into surrounding the unassuming entrance to the Grange with unassuming security.

There was a clear area with a forty-meter radius around the shack that looked like beaten earth. Actually, it was filled with motion sensors. Laser beam emitters were mounted on what looked like overly tall light poles.

For another forty meters back, all around the shack, the area was clear, but had camouflage netting that was indistinguishable from canopy from the sky. Nick had a clear view if he could make himself invisible.

No problem.

He ran to the outer edge of the perimeter and held up military-grade binoculars, scanning the sky. There! A small metal frame, maybe ten meters long. It was dull metal, non-reflective, but he saw it nonetheless. You had to look hard, but there it was. It was probably only semi-visible to radar but that was the thing about stealth. You couldn't make something invisible to the naked eye unless it was dark. But right now, a bright sun shone as it sank to the west. And the drone was slowly circling east. Cool. Its cameras could compensate for sunlight shining directly into the lens but the resolution would be compromised.

Nick came to a stop under the camouflage netting and looked for a hide to set up. His internal clock told him he had a little under three minutes. Okay. If he couldn't find or make himself a hide in three minutes, he deserved to have a bomb dropped on him.

He walked quickly south, checking the perimeter where the forest started, and almost immediately found a perfect hide among the massive roots of an ancient oak, a real rarity this high up.

He spread a thin foam mattress over the root, stretching it out on the ground, put the TAC-50 and ammo carefully on the right and sat down cross-legged, the thin foil blanket over his head and shoulders.

"Wow," Felicity said over the open line. "Just lost sight of you, Nick. Except for a small heat signature which might be your nose. But would probably be read as an animal. Well done."

"Take out that bastard," Metal growled.

"Roger that." Nick settled in, making sure nothing bit into his backside.

He carefully perused the immediate area. The shack was blown to bits, a blackened crater, with rubble emanating from it like a starburst around a black hole.

His SUV was lying on its side like a wounded animal. But ASI vehicles were armored. Maybe if the vehicle could be pushed onto its wheels, it could still function. It had the opposite of a soft underbelly. The chassis was hardened, the tires run-flat. If whoever had remotely pulled the trigger thought he'd taken out whoever was in the shack and had destroyed transportation for anyone who survived the bombing, they were in for a surprise.

He lifted the rifle to his shoulder, then frowned. What was that noise? Like...the rustling of leaves, only there was no wind. And it was regular. What the fuck—

Metal's voice came over his comms unit. "Nick! Get out of there! Fuck, it's a sniper drone, too! *Gogogo!*"

"Negative, Metal," Nick said calmly, shouldering the rifle.

"Fuck, man! That drone's big enough to carry a chain gun—one of those bullets catches you, you'll bleed out in seconds."

"Kay's in the Grange. Would you leave Felicity there with the possibility of another missile strike? And with a strafing gun on over-watch?"

Silence. "Okay, man, I hear you. Knock it out of the sky."

"Roger that." Nick put his eye to the scope. Someone rich and powerful was after Kay. Someone with the potential to do immense harm to a lot of people. That was Nick's usual target but this guy's real mistake was going after Kay. He'd have to get through Nick, and he'd have to get through the entire ASI team first.

Nick knew that if he was killed, Kay would be protected by ASI, and they would pull out all the stops. She was Felicity's friend and she was Al Goodkind's granddaughter. They wouldn't let anything happen to her.

But it so happened that Nick wanted to live and take care of Kay himself. They were both going to live through this and then he'd go after the fuckers with everything he had. He'd—

There it was!

Circling back slowly like an oversized eagle. When Nick put his eye to the scope, the drone jumped, looking as if it were right above Nick's head. The optics were very clear. While the shooting lobe in his head set up the shot, the analytical part of his brain was drawing in info.

It was a pity that the scope didn't have a camera, because he'd love to be able to study the underbelly once they got back to HQ. But it didn't. He only had time to see that there had been two missiles attached, only one remaining. The drone was circling back.

Suddenly, a *whap whap whap!* sound came from the bushes again. The drone was clearing the terrain with bullets before letting fly another missile.

Whoever was operating the drone wasn't seeing signs of life, but the motherfucker wasn't taking chances. This guy wanted Kay dead.

Not on my watch, motherfucker.

Nick slowed his breathing, finger tight but not too tight on the trigger. Breathing slowed, he slowed his heartbeat, watching the silver bird circle around to him. The bullets chewed up the undergrowth but didn't interfere with his view of the drone itself.

Closer, closer.

His heart was beating steady and slow.

The drone filled his scope. He tuned out the sound of the bullets chopping down trees, digging up the earth, striking the SUV, coming closer. The bullets so close now he could see shards of wood fly up.

He slowed his heartbeat more. Thump. Pause. Thump.

Between one heartbeat and another, Nick pulled the trigger. And watched the drone blow up.

The bullet had 220 footounds of force. The drone was made of lightweight metal to increase its flying time. No way it could withstand such an impact.

Nick crouched behind the tree trunk for ten seconds, waiting for all the hot shards of metal to drop to the ground, then took off for the secondary exit at a run.

"Excellent shot," Metal said in his ear. "The FBI didn't destroy your aim."

Nick ignored him as he ran. "Felicity," he said urgently. "Any other drones?"

"No." She paused. "But I can't guarantee that this guy doesn't have satellite access. Can you find the entrance that's under the camouflage netting?"

Nick swerved. Yes, there was another exit that had been placed under the cover of the netting. "Entering now. I want to exit as fast as possible with Kay. Find us a path out that's not open to eyes in the sky."

Clickety-clack. "Metal's taking care of that right now," Felicity said. "He and Jacko will be contacting you. I'll stay on over-watch."

A minute later, Metal was on comms. "Nick, make it to the very end of the second server farm. Matt will be waiting for you."

The third exit also had a ramp, and Nick hit it running, figuring he could run down the four flights faster than the elevator could take him. He exited into another section, but he had the floor plan in his head. A minute later he was placing his hand on the wall outside the safe room.

"Nick!"

Kay was sitting at a desk, still working at the computer, but at the sound of the door opening, she looked up. And her face changed. It was as if him walking into the room brought her Christmas and Easter and her birthday, all at once. In the midst of death and danger, her world falling to bits around her, he brought her joy.

Kay sprang out of the chair and ran to him and he caught her, held her. He buried his face in her hair, feeling her warmth all along his body.

He imagined what it would have been like, burying her. All that warmth and beauty and intelligence—lost forever. He held her even more tightly, resting his cheek on the top of her head for a moment.

Whoever was after her was smart and with resources. They had to get going. But he needed this—just for a moment.

Kay pulled away and looked up at him.

"You made it back! Thank God. What happened up top?"

"Drone," Nick said. "Big enough to carry a missile. And it had a machine gun."

Her face had gone pale, eyes huge. "Is—is it still up there?"

"Nope." Nick shook his head. "I shot it out of the sky. Felicity and Metal are keeping an eye on the sky but there's no guarantee that another drone might not be coming. So, we gotta go. Now."

Kay searched his eyes for a second, then nodded. "Will we ever come back here?"

"Maybe." If he had anything to say about Kay's life after they nailed the fuckers who'd attacked her, she'd never leave his side again. "Definitely. We need to go now, fast. Can you run?"

She smiled. "I can run. I can't outrun a Navy SEAL, but I can run for a while. I won't hold you back."

He smiled back at her as a wave of…something washed over him. Something hot that made his knees weak. This was some woman. This was *his* woman. She wasn't complaining, she was doing her very best.

Well, he'd do his very best by her.

"We're going to run down a long tunnel and through two huge server farms. The tunnel's going to be fairly dark and the server farm will be cold. But we'll exit pretty far away from here. When we exit, a guy will meet us. That guy I told you about."

"Matt Walker? The one who broke the jaw of the pedophile warlord?"

"That's the one. He's been taking some time off, but ASI contacted him and he'll be waiting for us. So—ready?" He held out his hand.

She put her hand in his, that beautiful face set and fierce. "After we get clear, I am going after whoever is behind this. I have an idea, but I wasn't able to finish the files. If what I suspect is true, he is going down if I have to take him out with my bare hands."

Whoa.

She must have seen the alarm on his face. She squeezed his hand. "Let's go, Nick."

She was right. They had to go. He took off at a jog. They had several miles to cover, but he didn't want to exhaust her right away. To his surprise, though, she kept up.

The living complex was huge. They ran down its entire length to a small door at the end wall. Nick keyed in the code and entered the dark corridor at a run when the door slid open.

It was designed to be traversed by automated cars and was dimly lit. The cars for this stretch weren't yet installed. At least it wasn't dirty and cobwebby. Automated sweepers cleaned it every week.

They reached the end of the corridor and entered into the server farm, which was kept at a constant forty degrees. Their heads were wreathed in the white condensation from their breath. It was like running through snow in winter. Nick ran them down the big central aisle of the server farm, heading straight for the opposite wall. He glanced to his right. Kay was breathing hard but keeping up. He wasn't running flat out, but that was okay. They were making good time.

At the other end of the huge server farm, Nick entered another code and the door slid open. Kay was about to sprint forward but he held her back.

"This next part will be easier," he said. Behind the door was an electric cart sitting at the end of a corridor so long the other end was lost to view. He opened the palm of his hand. "Madame, your carriage awaits. Hop on."

As soon as they were both settled, Nick switched the engine on by a button. No need to steer, it was programmed to shuttle back and forth down the three-mile corridor. It wasn't fast but they wouldn't have to run the distance.

The temperature was dry and very cold. Perfect for computer equipment, bad for people. Not many people used the shuttle.

Kay shivered and leaned into him. He reached into the back. "Here, honey." Two super-warm blankets. He placed one across their knees and the other across their backs then put his arm around her shoulders.

"Thanks." Kay looked around, in back of them and in front. From whatever the angle, the view was the same. A long, featureless corridor, dimly lit. "What is this?"

They had time. They were still in danger, but there was nothing they could do until the shuttle reached the end of the corridor.

"This is Felicity's genius idea. She wanted ASI to get into the cloud business and wanted to assure clients that it was super secure. So, we have two server farms, but one is air gapped. The client info streams into the first server farm, is thoroughly checked for viruses and is super sensitive to attempted hacks. Every half hour, after the check, the shuttle automatically carries powerful flash drives to a second server farm, which isn't connected to the internet, as it's air gapped. We've never had a hack, and I think we never will."

Kay gave a half laugh and shook her head. "Felicity's amazing. I hope you guys treat her right."

Nick smiled. "Like royalty. And if we didn't, Metal would whup our asses. The bosses really appreciate her. This business alone brings in over ten million per annum and that number is rising. It'll be more like fourteen million next year. Not to mention what she does at HQ."

"I wonder what'll happen when she gives birth. Twins. Boys." Kay shook her head. "That's a lot to take on."

"She'll manage. And the bosses have been talking about setting up a daycare center."

Kay blinked. "A daycare center? At *ASI?* The place made up of tough guys?"

"Well, there are areas where the tough guys aren't so very tough. You should see John with his two daughters. Toughest dude in the world has a spine made of pudding when it comes to his girls. Thank God Suzanne is tough. And I just heard the Senior's wife, Allegra, might be pregnant. And Joe and Isabel are talking kids. It would make sense to have a company daycare center, then everyone's mind would be put at ease. It would be off premises but nearby. On the same block."

"Who'd be responsible for bulletproofing the walls?" Kay asked.

"Metal and Jacko." He glanced over at her. "Oh. You were kidding."

"I was, but whoa. And I'm sure they'd ask for the employees to all have combat training. I am absolutely certain that ASI's daycare center would be the safest daycare center in the country. In the world. In the history of the world. There was a little movement starting up to have a daycare center at CDC, but, you know. Deadly viruses."

This was going to be tricky. Nick looked down at Kay's hand in his. Long, delicate but strong fingers, fingers that dealt with potential death daily and did it superbly well, in her mission to save human lives.

"You know," Nick said, toying with her fingers, "you're never going back to the CDC. It's lost to you."

It was true. Even if they nailed every single bastard involved in the bio-weapon scheme, whistle-blowers never had an easy life. She'd be looked at with suspicion for the rest of her days. Nobody would trust her. She'd slowly be shut out of doing sensitive, interesting research. She'd end her days there shunted to some basement office doing scut work. If she even kept her job at all.

She looked down at their joined hands. There was a long silence then she sighed. "I know," she said quietly. "I think I knew right from the start."

And yet she planned on blowing that whistle anyway. Even knowing that it would wreck her life.

It didn't seem possible but his respect for her went up another notch.

"You know," Nick said again, bringing her fingers to his mouth, kissing the soft skin. "ASI is looking to beef up its ability to deal with bio-weaponry. We've had a few offers for missions in the Congo and Pakistan, but we had to refuse because we don't have the equipment, and we don't have the expertise to *buy* the right equipment. We've got some ancient MOPP suits, but nobody trusts them. I think ASI would jump to have you as a consultant."

She smiled faintly. "You think?"

His heart leaped in his chest. "I do. In fact—"

The shuttle came to an abrupt halt and they both jerked forward. Kay would have fallen off the seat if he hadn't shot out an arm.

Goddamn. *Keep your head in the game.* He'd been so excited at the thought that maybe she'd stay in Portland, maybe she could work even just part time for ASI, maybe they could live together…

And he'd completely lost sight of the fact that to do all that, she had to be alive. No good mooning over Kay staying in Portland if she was doing that six feet underground.

The shuttle stopped. They'd reached the end of this server farm, too.

So, he pulled his head out of his ass, helped her down from the shuttle and pointed at the door ahead of them. She pushed the panic handle on the door.

And screamed at the top of her lungs.

Nick nearly had a heart attack as he lunged forward.

Eleven

Kay's thoughts were buzzing around in her head, together with her emotions. Fear, pleasure, terror, warmth, she felt them all, all at once. It was enough to give anyone whiplash.

Nick had just reminded her that her old life was gone. Her friends, the job she loved—gone. The place she worked for, which to her had been the very epitome of virtue, everyone working hard to save lives…well, that place was compromised. Stained with blood and greed.

She mourned losing the CDC while anger burned hot in her heart. Corrupt men had tainted its mission—and they were going to pay. One man in particular if what she suspected was true.

But in the meantime, she'd been…orphaned. It was an odd word for what she felt, but it fit. She remembered the moment she heard that her parents had died. It had felt like that. Like the bottom of her world had suddenly disappeared, leaving a cold and empty abyss. Things she'd loved and counted on were gone.

But Nick's mention of a possible job at ASI, even a consultancy job, filled her with hope. She could do a good job for them, save lives. She knew most of the operators at ASI and she liked each and every one of them. She knew Suzanne and Allegra. Lauren, Isabel, Summer—they were all great women. And Felicity was one of her best friends.

Up until now the future hadn't been in her thoughts. The future was a great gray wall and she couldn't see over it or around it. The present was bad enough. But Nick had made her think of the future.

A future with ASI. Maybe. A future with Nick. Maybe.

If she survived the next 24 hours, which wasn't a given.

Bad men were after her, using the same high tech and ferocity armies used to hunt terrorists. Relentless and unyielding. Who knew how long she had to live?

Kay pushed open the door, expecting to find another huge server farm—and instead encountered a huge human wall with a ferocious scowl.

Adrenalin shot through her body.

Oh my God! This was the end! They'd found her!

The air whooshed out of her lungs as her heart set up a frantic tattoo. She screamed and tried to scramble back and met Nick. He held her arm.

Kay tried frantically to free herself. Didn't Nick understand that they'd been found? Why was he holding her back? Why weren't they running for their lives?

She scrabbled with her feet to get away from the huge, menacing man looming in the doorway. He was looking at her narrow-eyed, his enormous hands curled at his side. He wasn't reaching for a gun but with those hands, he didn't need one. It looked like his entire body was a weapon.

Fear tightened her throat. "Nick!" she croaked, her voice raw.

Nick's hands fell on her shoulders and he squeezed gently. His head bent and his lips brushed her ear. "It's okay, honey. He's one of the good guys."

Kay's eyes widened. Her heart was still hammering its way out of her chest.

One of the good guys?

He looked terrifying.

A few things broke through her terror. The man in the doorway wasn't moving; he was completely immobile. Surely if he was going to attack her, he'd move. Wouldn't he? And Nick wasn't attacking him. Nick was almost *overly* protective. If he felt the man was dangerous, wouldn't he do something? But Nick simply stood still, holding her shoulders. Against her back, she could feel his heartbeat, strong and steady and slow.

She stopped pressing against him, stilled her feet and simply stood, trembling.

"Kay, meet Matt Walker, the new guy at ASI. I've known him for ten years. He's a friend. I told you about him."

The terror in her calmed. Oh God. She'd lost it, totally. Nick had told her about Matt Walker, but she'd completely forgotten.

She tried a smile. "The guy who knocked out the warlord."

The man's face didn't change, but he nodded gravely. "Broke his jaw and three teeth."

"Excellent." She relaxed. "Yes, Nick told me about you." She hesitated then offered her hand, hoping he wouldn't crush it. She needed her hand for work. "How do you do?"

He shook her hand, taking it gently in his, giving a little up-down shake then giving it back to her.

Time to make amends. "I'm sorry I...reacted the way I did. Please accept my apologies."

He dipped his head in acknowledgement but said nothing.

Now that her mind wasn't rattled by panic, she saw he wasn't as huge as he first appeared to be. He was taller than Nick, but Nick was of average height. He was broadly built like Nick. But unlike Nick, he gave off an aura of menace. Or, if not menace...something. Something that made her want to take a step back.

The man, Matt, looked over her head to Nick. "Got a shuttle right here to get through this farm. Then a vehicle at the other end. It's shielded." He had a deep voice, like Nick, but gravelly, as if he didn't speak much.

"There another drone up top?"

"Negative. So far at least. Felicity's keeping watch."

"We'll get out of here and come after them," Nick said

Matt nodded. "Fuck 'em." His eyes moved to Kay. "Sorry."

Nick took her hand and walked her into the server farm. This place was as impressive as the previous one. She could see down one row and it was like those exercises in perspective, where two lines narrowed to a point in infinity.

Beside the door was another shuttle. She knew the drill by now and got into the front seat. Nick sat beside her, and the whole vehicle dipped heavily when Matt got in the back. Not only did he look menacing, but he seemed denser than normal humans.

Nick draped a blanket over her completely but not over himself. The farther along they made their way to wherever it is they were going, the tenser he became. He leaned an arm along the back of the seat and leaned over to talk to Matt behind them.

Kay tried to listen, but the shuttle's motor made a buzz and she was too tired to focus. After a moment, their voices turned to bass murmurings and she found herself nodding off, only to jerk awake when the shuttle stopped.

They'd made the entire trip in only a few seconds? She looked back, astonished to see that she must have dozed the entire journey, because they were at the other end of the huge building.

Then they entered a ramp that carried them up several stories stopping at a big steel door. Matt got out and held the door open.

She could see a stretch of sky beyond an overhang, and about a billion miles of pine trees scented the air after the smell of the server farm, ozone and electronics.

The air was also warm compared to the chill in the server farm. Oh God. Sunlight and warmth! Kay made a beeline for the outdoors when Nick's hand grasped her elbow.

"Sorry." He didn't look sorry. He just looked grim and as dangerous as Matt. "HQ says there aren't drones, but let's be careful."

"What?" Kay looked again yearningly out the door at the enticing scene of sunlight and greenery.

"From the farm straight to the vehicle, ma'am," Matt said. "Safer."

"Kay." She looked him in the eyes. They were dark like Nick's but not warm like Nick's.

"Excuse me?"

"Kay. My name is Kay, not ma'am."

"Kay." He inclined his head, handing a tablet to Nick. "I was going to call you Dr. Hudson, but Kay it is."

Nick studied the tablet, swiping his way through what looked like maps, then lifted his head. "Got it. Let's go." Nick lifted her up into the high SUV and got into the driver's seat.

Kay looked back but Matt had already disappeared. She glanced over at Nick. "Sorry I screamed, but he looked really scary."

"Yeah, he doesn't give off warm-and-fuzzy vibes. But he's a good man."

"If he broke a pedophile's jaw, the best."

Nick slanted her a glance, his mouth lifted in a half smile. "I'm glad you can see that. Matt's world is divided in two right now—those who can see beyond the OTH discharge and those who can't."

"The world has a lot of stupid people in it," Kay answered.

"Amen."

Instead of pulling away, the SUV plunged down into a tunnel that curved away then righted itself. She watched the odometer. The tunnel ran for five miles.

"So—this tunnel is another safety measure?"

"Hm." Nick was driving fast, in complete control of the vehicle. "The entrance to the server farm is meant to be difficult to find and, as luck would have it, difficult to follow from the sky."

"You guys take paranoia to an art form."

"That's a compliment."

"Yes, I guess it is. Helpful, too. So far that paranoia has kept me alive." She could imagine all too well what would have happened if she hadn't been able to call Nick. Where would she have gone after watching Mike die, knowing that drone was overhead?

They came to the end of the tunnel and ascended fast, up into a well-maintained two-lane blacktop in the middle of the forest.

Nick tapped a spot on the steering wheel. "Felicity, Metal, talk to me. Do we have eyes in the sky on us?"

"Negative," Metal answered. "We're working now on backtracking to where the operator is. Morrison's involved, since there's been a homicide and attempted homicide. We're going to have an address soon."

"Okay. We'll be at the staging area in about an hour and at HQ half an hour after that."

"We'll have news by then. Morrison doesn't like murderers in his town."

"Roger that. Out."

The blacktop merged into a county road that was much less well maintained. If the big SUV's suspension hadn't been so good, it would have been a bumpy ride.

"So the Captain will be there, too?"

"Yeah. He'll be with his team when they get to that address. He's really good friends with Midnight and the Senior. He's going to nail this guy."

"Or guys," Kay said softly.

Nick let that swirl in his head. "You think it's a big conspiracy."

"Not big," she answered. "But powerful, yes. Any chance there'd be a laptop in this vehicle?"

Nick turned to smile at her briefly, then brought his attention right back to the road. "Honey, if we didn't have a laptop in this vehicle, we wouldn't be ASI and the terrorists will have won. Reach around to the back-door pocket."

Kay unlatched the seat belt, found the laptop, pulled the seat belt around her again and opened it. She tooled around a little. It was a good laptop, top of the line. Enough power to work on.

"We have wifi?"

"Honey, please."

"Okay." She waved her hand bye-bye. "I'm going to disappear, Nick."

She did. Sitting right beside him, she just disappeared. It was the weirdest thing. Kay stuck her pretty nose closer to the screen and just—poof!—went away. She could have been on the moon, even though she was sitting close enough to him to touch.

Well, she was doing her smart-girl thing, so he'd do his tough-guy thing. Felicity and Metal assured him there were no more drones and he believed them. But the guys after Kay hadn't given up. A weaponized Spanish flu would be worth millions, maybe billions, and they weren't going to be deterred by one slender virologist. They didn't know yet that she had ASI behind her.

Kay would get their names and he and the team would go after them, and then…and then…

He and Kay could continue whatever it is they had going.

Oh hell, who the fuck was he kidding?

He wanted her, forever if she'd have him. He wanted it all. He wanted them to live together, he wanted marriage and maybe even kids.

Definitely kids.

He slanted her a glance. Super-smart, incredibly pretty red-haired girls. Or Mancino-tough little guys. Either way. Or both.

The ASI guys were all getting broody. Jacko, now Metal. Soon Joe and Isabel. Definitely Jack and Summer, once Summer got over her skittishness. Though Nick had a huge family back home—over fifty people between first and second cousins and their kids—he wanted to establish a family here, too. His and Kay's kids would grow up surrounded by family. Family of choice here and blood family on the other side of the country.

Nick had grown up inside a big, loving family and it was the only way to go.

He hoped Kay was on the same page. If not, he'd convince her. If he had to, he'd do the dirty and say Al wanted great-grandkids before he died.

She loved her grandfather fiercely, that might do the trick. Because no way was he letting her go. No way was he losing her, either to the fuckheads after her or after the danger was over.

Nick could almost feel things slotting into place. Now he knew why he'd always kept things very light with his lovers. Not exactly slam-bam, thank you, ma'am, but more—don't leave your toothbrush at my place. It's not that he didn't like the women he slept with, it was just that they hadn't touched his heart. And he'd gotten bored really fast.

Not with Kay.

Kay touched his heart, his head, and definitely his gonads. He couldn't ever imagine getting bored with her. If anything, he was worried that he might not keep up with her. A scientist with a PhD in virology? Christ. She wouldn't want him to study biology or chemistry or virology, would she? He hoped not, because his thing was the law and guns and he'd basically sucked at science, except for math, all the way through school.

But if he wanted to marry Kay and have kids with her, he needed to keep her alive. So, first things first.

He gave a little beep to HQ and got an immediate response: negative. They were still clear. But if the bad guys had access to satellites like HQ did, then they were in big trouble.

But fifteen minutes later his comms beeped.

"Nick." Metal's quiet voice came on.

"Yo."

"We've got the address."

Nick was electrified. He shot a glance to Kay, who was still engrossed in her laptop. "Copy that. Will someone be at the staging area to hand her off? I want to be at the takedown."

Fuck yeah. No way was Nick going to be somewhere else when they caught the guy after Kay. If necessary, he'd leverage the fact that he was ex-FBI. He could even fudge the "ex" part, act like he was there from Washington.

He didn't care if there'd be fallout. All that mattered was that he could watch them smoke the guy. The guy had to be *gone*. No longer even a remote threat. Once he was indicted for treason, for terrorist activity with bio-weapons, for homicide and attempted homicide, he'd be put away until the sun went dark.

Though Nick would prefer him dead.

So, step one, make sure Kay made it safe and sound to ASI undetected, then step two, get the motherfucker who'd targeted her.

It felt good to have a plan.

Kay was still pounding the keyboard, frowning, when he pulled up in front of a ten-story city-run garage, then turned into it. Joe and Jacko were on the second story, as arranged. Jacko was wearing his usual scowl. He saved all his smiles for his wife. Joe—who'd nearly died on his last mission and had lost so much weight his kidney had slipped—was back to fighting weight. Of course, living with a world-class chef didn't hurt.

"Honey," Nick said as he pulled up beside the white Transit van. She hadn't even heard him, peering into the screen as if it held the secrets to the universe. Well, maybe it did. "Honey," he said again, touching her shoulder.

Kay blinked and surfaced. "Oh!" She looked around at the garage, puzzled. "Where are we?"

"We're switching vehicles. You're going on to ASI and I...have a few things to see to. I'll join you at ASI later."

She stared at him, her eyes so very blue, the only spot of color in the gray garage. "You guys have found out where this guy is, haven't you? And you're going after him."

Goddamn. Nick sighed. It was going to be hard living with Kay if she was going to be able to read his mind so easily. "Yeah, I'm tagging along with the police. And you're going to ASI to do your thing with Felicity."

She nodded. "Fine. There's some data I'd like her to help me with."

Oh God, he could have kissed her. She wasn't clamoring to go with him. She was letting him do his thing while she did hers. He was really good at what he did and she was really good at what she did.

Teamwork.

He could have kissed her on the mouth. Then thought—what the hell. Leaning over, he gave her a noisy smack on the lips. It was so fast, she didn't have time to react, just stared at him with that luscious mouth slightly open.

"What was that for?"

"Oh, nothing," he said casually. "Just that I love you."

Nick got out and walked around to the passenger side of the SUV. Kay was looking slightly shell-shocked as he helped her down.

She was off balance. Good. He'd been off balance since he'd met her. Evened things up a bit. Why should he be the only one stumbling?

"What did you say?" she demanded.

Nick gave what he hoped was a mysterious smile. "You heard me." He held her arm while walking her to Joe. It wasn't just a gentlemanly gesture. He liked touching her, he liked the idea of delivering her over to Joe's care, like precious cargo. She *was* precious cargo, the most precious in the world.

Nick speared Joe with a cold glare. They'd fought in Afghanistan together and they understood each other just fine without words.

Take care of her. If anything happens to her, I'll hold you responsible.

It's okay. I got her.

Kay was watching their faces, eyes flicking from his face to Joe's.

"You got the place?" Joe asked.

"Yeah." He did. On his cell, he had an address and GPS coordinates. He also had where the SWAT team was staging, with a detailed map of the area.

Kay got into the van with Joe, watching solemnly as Nick crossed to get into another SUV driven by Jacko. This one rode lower than the one he'd driven. It was heavily armored.

Kay mouthed, *I love you too.*

Nick nodded and Jacko pulled out. It took all of Nick's willpower not to turn around for one last glimpse of her.

"She'll be okay," Jacko rumbled in his basso profundo voice.

"Yup."

"Doesn't make it any easier."

"Nope."

They rode in silence, Nick reading over what intel they had as Jacko navigated the streets. They were all good drivers and in SEAL training, they'd all taken combat driving lessons. But Jacko had lived in Portland longer than Nick, who was a newcomer. He was driving.

"Bud's planning on going in hot," Jacko said after fifteen minutes of silence. They were driving through a light industrial area, mostly warehouses, most of them rundown. Every once in a while, Nick caught sight of the river, steel gray, white-capped.

The weather had turned unexpectedly cold and windy.

Nick didn't give a fuck, barely noticed. The only effect it had on him was ballistically—recalculating windage if it came to snipering.

Because the cops might have rules, but Nick didn't.

That sick fuck was going *down*.

Twelve

ASI Headquarters

Kay had almost forgotten how beautiful ASI headquarters was. Well, of course. John's wife Suzanne was amazingly talented. At one point, John and Suzanne had lived on the premises but as ASI grew, it took over the building, which had once been a shoe factory.

Suzanne and John had built a beautiful residential complex on the same street, and Felicity had had Kay in stitches describing how John had wanted to turn it into a high-tech fortress.

ASI was super high tech, but with soothing colors, everything elegant but as comfortable as possible with every perk under the sun.

Felicity was very happy here. Of course, her fiancé worked here, which made her loyalty ironclad. Felicity had received head-swimming offers from headhunters and had never been tempted, not once, not for one second.

She loved her job, she loved her co-workers, she loved her bosses and their wives, and she loved Metal. Kay had watched her blossom from a shy nerd to a confident woman in the time she'd worked at ASI.

Kay had even envied Felicity, just a little.

Kay loved working at the CDC. Or had loved it until the troubles started. But no one could accuse CDC employees of being friendly or being teammates outside work. ASI guys and their women were really good friends outside work. Strong, steadfast friends, friends for life.

And at work—Felicity was making the company a lot of money. The server farms, for example, which were her idea, were bringing in income like a river pouring cash, Nick said. But Felicity was clearly valued beyond her success as a rainmaker.

While Kay sat beside Felicity studying Priyanka's files, almost every single ASI operative stopped by, some just to say hello, some to ask her if she needed anything, some to ask how she felt. The news of the pregnancy was now official, and it was amazing to see all these really hard-bitten men all but offer to rub her feet for her.

Felicity had to beat them off.

At which point, they turned their attention to Kay. Some jungle drumbeat had somehow made the rounds that Kay belonged to Nick and might become a future consultant or even employee, and they were rolling out the red carpet. If she'd accepted everyone's offer to make her a cup of tea, she'd drown. Pillows had been thrust at her, two operatives came in to ask her opinion on which gas masks to purchase, and everyone had stopped by to introduce themselves.

Her first day at the CDC, she'd spent completely alone in her office.

Sometimes life gives you gentle hints.

Sometimes life gives you a punch in the back to make you stumble forward. This was one of those times.

Her life was in total disarray. Very bad things were happening at her workplace. It was clear that people she implicitly trusted, people who were supposed to work tirelessly for the public good, had betrayed the trust given to them. Why had they done it? For money, for power, for both? Who knew?

The one thing Kay knew was that she would never again be able to drive onto the CDC campus and feel good about what she was doing.

For her, whatever happened, the CDC was gone. Her dream job since she was in high school had turned into a nightmare.

She was under threat. It was true that she was being protected by an amazing man and an amazing company. They had spread their umbrella of protection over her and it would take a lot to pierce that protection.

Nonetheless, pure evil had taken a swipe at her and she'd been nicked by its claws.

For the moment, there was no past for her. No job to go back to; she couldn't go back to her apartment; she didn't dare visit her grandfather for fear that he'd be caught in the crosshairs.

Though now, maybe, she was being given a future.

But first, unfinished business.

"I have something," Felicity said. "Anomalies. But I don't have any context. Don't know what they mean."

"Show me," Kay said, and Felicity did. The worst possible news. As they proceeded, Kay could feel her heart breaking.

Felicity's findings corroborated her findings of use of the CRISPRs at the CDC in Atlanta.

Kay went over the data again and again. Told Felicity to try to prove her wrong. To find data that disproved her thesis. But Felicity couldn't.

In the end, they sat back and looked at each other.

"I can't believe it," she whispered, sick at heart.

"Yes, you can," Felicity answered sadly. "I can read it on your face. This isn't a surprise. You don't want it to be true. But it is."

Kay nodded.

Felicity touched her hand gently. "I can look into him. Hack into his finances. I'll bet you anything we'll find a sudden flow of money. Big money, to do what he's done. It always comes down to money."

"It wouldn't with me or with you."

"Or with Nick or Metal or Joe or Jacko or any of the rest of the guys at ASI. There wouldn't be enough money in the world to have them do something like this. Betray their consciences and their country. But that's not the case with this guy. He sold his soul to the devil, probably for a lot of money."

Kay opened her mouth, closed it.

Sat, while the anger grew. And grew and grew until she thought she would explode.

"He's my boss." A fierce, fiery lump was in her throat. The words hurt.

"I know." Felicity put a hand on Kay's shoulder.

"Dr. Frank Winstone. The *head* of the CDC."

Felicity nodded.

Kay couldn't move, could barely breathe.

The head of the CDC was a person charged with protecting the nation's health. Protecting it from harm. Protecting it from exactly this kind of danger. The CDC was filled with professionals working their hearts out to protect the public, often by risking their own lives.

The Viral Special Pathogens Branch regularly sent officers into the heart of outbreaks of Lassa and Ebola and they went uncomplainingly, their sole purpose to help.

Every cell in Kay's body and every neuron in her brain rejected the idea of the head of the CDC helping to engineer a weaponized Spanish flu and genetically engineering it to hit specific people or peoples. It went against everything she believed in, had worked for all her life.

Her mouth tightened. This was the evilest thing she'd ever heard of. She knew there was evil in the world. Hell, her grandfather was a former FBI agent. He'd shielded her from most of the horrible things he'd seen, but enough got through for her to understand what was out there.

True, a lot of evil came from ignorance. But it took a special kind of evil to spend years and years studying science and turn around and use that knowledge to kill people. While heading an agency dedicating to saving lives.

He'd betrayed her, he'd betrayed the thousands of people working for the CDC, he'd betrayed the thousands who'd risked their lives. He'd betrayed the millions of Americans who trusted the CDC to keep them safe.

It was betrayal on an epic scale—and she wasn't going to sit still for it.

Felicity eyed her. "You're getting mad, now."

She turned her head. "Damn right."

"You're over the sad and into the mad."

Kay grunted an assent.

"What are you going to do about it?" Felicity cocked her head and studied her.

Kay froze. *Was* she going to do something about it?

She straightened in her chair. Yes. Yes, by God, she was.

Frank had taken something sacred—science and the worldwide effort to improve human health involving the sacrifices of generation after generation after generation of men and women—and turned it into something filthy. Dangerous and dirty, calculated to do harm.

For *money*.

To let it stand would be to betray the memory of scientists she revered.

Not going to happen.

But... "I don't think we can prove anything, or at least anything that would stand up in court."

Felicity sat for a moment, thinking it over. "No," she said finally, mouth turned down into a frown. "You're right. I mean, I think I understand what he did, but only because you explained it. It makes sense to you, but you're one of a handful of people in the world who can see it. For everyone else, it's all circumstantial. A good lawyer, and he'd have the best, would throw out so much smoke nobody'd understand. The DA would follow the money, but I'll bet the money disappears into opaque accounts very soon. We don't have a smoking gun."

They didn't. A terabyte of data, and though it pointed down to Frank Winstone like a huge red arrow in the sky, there wasn't enough evidence, clear evidence, a DA could follow. It was too technical.

Everything inside Kay rebelled. She shuddered with disgust at the idea of Frank getting off scot-free, continuing his path of destruction. He'd killed her best friend, he'd probably killed a researcher, and he'd killed a fine journalist. He'd tried to kill *her*, and he'd been responsible for the death of who knew how many people via the genetically edited flu.

If it served his purpose, he'd no doubt keep on killing. There was no one who could stop him.

Except her.

It was dangerous, and she'd have to depend completely on Felicity's hacking skills and her acting skills and Frank's greed. But if it could be done...

"Felicity, do you think you can do something for me?"

Felicity's pretty face was serious. "Just ask."

"It's dangerous and probably illegal."

"Will it bring this guy down?"

Kay smiled. "Oh, yeah," she said softly. Down. Down forever. With luck, six feet under.

"What do you need?"

Kay told her. Felicity turned pale.

Kay froze. She was asking too much. "Oh God. Can you do it? *Will* you do it?"

"Absolutely. Count on me." Felicity covered her mouth.

"I'm sorry if the thought makes you sick." Kay touched Felicity's arm.

"Not that. Morning sickness." And Felicity bolted for the bathroom.

"Three," SWAT lieutenant Rand Wilson said, and tipped his ruggedized tablet toward Nick.

Nick could see the heat signatures of three men. He nodded gratefully, glad that Wilson was happy sharing intel. He knew that Wilson had been given explicit instructions to cooperate with him, but he didn't get any sense that Wilson resented that. Cooperation was fully and freely given.

The eternal brotherhood of soldiers. Wilson had been a Ranger and two guys in his team were former SEALs. One was a former FBI special agent.

Nick fit right in. But he'd have been there even if they were one-eyed green-haired mutants who hated humans, because no way was he not going to be there at the takedown. Whoever was in the warehouse, behind those metal walls, had tried to kill Kay. He wasn't going to miss anything.

Bud Morrison was at TOC, the Temporary Operational Command, another warehouse farther down the street. Command and control, everyone bunched around computers hooked to their comms units. They were all connected via an internal comms system ASI had perfected. Or rather, Felicity had perfected, with the help of some mysterious guys in Asia with sky-high IQs and minimal social skills.

ASI had tried to recruit them, but they preferred to stay in their hobbit burrows in Singapore and Taiwan. All Nick really understood was that soon there would be a blackout inside the target building and that, inside the building, cell phone coverage and their connection to their overhead drone was already gone.

On the tablet, they could see the drone overhead, uselessly beaming down intel the fuckheads inside the warehouse couldn't see. In the meantime, the PDP's own drone was circling. Its FLIR showed the SWAT team with reduced profile, since they were crouching, the three upright figures inside the building, and cold emptiness all around.

The guys inside were deaf and dumb and soon would be blind.

Wilson and his guys were crouching outside, ready to infiltrate. Each had IR tape on their helmets so they wouldn't shoot each other. The tape would easily show up in their night vision/IR goggles.

God bless technology. Though of course the principle hadn't changed since the dawn of time. The man with the biggest club won. Now it was a battle over who had the fanciest toys.

It was also true that the most determined won, and Nick was determined. He respected Wilson and his boss, Morrison. This was their job and they did it well, with bravery and training.

But they didn't have Nick's motivation. The men inside that warehouse had come after Kay, the love of his life and his future. He would never let on to the SWAT team leader or to Morrison, but he was determined that none of the men come out alive from the warehouse.

Whoever their leader was, he was smart and resourceful. The kind who even from prison could enact revenge. Nick was not going to live checking his six constantly to make sure bad guys weren't behind them, ready to kill or kidnap Kay.

Not going to happen. Not in this lifetime or any other.

Once they breached, Nick was going to have to tap dance fast to ensure that there were three kills and three dead bodies were ferried out, and those dead bodies wouldn't be the guys on the SWAT team.

He had various ideas how that could happen but it all depended on the flow of combat. So he was going to have to stay sharp and use every single opportunity to engineer the deaths of the three guys inside without having to go to prison for the rest of his life.

Not easy. But then nothing in his career had been easy. And he'd never had so much at stake before.

"Three." Wilson began the countdown. On three, the lights would cut out and they'd breach the door, wearing night-vision goggles, and mop up.

Nick was supposed to stay outside until the mopping up had finished, but he intended to wait until the SWAT team made it inside, then would follow on their heels in case they needed help.

They probably wouldn't. Nick had observed the behavior of every team member, and he approved. They all had the smooth, easy grace of athletes at the top of their game and they communicated without words, good signs. Their moves were smooth, not jerky. No panic in these men, no confusion. They knew exactly what to do.

Nick could visualize in his head the moves. The sudden darkness as the lights cut out, the cops bursting in screaming, "Police! Down on your knees!" They'd have HK G36s at the shoulder, Beretta 92s in quick-draw thigh holsters for close work.

"Two," Wilson said.

They'd burst through the door in a controlled way guaranteed to cover the entire area. High, low, left, right, as choreographed as the dancing in *Swan Lake*, only prettier as far as Nick was concerned. Anything planned to put down bad guys was as pretty as could be.

Two guys would be stationed out back in case they were able to make a run for it.

"One, gogogo!"

The door blew open and the men moved as one, swarming into the space.

And the three red figures on Nick's tablet disappeared.

Fuck!

He looked up from the tablet and saw an immensely bright glow coming from the door. The inside of the warehouse was lit up like day. Light that bright would blind the SWAT team members, who had on night vision. Night-vision goggles magnified ambient light sometimes a thousand fold. In the sudden presence of a very bright light, they'd automatically switch off but not before causing temporary blindness.

His guys were now blind.

The shooting started immediately, careful single shots. No spraying and praying, these guys were pros.

Someone screamed.

There was an explosion in the back of the building. The two SWAT team members stationed in the back were gone.

Nick ran, a clock ticking in his head. The SWAT team would know to go to ground and seek cover, even while nearly blind. But right now, right this instant, they were sitting ducks.

Another shot, another man screamed.

"Down!" Wilson roared. Then screamed as a bullet hit him.

Fuckfuckfuck!

"Morrison!" he yelled into his comms. "Men down!"

"Incoming," Bud's calm voice replied. "Two mikes." A car door slammed in the background and an engine revved.

Two minutes were an eternity. Plenty of time for the good guys to die, for the bad guys to escape.

Nick rounded the corner to the back, briefly eyeing the remains of two brave police officers. Rage burned in his heart. He toggled the handle of the back door, but it wouldn't open. There was a lot of noise coming from the warehouse, so nobody would hear the bullet that struck the handle unless they were right on the other side.

If somebody was right on the other side, and heard the shot, then they'd be standing right there, armed and waiting for him.

Nick shot out the lock, kicked the door open, went in low, almost hoping someone would be there.

Nothing.

He could see at a glance the situation. A three-sided wall of glass had been erected around what was a command station. Glass explained why the three heat signatures had winked out. It didn't allow IR through. The men had stepped into the cubicle when the lights went out.

Two huge spotlights had been mounted on stanchions. A generator buzzed. They'd expected the lights to be cut.

The SWAT team was recovering, shooting back from behind makeshift cover. An overturned table. Ominously, two of the SWAT team members were on the floor, still.

The spotlights were aimed at the door, so Wilson and his men were still blind. They couldn't see what Nick saw, the three men retreating, firing steadily to keep Wilson and his men under cover.

The way the bad guys were retreating showed discipline and training. One would keep up a steady fusillade of bullets while two retreated, then another one would take to a knee while the shooter fell back. It was disciplined and well thought out. Nick knew from the drone footage that out back was an SUV, which would no doubt be armored. They had their escape planned, already probably rejoicing that they would make it out and disappear.

Nope. They were not leaving this building alive.

To hell with the order not to shoot to kill. Two men were down, two others were dead. Nick hoped with all his heart that the SWAT team members lying so still in the warehouse were alive, but the bad guys had shot to kill and had forfeited anything resembling mercy. There were two dead men out back.

And they'd tried to kill Kay.

The first of the men was almost at the back door. Wilson and his guys were still shooting blind, the bright light directly in their eyes. Their bullets went wide.

Calmly, Nick took a knee, shouldered his weapon, selected single shot. This required precision shooting.

So far, they hadn't realized he was there. They were too busy trying to kill Wilson and his men.

Nick took careful aim and fired three shots. One after the other, spaced not even a second apart.

One by one, the escaping men fell. The first one grabbed his neck and looked astonished before falling to the ground. The other two realized there was another shooter but they couldn't tell where. They were still looking when they fell, red mists where their heads had been.

The shots from the back of the warehouse ceased and so did those from the SWAT team. Wilson stood from a crouch and limped forward. The front of his tactical pants was red with blood, but you wouldn't know that from his face.

"Mancino?" he called, shielding his eyes with the palm of his hand.

"Yo." Nick stood just as Bud rushed into the room.

It was unusual for someone as senior as Bud to be part of an op, but Bud wasn't a desk jockey. He looked around, noting everything. The three dead guys clustered at the back. Wilson and his team around Nick. The two men on the ground. They were wounded but breathing, Nick was delighted to see. And the bad guys were dead.

"Mancino saved our asses," Wilson said quietly to Bud.

"No, no man." Nick pushed that away with a gesture of his hand. He didn't want the credit, he just wanted the dead guys dead. As a matter of fact, things had gone his way, because he'd have killed them anyway. The fact that he'd done so and wasn't going to be charged with homicide was icing on the cake. "I happened to be outside and could make a lateral entrance. Your team softened them up, I was just on mop-up detail." He looked at Wilson and allowed the grief he felt to show. "Your two guys out back. They're gone. They had explosives ready to blow."

Wilson staggered, almost lost his balanced. His head hung low, then he raised it. He turned to Bud. "Medics on the way? Eisner and McBride are wounded. Eisner's losing a ton of blood."

"Yeah." Bud tapped the comms unit in his ear. "They should be here right—" A loud ambulance siren filled the air, cutting out as the ambulance drew up outside with a screech of brakes. "Now."

Two guys wearing EMT jackets jumped out of the back of the ambulance while it was still rocking, carrying a gurney. They carried out a stabilized Eisner, already transfusing, then McBride. Both men held thumbs up, Eisner's hand shaky, McBride's firm.

Everyone stood silently as two body bags were carried out.

The ambulance drove away, the PPD crime scene unit showed up and Nick groaned.

Bud's heavy hand landed on his shoulder. "I know," Bud said sympathetically. "But we have to do this by the book and I need to get your testimony, together with that of the SWAT guys still standing. We can get Eisner and McBride's testimony later when they're out of surgery."

Nick quivered. He wanted to get this over with as fast as humanly possible and get back to Kay. He wanted to hold her, reassure himself that she was all right, then get her into bed as fast as he could.

He was pumped with adrenaline, and the handiest way to vent that was fucking. Way out in the desert in Afghanistan, there hadn't been any women available who wouldn't have been stoned to death for talking to him, and he didn't fancy goats. None of the team members did, so they all beat off in the barracks.

So yeah, he wanted Kay, because he was about ready to explode.

He wanted *her*. Not just any woman with the right plumbing but her, Kay Hudson, beautiful and brilliant and all his.

It was way too soon to propose. He knew that. But he wanted to stake his claim. Nail her and nail her down at the same time. Make sure she'd stay with him in Portland. Nick wasn't one to think much about the future, because usually the present was enough to handle. Or that was the old Nick.

The new Nick wanted to make plans, be absolutely certain that Kay would be part of those plans. He wanted to look into the future and see her in it.

Right now, he'd give anything to be with Kay, holding her, kissing her, being inside her. He didn't want to be here in this abandoned warehouse, walking Bud and his crime scene team through what had happened. But—Nick was a professional. He'd had patience beaten into him when he'd joined the Navy as a hotshot hothead. Patience and control and discipline had been pounded into his head and muscles.

So he answered Bud's questions patiently, walked him through it, basically did an after-action review, like he'd done countless times after a battle.

And it *had* been a battle, no doubt about that. A hundred bullets fired, five dead, two wounded. Yeah, that was a battle.

They'd discovered the laptop that operated the drone and one of Bud's techs would go through its entire history. About an hour into the debriefing, IDs on the dead guys came in from the facial-recognition databank.

The head guy was a surprise—Oliver Baker, himself.

Nick looked at Bud in shock, and saw his surprise reflected in Bud's face.

"Oliver Baker," Bud said slowly. "Huh."

Huh indeed.

Baker wasn't quite a security contractor, not in the sense that ASI was. He was more a power broker, the "Fixer", as his nickname suggested. So, he was the one who had used the bio-weapon?

The two other men were in his employ. Basically his only employees, so his company, Solutions International, was effectively no more. Nick wasn't too clear on what exactly Baker did, and didn't care. What he cared about was that for whatever reason, Baker and his guys had gone after Kay and now they were dead. Everyone who wanted to hurt her was dead. That was good enough for him.

Nick looked at Bud. "Kay has about a terabyte of data that she's studying. What he was up to will be in the data. Kay will figure it out, if she hasn't already." He met Bud's sober gaze. "What I *can* tell you is that he was messing around with bio-weapons, with some kind of weaponized super-flu. Something that had Kay scared shitless. She's a virologist and doesn't scare easy."

Bud's face tightened. "Bio-weapons, huh? Give me a gunned-up mobster any day." He shuddered. "Don't ever want to puke up my insides."

"I think that's Ebola, but what this guy was messing with was potentially worse. Could have caused a pandemic. Millions dead."

Bud made a sound of disgust deep in his throat. "Then we owe Kay our thanks."

"That we do. Okay. We done here, Bud? I'd like to—"

"Get back to her," Bud said. "Yeah. Get out of here. If we need you again, we'll call. Get back to your woman, she's been through a lot. We might need to depose her, but not right now."

"Not right now." Nick pulled out his cell. "Felicity, Nick here. It's all taken care of."

"I heard." Nick could hear the smile in her voice. "I imagine you want to know where Kay is."

"Like my next breath."

"She's waiting for you back in her room at the hotel. I heard mention of room service and champagne.

If I were you, I'd get there before she changes her mind."

"Oh, yeah. I think I can hitch a ride with the PPD." He raised his eyebrows at Bud. Bud nodded. "Great." And he took off at a run.

"Nick!" He turned at Bud's call. Bud held his thumb up. "Good work!"

Nick gave a thumbs-up in reply and ran.

Kay was just lighting the candle on the room service dinner table when she heard a sharp knock on the door. No time to ask who it was because she heard Nick's voice.

"Kay! It's me! Nick!"

As if she wouldn't recognize that deep voice.

Smiling, she opened the door, held her hand out. "Hi. I ordered dinner. I didn't know what you'd want so, I just went with steak and—umpf!"

Like before, like that night that changed her life, Nick backed her up against the wall and took her mouth in a kiss that she felt right down to her toes. As before, ferocious and hungry, but this time with something else.

He'd killed three men, Felicity had said. Kay led a scholar's life, but something deep in her DNA told her that coming straight from a kill meant his blood would be up. Mankind was about a hundred thousand years old, and had only been civilized for about two thousand of those years.

Right now, Nick would be in a pre-civilizational state. His movements were jerky, fierce, fast. Totally unlike the cool operator he usually was.

He was pressing against her so hard, she found it difficult to breathe.

Kay put her hands on his shoulders and pushed, just a little.

He pulled away, head back, eyes closed. "Sorry," he whispered, then brought his head back down to look her in the eyes. "Sorry, sorry. I don't want to be out of control."

She could see that. She could see that he was fighting a fierce battle with himself. "It's okay." Kay smiled at him. "You're just back from the wars."

Nick leaned his head forward until his forehead touched hers. "That's why I love you. One of the reasons why I love you. You're both beautiful and wise."

"Hmm. Let's try this again, from the top."

He cupped the back of her head and kissed her again, more tenderly, less ferociously. "Like this?" he murmured.

"Exactly like this."

He kissed her from every angle. He'd plunge into her mouth, tasting her, then lift and kiss her again from another angle. She welcomed him, glad that he was here with her, alive and safe.

It could have gone differently. He could have been shot, as two police officers had been. Nothing about what had happened had been safe. She could right now be looking down at Nick's dead body in the morgue, mourning him and mourning what might have been.

She didn't have to mourn him now. She would, one day, about seventy years from now if they were lucky. But not today.

"I'm so glad you came back to me," she whispered when he lifted his head.

"Always." Those dark eyes looked deeply into hers. "I'll always come back to you. So." He winked at her. "Are we done talking?"

Kay laughed. "Yeah, we're done talking."

"Good," he said, and started unbuttoning her silk shirt, focusing narrow-eyed on the task as if he were defusing an atom bomb. Slowly, taking infinite care with each button, down to the last one. He looked up into her eyes, asking permission.

Kay said nothing, just held her arms slightly out from her sides.

He brushed it off and it fell fluttering to the floor. One of her expensive Ralph Lauren pastel-silk blouses from the suitcase Portland PD had delivered back to her. She glanced down at it, at her feet. Normally Kay kept her things well, but right now, the sight of the soft sage-green silk abandoned on the floor pleased her, a symbol of her normally fastidious organization gone a little loose because she had Nick in her life.

She foresaw a lot of silk blouses on the floor in her future. Maybe.

Her black gabardine pencil skirt was next. It was closely tailored so it required her to shimmy a little to get it down and off her, and Nick shuddered at the sight.

"You're a cheap date if that excites you," she said.

The muscles in his jaw jumped. "It all excites me. Undressing you, thinking of undressing you. Listening to you breathe excites me."

"How about this?" She reached behind herself and unhooked her bra. It fluttered to the floor, landing on top of the silk blouse and the skirt.

"Jesus," Nick muttered. He curled his hand around her breast and took her nipple in his mouth, suckling so strongly his cheeks hollowed.

"Oh!" Kay had been feeling so smug and so in control, but all of a sudden, the control left her in a whoosh. She clutched his head, fire shooting from her breast to her sex. Her legs could barely hold her up.

"Okay, that's it." Nick picked her up, strode the few steps to the bed and laid her down. Jacket, shirt, tee shirt, boots, socks, briefs, jeans. All dropped to the hotel carpet in seconds. His hard penis bobbed, already shiny. He closed his eyes, opened them again, gaze fierce. "God, you're beautiful."

"So are you." He was. The epitome of male beauty. Broad shoulders tapering down to a narrow waist, strong thighs, and what was between them...wow. She curled her fingers in a *come to me* gesture.

His face lightened and one side of his hard mouth lifted. "I thought you'd never ask. But first..."

He slid her lace panties down her legs slowly. Down her thighs, knees, ankles and threw her panties over his shoulder.

"At one point, we're going to have to treat our clothes better."

"Yeah," he answered. "When I get a little less worked up at the thought of having you. Maybe in about a hundred years. And speaking of being worked up..."

He climbed onto the bed, covered her body with his.

"Yeah?"

He kissed her while spreading her legs with his own hairy thighs. "I'm afraid that's it for foreplay. It has to be now, otherwise I'm going to explode."

"Now, Nick," she whispered, watching him closely, seeing the moment his eyes lit up.

He entered her immediately, one long, deep stroke. He didn't use his hands, but he didn't need to. Kay had had more than one lover who'd needed to stuff themselves inside her. Not Nick. He slid in, and he found her more than ready.

He lay his head next to hers on the pillow, mouth next to her ear. Cupped her hips. "Now." And started moving so strongly, the headboard beat against the wall in a pounding rhythm.

Kay closed her eyes, concentrated on where they were joined, feeling him thrusting so hard and fast inside her, and surrendered almost immediately to her climax. The pressure was almost too much to bear, so much heat, that slick rhythm that echoed her pounding heart—she erupted with a cry, holding him so tightly to her.

Nick bucked and moved in her even faster, harder, then held himself deeply inside her, grinding, groaning as he came, too.

Long minutes went by as she slowly came back into herself, drifting back down to earth. Who knew where she went when she had an orgasm with Nick? She had no idea. Somewhere really nice, though.

Coming back to earth was always a jolt. Nick's heavy body crushing her so that she had to consciously expand her lungs to breathe. Her sex and thighs were damp and the smell of sex was sharp in the air. Her knees fell to the sides, her arms dropped down to the mattress. She had no strength left.

"Whoa." Nick lifted his head. "That was fast."

"But furious." She smiled.

"I'll make it up to you once I eat something. You were saying something about room service when I walked in."

"There's nothing to make up for." Kay made a real effort and lifted her hand to caress one sharp cheekbone. "But yes, I did order room service. Steak and salad. And it should be arriving right about—"

There was a knock on the door.

"Now. There's a robe on the armchair. Can you put it on and open the door? I'm going to take a quick shower."

"Sure." Nick rolled easily out of bed, found the bathrobe, walked to the door.

Kay hoped the room service meal would be good. Considering she was going to leave Nick tomorrow morning.

Deja vu. The next morning, Kay slipped out of the hotel room like she had…what? Only a couple of days ago? Was that possible? It felt like a lifetime ago. So much had happened, everything was different and yet here she was, slipping away from Nick. Again.

He was going to be so pissed.

If she was successful, she'd have to calm him down.

If she failed, it wouldn't matter because she'd be dead.

This time, walking out the door, she didn't pay attention to the cameras. She didn't need to.

There was an internal passageway to the auditorium and conference venue, but Kay wanted to walk along the road. Feel the sun and smell the air. Because maybe it would be the last time she ever felt the sun on her face.

No. No use thinking like that. She was sure of her reasoning and she was sure of Felicity's skills. This was going to work and her revenge was going to be complete.

And then she was going on to lead a long and happy life with Nick.

But still, she gulped in the fresh air, lifted her head to catch the sunshine, glanced in shop windows on the way. Feeling terrified, determined and angry.

The conference hall entrance was around the corner from the hotel. The building itself was stepped back and the entrance was a two-story atrium. Inside was a reception hall where conference attendees met and mingled. Poster sessions lined the walls.

It was the last day of the World Virology Conference and the place was buzzing.

Inside was all virology, all the time.

Her people.

She looked around fondly at the very unlovely people who prized brains over looks. The men all but wore lab coats. Lab coats probably would have been an improvement over the wrinkled, rumpled polyester sports jackets that male scientists seemed to privilege. The women were frumpy, too. Most with messy hair and no makeup and not a malign thought in their heads. Friendly souls, mostly, who worked themselves into the ground in the hopes of providing a tiny brick in the wall of human knowledge.

Her tribe, and she loved them.

It was early. She walked around, greeting people she knew. It wasn't that big a world. Most of them knew each other from their graduate student days and she caught up on work and life with a number of people. One woman, a researcher for NASA's extraterrestrial life program, gave gentle condolences for Priyanka's death. Unexpectedly, tears sprang to Kay's eyes.

Oh God. She still wasn't over it. She looked away, blinking furiously, then brought her gaze back to the woman, who was looking at her kindly. She placed a hand on Kay's arm, a gentle touch. "She will be missed," the woman said, and Kay nodded, a lump in her throat.

It reminded her why she was here. Because evil men had killed her best friend and removed a bright, wonderful soul from the world.

For money.

And they were playing with a fire that could burn down the world.

For money.

Goddamn them.

She stood in front of a poster. **Mutation Analysis of the ATP7B Gene**. She knew two of the authors, genial nerds working at a research center at Biopolis in Singapore. Hard workers, very smart.

Her cell pinged. An incoming text.

She swiped, read.

Where R U?

Asshole. Trying to be young and hip. Two could play at that game.

@ poster sessions

He'd want to be private. Sure enough…

Meet u @ Rose Bar in 10

The Rose Bar was the evening cocktail hour gathering hole. No one would be there this morning. Most would either be in the breakfast room or the coffee bar, chatting, networking before the sessions began.
She replied.

Gr8

Ten minutes later, she felt a tap on her shoulder, turned and smiled into the bright blue eyes of her boss, Frank Winstone.
The director of the CDC.
"Hello, Frank. Thank you for coming."

Nick smiled in his sleep, opened his eyes a crack, then closed them again. They wouldn't stay open.

Post-op collapse. Not to mention post-op sex. Though sex with Kay was anything but routine, he knew enough to realize that every hormone in his body was wrung dry. No matter, he could relax. His mind wasn't functioning well but he knew he wasn't on duty, today or tomorrow. Tomorrow was the furthest he could stretch his mind to anyway.

Lazy thoughts flitted through his mind, in no particular order. He was hungry. He wanted pancakes for breakfast and a whole pot of coffee. He really needed a shower. His dick was hard. You'd think it wouldn't be but it was. Maybe because of the smells in the bed. The smell of Kay and sex, a unique combo he was going to relish for the rest of his life. Today at some point, they needed to get home.

He reached out his hand to pull in warm woman and found a long stretch of cool sheet instead.

Hmm.

She was in the bathroom. He needed to go, too, but it could wait. First, he wanted an early morning kiss. And, well, his dick was hard. It shouldn't be, but it was.

Finally, his senses kicked in, one after the other. There were no sounds coming from the bathroom, none. People made sounds in the bathroom. The usual, plus water splashing, either in the sink or the shower.

He rolled time back in his head. He'd been sort of awake for about ten minutes now, and ten minutes with no sounds in the bathroom was weird.

He opened his eyes and confirmed that Kay wasn't with him or anywhere else in the room. Dirty dishes from last night's late meal were still on the table. He could smell the steak and potatoes and a hint of the wine. There was still a finger in both their glasses.

He was hungry but the smell of food sparked a curdle in his stomach, because he was starting to get suspicious.

Nick threw the covers off and walked naked to the only place she could possibly be if she were still in the hotel room. He rapped a knuckle against the bathroom door.

"Kay?" he called softly.

Silence.

Goddamn.

He jerked open her closet door. She'd gotten her suitcase back. She'd mentioned it last night. He had a good memory for what had been in it, and there was a suit missing. It was emerald green and it wasn't there. It was on her, wherever the fuck she was.

Snatching his cell, he punched in Kay's number. It went to voice mail. Then he punched Felicity's number, on videochat. It was Sunday morning and she was pregnant.

Tough shit.

She had to know where Kay was.

The cell rang a couple of times, then he saw Metal's sleepy mug. "Dude," he slurred. "The fuck? It's Sunday."

"Ask Felicity where Kay is."

Metal's eyes popped open at Nick's tone. He never allowed anyone to speak with disrespect to Felicity, not that anyone at ASI ever would. Felicity was a goddess. But right now, Nick was pissed at everyone, and that included Felicity.

Metal's eyes narrowed when he saw Nick. "Cover up, man. You're not talking to Felicity naked."

Nick looked down at himself. Yeah, he was naked, not that Metal could see Nick's good parts. He kept the cell aimed at head and shoulders. Still. He put the cell face down on the bedside table and pulled on a tee shirt and briefs. Picked the cell back up, still royally pissed.

"Kay isn't here," he said bluntly. "Where the fuck is she? Does Felicity know?"

Metal scowled. "Kay's not where?"

"In the hotel room. We spent the night here and I woke up and she's gone. She wouldn't go somewhere without telling me, unless she was kidnapped or decided to walk into danger. So, you can see I need to talk to Felicity."

"Yeah. You must be freaking." Metal leaned closer to the screen. "You *are* freaking. Can't say I blame you."

Nick's teeth ground together. "Put. Felicity. On. Please."

"Can't." His face pulled into painful lines. "She's busy projectile vomiting last night's dinner. Maybe yesterday's lunch, too. You have no idea—"

A slender hand appeared on his shoulder. "Give me that," Felicity said, and her face appeared. She was paper white, including her lips.

"Felicity, I am so very sorry to bother you," Nick said, all of a sudden feeling like a shit. "But Kay's gone and I have no idea where to find her."

Felicity bit her lips.

Metal's head swiveled. "Honey?"

She sighed just before Nick would have growled at her and Metal would have challenged him to a duel. Nick was a really good shot, but so was Metal. They'd have killed each other.

"She, ah... She figured out who else was involved and emailed him to meet her this morning."

Every single hair on Nick's body stood up. "She *what?*"

Felicity nodded and swallowed heavily. "Yeah." She checked her *Green Lantern* watch. "She's meeting him right about now."

Nick was struggling into his jeans. "Where?"

"The hotel, the conference center. But don't worry because...God. Sorry Nick, gotta go."

Nick jammed his sockless feet into his boots, picked up his gun and holster and ran.

"So." Frank smiled into Kay's eyes. "Do you have a problem I can help you with?"

Blue eyes affable. Good guy, good boss attentively listening to valued employee. And underneath, a monster.

She remembered every word of the email she'd sent him.

Frank, I have some data Priyanka left me. She was working on something before she died and was very worried. I'm going through her data now and there are some anomalies. Do you think we can talk about this tomorrow? I'll be at the conference around ten.

Kay looked around. The Rose Bar was a good choice. It was on the north side of the building and the morning light was dim. Though she could hear the voices of hundreds of people out in the corridor, it was quiet inside the cocktail bar. They had complete privacy.

She looked into Frank's eyes, watched them carefully. The skin around his eyes was taut and smooth. No bags under them, the sclera clear and white as a baby's. Treason and crime on a massive scale clearly did not disturb his sleep at night.

She stepped a little closer to him, slightly inside his perimeter. In her pocket, she switched on the recording function of her cell phone.

And she knew that she had backup. He was hidden and he was an excellent shot.

"Yes, I have a problem, and yes you can help me with it. Let me tell you what Priyanka thought, and what I think. I think Bill weaponized H1N1, made it fast-acting and even more lethal. And then I think you used our CRISPR-Cas9 to splice specific DNA to the virus so it would only affect one person, or one person and his or her family. Or an ethnic group or tribe. And I think you did that as a *service* to be sold. For money. And I think you are despicable beyond words."

Frank's expression didn't change, except for a slight narrowing of his eyes. "Well," he said, rocking back on his heels and putting his hand in his pocket. "That's—that's quite a series of accusations. Do you have any proof?"

"Yes," she said, happy to see him pale.

He'd stopped smiling. "You don't."

"I do. On Priyanka's data. Clear evidence of use of the CRISPR, at night. Unrecorded, unregistered, but she has proof."

"Experiments," he said. "Nothing wrong with that."

She edged closer to him. "Maybe. Maybe not. But you're going to find it hard to explain the accounts in

Panama and Aruba. Worth millions of dollars. That's impossible on a CDC salary."

His face splintered, then rearranged itself, only this time the affable good guy was gone and Kay's heart beat faster, because she was looking into the face of pure evil.

"You little bitch. You and that Indian whore, meddling in things that are none of your business."

"Oh, but it is my business, and it was Priyanka's. We didn't dedicate ourselves to science to have scum like you spread disease and corruption. You've defiled everything science and the CDC stand for."

"Spare me the sermons, you bitch. Whatever you think you have on me can't touch me. And you won't be alive anyway."

He pulled his hand out of his pocket, lifted a cylinder, and sprayed her with a liquid. It coated her face, dripped down off her chin.

Kay gasped. Held out a hand to keep her protector at bay. She had this.

Frank's eyes glittered with malice, with triumph.

Kay gasped again, stumbled, grabbed on to his shirt front. With every ounce of strength in her body, she jerked him toward her until they were nose to nose.

Snaking her hand around his neck, she brought his face closer, closer still…

And kissed him full on the lips, lingering. Rubbing her face against his.

She could feel surprise in his body. Could feel something else, too—his lungs starting to heave.

Kay pulled away just enough to be able to speak, watching him so carefully. She wanted to see every expression, every nuance. Her heart was pounding but it wasn't with fear. Oh, no.

"The DNA was switched. The wrong DNA was flown out to you, so when you worked the CRISPR you also had flown out—you were working on your own DNA. You matched *your* DNA to the weaponized H1N1 virus. You're dying, Frank."

His eyes bulged. She was so close, she could feel his heart beating hard in his chest. Hear his lungs struggling uselessly for air. "No!" he wheezed.

It would be the last word he ever spoke.

"Yes." Kay smiled right into his eyes, her face an inch from his. "Oh yes. It's filling your lungs with fluid right now. You can feel it, can't you, Frank? Such a vicious little virus you and Bill created. But effective, very effective."

He was turning blue, choking. Kay was holding him up by his shirt front as his feet scrabbled for purchase. He was falling, but before he fell, she had something else to tell him.

"This is for Priyanka, you son of a bitch. And Mike Hammer. Die, you bastard."

His face was below hers, now, desperation in his eyes. The choking sounds grew loud.

"*Kay!*"

She turned, letting go of Frank. He fell at her feet, hands desperately scrabbling at his throat.

And suddenly she was in Nick's arms, held tightly, his head buried in her neck. "Oh God, oh God!" He pulled back, lifted a finger to her face and looked at the liquid in horror. "God no!"

Frank's heels were drumming on the floor. Neither of them paid him any attention.

"Is this—is this the virus?" Nick asked hoarsely. She could see the whites of his eyes around his dark pupils. He looked like a madman.

"Yes," she said, and he flinched. "But I'm not the one who will die here. He thought the virus was tailored to me, but Felicity and I switched the DNA so he designed his own death."

Nick didn't look any less horrified. "You—you switched?" His Adam's apple bobbed.

She smiled, looked down. Frank's heels had stopped drumming against the slate floor. His legs twitched once, twice, and then he was still.

"Our DNA is kept in numbered vials in a carousel, so we simply gave Frank's computer the wrong number. So, he—"

Nick held up a big hand. "Do I want to know?" He looked down at the dead man at his feet, looked back up at her. "No," he said decisively. "I don't want to know. Is this the last of the bad guys?"

"The very last," she reassured him.

"You're not going to run off again and put your life in danger?"

"No. Definitely not. And I wasn't in danger. I *knew* he didn't have my DNA. Felicity and I tracked him giving orders for the wrong vial. And I had backup."

From a corner, Jacko lowered his pistol and gave a salute off his forehead. Then like smoke, he disappeared.

Nick turned back to Kay and blew out a breath. Punched a number on his cell. "Yo. Mancino. Another guy down, the head honcho, I think. Yeah, deader'n dirt. No, I didn't gun him down. Kay scienced the shit out of him."

Kay laughed. She felt light, free.

Nick just stared at her, breathing heavily. He glanced sideways, slid a linen napkin from a crystal napkin holder on the table.

"What are you doing?"

Nick kicked Frank's body out of the way and kneeled.

"Kay Hudson. Will you do me the honor of marrying me?" She gaped. He took her hand and slipped the crystal napkin holder on her left ring finger. It was so huge she couldn't close her hand. "If you're married to me, I have the right to keep you out of danger, yeah?"

"Uh, yeah." She blinked. "I guess."

His chest heaved. "Marry me. Please. Say yes. Before my head explodes and we have two dead bodies on the floor."

She felt even lighter, as if she could float away.

So this was what happiness felt like.

"Yes," she said softly.

The End

Dear reader, I hope you enjoyed this book. If you did, I'd appreciate a review on the Amazon page and/or on Goodreads. If you liked this book, you might also enjoy:

THE MIDNIGHT TRILOGY
1. Midnight Man
2. Midnight Run – Coming Soon
3. Midnight Angel – Coming Soon

The Midnight Trilogy Box Set

THE MEN OF MIDNIGHT
1. Midnight Vengeance
2. Midnight Promises
3. Midnight Secrets
4. Midnight Fire

MIDNIGHT NOVELLA
Midnight Shadows

Woman on the Run
Murphy's Law
A Fine Specimen
Port of Paradise

THE DANGEROUS TRILOGY
Dangerous Lover
Dangerous Secrets
Dangerous Passion

THE PROTECTORS TRILOGY
Into the Crossfire
Hotter than Wildfire
Nightfire

GHOST OPS TRILOGY
Heart of Danger
I Dream of Danger
Breaking Danger

NOVELLAS
Fatal Heat
Hot Secrets
Reckless Night
The Italian

About The Author

Lisa Marie Rice is eternally 30 years old and will never age. She is tall and willowy and beautiful. Men drop at her feet like ripe pears. She has won every major book prize in the world. She is a black belt with advanced degrees in archaeology, nuclear physics, and Tibetan literature. She is a concert pianist. Did I mention her Nobel Prize? Of course, Lisa Marie Rice is a virtual woman and exists only at the keyboard when writing romance. She disappears when the monitor winks off.

Made in the USA
San Bernardino, CA
11 February 2018